SPACE JUNK

Borgo Press Books by RORY BARNES

The Dragon Raft: A Young Adult Novel
Human's Burden (with Damien Broderick)
Space Junk: A Science Fiction Novel

SPACE JUNK

A SCIENCE FICTION NOVEL

RORY BARNES

THE BORGO PRESS

MMXI

SPACE JUNK

For Jo Habib

CONTENTS

PART ONE
THE DESERT

Em Talking

I spent three years—three of their years—on the planet Earth. By their counting I was sixteen when I arrived and nineteen when I left. I have never returned.

I'm old now. The Earth episode is a small, distant fragment in a rich and complex life that has been anything but placid, anything but simple. But they remain, those three Earth years, cocooned in a cartouche of pure memory—and they remain the most intense, most significant, years of my life.

Here is a mawkish trope, a literary cliché: as the old crone lies dying her mind wanders, the aches and pains of her decrepitude fade, she becomes a girl again, a young woman in the full vigor of her youth. The sun shines; perhaps she walks barefoot along a beach, her dress tucked up into her knickers to escape the waves, she hears again the voices of her youthful companions (long dead, long dead). She walks towards her lover (long dead, long dead), her limbs are lithe, her breasts firm, her vision unclouded.... And then the poor old girl dies, happy, if totally demented.

In the moments before I die—if I have any say in the matter— I won't walk along a beach. I'll regress instead to those long gone nights in the Dog and Harp, a dive so degenerate you could only find its like on the planet Earth. But as I die I'll laugh with my companions, lean on my brother's shoulder and whisper in his ear, call for another round of hooch, banter with my beautiful friend Quincy, and even exchange a kiss with the idiot boy. Then I'll snuff it, a happy corpse.

Oh, all right, all right, reader dear, I said it was a cliché. And it is. But it is no less affecting for all that. It is a vision, a cliché that informs my ancient days, that will inform my part of this narrative, whether you like it or not. And, quite frankly, comrade reader, I'm not yet that far gone in the brain—if I was I wouldn't have entered into a friendly contract with the idiot boy to write this memoir of both our lives, I would be lying prone on my deathbed. Enough. Let us start this story with the arrival on Earth of my brother and I in the year I turned sixteen.

* * * * * * *

Harri and I were the first ones down the ramp.

"Oh god," I said, practicing my English. "How long do we have to stay here?"

"Forever," Harri said, not bothering to speak English. "We've got to stay here forever."

"But just look at the place," I said.

"I'd rather not," Harri said.

But it was impossible not to look at the place. The complete absence of anything to look at made you stare. I looked around, desperate to find something to fix my eyes on. The landscape was totally empty—there was nothing in it. No hills, no rivers, no mountains, no trees, no buildings, nothing at all. No animals. Nothing. The ground was flat in every direction. It was made of dirty gravel. Horrid, spiky bushes about a meter tall grew out of it here and there. The horizon was a perfect circle with us in the middle of it. Us and the smugglers' runabout and a dirty conveyance on wheels. And that was all.

I looked at the conveyance, its back part had no windows, just two huge metal doors opened wide. I'd done some work on the types of conveyances used on Earth—I recognized this one as an articulated lorry. A short ladder was propped against the back of the lorry, half obscuring a painted message. I moved so that I could read it: *You toucha my rear, I breaka you face.* I was suddenly worried that the Advanced English course I'd done on Newharp wasn't as good as it was meant to be. I moved back to stand beside Harri.

"You can understand why the Ancestors left this joint," he said.

He's a gloomy individual, my brother Harri. Talk about looking on the darker side of life—Harri looks on the darker side of death. It's a wonder to me that he's actually alive. Although, given what we'd all gone through in the last eighteen months, I suppose it was a wonder that any of us were still alive. That old man the pirates had killed when we were in orbit around Castor, he certainly hadn't made it. And the two girls the pirates had taken with them: fate unknown, although you could guess. I'd had enough of pirates and rat holes in space—if this was Earth, it would have to do. I hopped from one foot to the other—the gravity was almost exactly the same as home. The air smelt a bit odd, but it wasn't as bad as the stuff we'd been breathing in the belt.

The last of our party straggled down the boarding ramp and now we all stood on the planet of our ancestors. A man climbed out of the cabin of the articulated lorry and dropped down to the ground. He didn't look very civilized. He had drawings on his face. He was the first native born Earthman I'd ever seen.

"Right oh, youse mob, hop into the container. Can't afford to pissfart about."

The man came towards us and waved towards the steel box. He seemed a strange, vulgar type, dressed in very dirty clothes.

"Come on, up the ladder, the cits will be here any minute. They'll bundle you straight back to the belt. All aboard, all aboard!"

"Err, excuse me," Mr. Sam Yang Rhee said with great dignity and bad grammar, "This conveyance appears not with any seating facilities to be equipped with."

"Get on board, you dopey mutant. Stop whinging."

"And where, pray, are we down to sit?"

"Park yer arse on the floor. Come on, get in. We're outta here. Now!"

We all stood and looked at the steel box. There was nothing in it. Nothing at all. Except dirt and rust.

"We were told an omnibus to expect," Mr. Sam Yang Rhee said.

"This buster, is a misery bus. It's what illegals like youse travel in. OK? Look, sport, it's a container. That's the beauty of it. It looks like every other container on the back of every other truck on the highway. Right? It could have fresh fruit and veg in it. It could have carpets from the fabulous East, it could have furniture, any damn thing at all. But what it's going to have in it are a mob of whining aliens. Now get on board. Before the smugglers take off. They'll cook the lot of us with their sotto-c."

Mr. Sam Yang Rhee looked at the people-smugglers' craft. I could see he wanted to run back up the gangway, hurl himself into the luxury of the webbed hammocks. Pirates or no pirates. But already the gangway was withdrawing. He shrugged and without saying a word climbed the short step-ladder and made his way into the steel box. Everyone followed. Most people took out handkerchiefs and tried to sweep the dirt from the little patch of floor on which they sat down. Those who had managed to keep a few possessions with them, sat on their suitcases. I was the last person to climb the ladder. As I did so, the man with the drawings on his face said, "Jeeze, you'd be a bit of orright. Wanna ride in the cab?"

"I beg your pardon," I said. "My English is not yet perfect."

"Don't worry about English," the man said. "Come and ride up the front. Forget about this mob."

He put a dirty hand on my arm and started to pull me back down the ladder. I pushed him away and bolted up the last couple of steps.

"Stuck up bitch," the man said and then said some other words I couldn't understand. He picked up the step ladder and tossed it into the container, I had to grab it to stop myself being hit. The man swung the doors closed. It was suddenly very black, blacker than space itself. A minute later an engine growled into life and the steel container started to sway and jolt.

Ned Talking

Morning, reader. I'm your other narrator. We'll do this tale together, me and Em, turn and turn about. But note this: Em might have spent a total of three years on Earth, but I was born there. All of my first eighteen years were Earth years, and I'm fucked if I'm going to regress to any of them when I die. A pox on the place. Alive or dead, I'm entirely comfortable where I am, thank you very much.

* * * * * * *

The day Em arrived on the smuggler's runabout was the same day Old Ma Harrison burned down the Mothers and Babies. I quit town. They'd hang the rap on me, sure as eggs. There was no way old girl Harrison was going to own up. No way at all. Blame the janitor, blame the fifteen year old—*he's already got a record as long as your arm, the little hoon.*

I walked along the side of the highway trying to hitch a ride while behind me the smoke from the Mothers and Babies rose in a dark column to the heavens above. The day was cold, the oil fields were empty of everything except flowers—a sea of puke yellow. The passing trucks were full of heartless wankers. Not that there were many trucks or cars. We don't get much traffic. Most of the drivers ignored me, pretended they hadn't seen me, but the driver of one rusty canola roller stuck his finger in the air, sneering. You poor suck. I knew the bastard: Jigger O'Grady, known as Tats. I stood in the back draft, buffeted by wind and rage, and raised my own finger to his rear vision mirror. Then for good measure I gave him all ten fingers at once. Jabbing them.

The last time I'd seen Tats he'd been swimming in the fifty meter irrigation ditch half an hour after chucking out time at the Tidy pub. He'd gone and convinced Maureen Neilson to go swimming with him—stark bollocking, the pair of them. Pissed as newts. Pile of clobber on the bank—Maureen's knickers as white as a skull in the moonlight. I'd knocked off Tats' jeans and high-tailed it over to the Mothers and Babies and run them up the flag pole. They were still there the next morning, flapping in the breeze. Filthy, grease stained pair of daks. The crotch half rotted away. God knows how Tats got home that night: wearing Maureen's skull-likes probably. Mind you, "home" for Tats was the sleeper compartment of his pig sty of a rig. A right little nest of sin—half the town's illegitimate had been conceived in there. Talk about poetic justice—the Mothers and Babies was just the right place to run his strides up the pole. The trouble was, somebody had seen me doing it. Dobbed me in. The word was that Tats was gunning for me.

I was about to drop my own daks, point me bum at Tat's disappearing mirrors. But the air brakes slammed on. The tires—all eighteen of them—locked. Smoke, burning rubber, dust, the works. Too right he was gunning for me. The canola-roller half jackknifed to a shuddering halt by the verge. It was a rusty, unwashed, greasy crate of a semi-trailer with some crap about *I Breaka You Face* painted across the back of the tray. It was carrying an even rustier forty-eight foot container. A faded sign said the container was the property of Solar Freight Lines. But I didn't have time to stop and stare. I reckoned Tats would be grabbing a tire lever, swinging open the driver's door, dropping down to the tarmac.

I didn't run away. I was brighter than that. I sprinted straight *towards* the semi. Shifting, legging it. I reckoned Tats would be coming back towards me, on the driver's side of the truck. If I could make it to the truck before he came into view, I'd be right. Jeeze I nearly bust a gut going that distance. But I made it. I got to the back of the truck before Tats appeared. I jogged past the rear wheels and dropped to a crouch. I was right, the guy was walking back along the other side of the truck. Jeans the color of axle grease—probably the same ones I'd hoisted—and steel-capped boots. I padded as quietly as possible along my side of the truck. Funny thing, I was sure I could hear alien music—off key, with a bit of singing, alien style. It was coming from inside the container. I snuck round the front of the truck. There were bull-bars on the rig as big as irrigation pipes. A plastic doll in a well filled bikini was tied with wire to the top bar. On the duco were the words *Miss Daisy*. Just the sort of stupid name Tats would give a rig. He was a bit of a no-hoper, Tats. I slowly stuck my head round the driver's side of the truck. I couldn't see much, the driver's door was hanging open, obscuring my view. I dropped to a crouch again. The poor mongrel was standing in the road about three meters behind the back of the truck, scanning the oil fields. He wasn't carrying a tire lever, he was carrying a monkey wrench. He had his back to me. He turned. He saw me. I moved, there was no time for fancy footwork. I was out into the road, round the open door, foot up on the step, hand on the rail, swinging myself up and in. Slamming the door.

Tats was screaming, cursing. His steel-capped clodhoppers were drumming on the road. I banged my hand down on the door lock. But the window was down. I looked for the fast-glass button. There wasn't one. Talk about primitive. I started winding like a madman, but I wasn't quick enough. The guy was clambering up the outside of the cab, trying to yank the door open. He'd had to drop his monkey wrench but—I'd heard it clatter on the road. I kept winding. Tats got one hand on the top of the glass and tried to pull it down. I kept winding, but it took all my strength. Slowly the gap closed. Tats' face was hard up against the glass, screaming with rage, his eyes were darker than the tattoos. My own face was only ten centimeters from my side of the glass. You could call our situation intimate. I felt the window start to press his fingers against the top of the door frame. He wrenched his fingers loose just as the winding handle broke off in my hands. He cursed and dropped out of sight. I took a deep breath. But there was a flash of movement: Tats was ducking round in front of the truck. I flung myself across the cabin, slammed down the door lock on the passenger side. My luck was holding—that window was up. I was locked in. Tats' face appeared in the passenger window, but I didn't have time to study the noble brow, the clean cut jaw line, the delicate artistry of the tats. Miss Daisy and I were going traveling. Time to shift.

Except I'd never actually driven a truck before.

Utes. Now utes I know about. Circle work. Born to it. There's paddocks and bits of scrub around our town that have circles burned into them like whirlpools. They appear overnight. Funny that. *News to me, officer, I was home in bed.*

But semis are something else again. Luckily the engine was still running, I didn't have to worry about starting the thing. Thing? I do apologize. *Miss Daisy*—I didn't have to worry about firing *her* up. The gemco was juicing along just fine. I just had to get her into gear. There were an awful lot of gears. There seemed to be two gear sticks and one of them had another lever on it. Split-shifter, I reckoned. I depressed the clutch. It put up a bit more resistance than the clutch on Johnno's old man's ute. But I got it down to the metal and slammed Miss Daisy into gear. Don't ask me which gear. It was just a gear, OK? I let in the clutch. The semi shuddered and juddered and half danced, half hip-hopped a meter or two down the road. The engine nearly died. I slammed the accelerator down. The engine howled back into life. The truck shuddered forward like an earthquake. Oh, yeah, the brake. Don't forget the brake.

I hauled the tension off the handbrake and let it go. There was a explosion of air somewhere under the truck. Yeeeeeha! We were away. We were rolling good and proper now. Miss Daisy, I think I love you. I experimented with the gear sticks and found a gear I liked, crunching a few cogs in the process. I looked in the big rearview mirror. Behind me the highway was a ribbon of bitumen. The column of smoke from the Mothers and Babies was rapidly diminishing in size. I looked at the passenger side mirror, but the view was obscured. Tats was still there.

I'll say this for poor old Tatters, he knew how to hang on. He was hanging on real good. I reckon we were doing sixty, seventy, maybe eighty—there were too many dials on the dash to see which was the speedo. Tats wouldn't want to get off now. Hanging on was his thing, hanging on was his reason for being. I reckoned I was doing ninety, doing a ton. We were into the desert now, well past the last irrigation ditch. No more puke yellow oil fields, just the old familiar desert: saltbush, spinifex, windblown weeds, salt pans here and there. A bit of roadkill, all feathers or squashed fur. Hooch cans that hoons have flung from moving vehicles. And the sky. The sky, the sky, like one vast, delicate china bowl—deep blue high above fading to washed out white at the horizons. And sometimes a cloud, pure white, nothing to do with rain. And beyond the bowl of blue, the heavens, the endless deeps of space. From which the illegal aliens came.

Oh yeah, I'd tumbled to friend Tat-face. I knew what sort of a load we were carrying. I laughed out loud and gave Tatters a grin, pointing my thumb behind me, in the general direction of the container. I narrowed my eyes and made a weird, alien face. Poor old Tatters didn't look too happy hanging onto to the mirror struts. But he knew that I knew. We both knew I'd just hijacked a people smuggling wagon. You wouldn't believe it would you, of all the rigs tooling up and down the highway I'd gone and grabbed a misery bus. Although, people smuggling was just the sort of get-rich-quick scheme that a born loser like Tats would go for. Not that there aren't plenty of smuggling opportunities in our neck of the woods—our neck of the desert. For good reason the smugglers favor our area. They can get their runabouts in and out with bugger all chance of detection. And the landscape is so flat they don't have to worry about putting down on a mountain range or something—tipping the things over, puncturing the skin, landing in a swamp, landing in the sea. They're a bit slapdash, some of the illegals, not too snap with their celestial navigation skills, not too precise with their landings. It's a wonder they even find planet Earth. Perhaps some of them don't. Miss completely, get burned up in the sun. How would anyone know?

But how would anyone know if the aliens are really people? If you ask me, the term *people-smuggling* might be a bit off beam. I mean, the aliens look a bit weird, they've done a bit of interbreeding out there in the cosmos, no doubt about that. They're not called space junk for nothing. The buggers say their ancestors—*some* of their ancestors—came from planet Earth. They go on and on about it. Homecoming they call it. Reclaiming the birthright. Bloody hell. What about disease? Some of the planets on the edge of the known population scatter are a bit filthy by all accounts. A bit on the nose. Rat infested lumps of rock orbiting some decaying sun. Cockroaches the size of dinosaurs. The aliens don't inhabit planets, they infest them. The scum of the galaxy. And they want to come here and take our jobs, marry our sisters and daughters! And breed. That's what they are good at, aliens, breeding.

At least that's the sort of ranting, raving spiel old girl Harrison goes on with. Her and the League o' Purity. You should hear Ma Harrison when she gets going. I had to hear her all the time. I worked for her, mucking out the Mothers and Babies after school. Mon to Fri—junior rates, casual, no holiday pay. The way Harrison went on and on you'd reckon some diseased alien had come and run off with her very own daughter, the precious Sue-Ellen Harrison. You'd be right. The only trouble was, young Sue-Ellen had been keen to go. Desperate for it.

A vicious kidnap according to old girl Harrison.

Done a bunk with space junk according to the town. A girl like that—what can you expect?

Blessed escape with Prince Charming himself according to Sue-Ellen. For months after she'd disappeared, we'd get emails from her. Showing up on the school's computers, lobbing into the town's terminals. Not that she hadn't used a cut out. Used several. Sent the damn messages to the Moon and back three times before they hit good old Tidy Town. God knows where she really was. There was no tracing her. But she was with Prince Charming the Alien that was for sure. And she was well on the way to becoming the mother of a dear little baby alien. Which made old girl Harrison grandmother to a baby space junklet. That went down a bundle with the town's gossips. But not with old girl Harrison. She had the answer: the emails were fakes. Her daughter couldn't possibly have written that sort of filth. It was the aliens. It was a fiendish trick designed to cover up the awful truth: actually the aliens had eaten Sue-Ellen in one of their revolting rituals. Had her for a midnight snack. They did that, you know, the aliens, the space junk.

An oncoming truck blasted its klaxons. Flashed its lights. I swerved Miss Daisy back onto the proper side of the road.

The oncoming blazed past, the driver going ape in his cab. The smack of the wind, the shock of its passing. Center-road creep—it's a killer on the desert highways. It's true what they say. The road was as straight as ruler—looked like it went on for ever. That was the problem. Even a new-comer to semi driving like me could get a bit bored, allow his attention to wander. There was a banging on the passenger window. Tatters was getting alarmed. He was looking a bit off color, poor Tats, not a shadow of his former self. He had one arm wrapped round the mirror struts and was making gestures with the other. He was trying to say something but the wind was ripping the words out of his mouth, distorting the flesh. *Good grief! I do believe he wants me to stop, he wants to be let back into the cab.* No way, José. This is a decent misery bus.

The day was dying. Night comes quickly in the desert, but the brief minutes of twilight are a time of peace and solace. A time for reflection. At least that's what they say. The Reverend Robbo used to say it all the time—*we're nearer to god in the desert, lads and lasses, nearer to the almighty. Feel that spiritual tug, lads and lasses, feel it pulling at your heartstrings.* Yeah, well, there was a bit of tugging and pulling at the Junior League o' Purity all right, but it wasn't at any heartstrings that I knew about.

The sunset was off to my right, glowing like a volcano. I felt real good—I was tooling down the highway, shaking the dust of Tidy Town off my boots. And all was right with the world. Except for poor old Tatters out on the wing. I'd have to get rid of Tatters. There was no way I was going to stop Miss Daisy and get out to meet Tats, have a bit of a chinwag with him. I supposed the thing to do was slow down just enough for him to jump off. Trouble was, if I slowed down, I'd need a slower gear. I wasn't too sure where all the gears were. Still, it was worth a go. I took my foot off the pedal. Miss Daisy began to slow. I looked over to where Tats was hanging on for grim death. I made bugger-off motions with my hand, getting the message across: time to mosey along, Tats old son. The desert is good for your soul. Tats could do a bit of meditating, repent his sins. Miss Daisy was rolling real slow now, the engine was hiccupping. I put in the clutch and just let her glide.

"Go on. Hop it!" I yelled at Tats, but I don't know if he heard me through the glass.

I got Miss Daisy down to walking pace—well maybe running pace. Tats could easily jump off now. Maybe he'd roll a bit when he hit the ground, but he wouldn't break a leg.

"Bye bye," I yelled, waving a cheery hand.

But the old Tats was proving a hard customer to shift. He glared at me through the glass, his face glowing in the last rays of the sinking sun. What would happen if I stopped? There I'd be, sitting in the cab, ready to plant the foot. And there Tats would be, gawking through the glass like a shark in an aquarium. I reckoned he'd try to bash the window in with a rock, but he'd need to jump down to grab the rock first. That would be my chance: I'd flatten the pedal. I'd be away. It was a risky plan but I thought I'd give it a go.

Then I looked in my mirror. A powerful set of double headlights was closing fast. There was still just enough daylight to see the outline of the vehicle behind them. A cruiser! Big monster, low to the road, radar dome on the roof, aerials like a fishing competition, heaps of oomph. It was the sort of thing the citizenship police drive. Just what I needed, a pair of nosy cits asking questions. *You got a license to drive this thing, son? Who me, officer, sure. All the fifteen year olds in our town have semi licenses. Don't get smart with us, son.* There are some conversations you can do without. Lights on the cruiser's roof started to flash, a siren wailed. Oh gawd. I took Miss Daisy out of gear completely and moved my foot to the brake—not an instrument I'd had any occasion to use in my truck driving career. The cruiser cruised past. The sirens died but not the flashing lights. A holograph began to flash in the air above the cruiser's rear end. STOP POLICE. Sure, sure, I'd dearly love to stop the police—I'd love to stop them hassling poor runaways like me. But I'd have to do what they said. I rammed my foot down. Poor Miss Daisy, she stopped all right. Nearly ripped the road to shreds, jackknifing all over the shop. The engine stalled. It was suddenly very quiet. Behind me I could faintly hear the aliens in the container yelling and shouting and banging the sides. Poor bunnies. I looked at the passenger window. Tats had disappeared. Hardly surprising. About a hundred meters down the road the cruiser came to smooth halt and then began to back up. The hologram changed: REMAIN IN CAB—HANDS ON WHEEL.

The cruiser came to a second halt and the two cits opened their doors and clambered out real slow. They had all the time in the world and they were keen that I knew it. They began to walk towards me, swaggering slightly. They were big bastards in uniform, carrying things that might have been firearms, but were probably just spotlights. There was a sudden flurry of movement off to the side. Tatters! He was doing a runner. The two cits stood and watched. I watched too. It was almost dark now, but the sky above the horizon was still a shade or two lighter than the desert. Tats' silhouette could be seen hurtling towards the skyline, ducking and weaving through the clumps of saltbush. I reached for my window handle. But it wasn't there, I'd snapped it off a couple of hours ago. I opened the cab door and yelled at the cits.

"He's an alien, he's an alien! He's come to breed like rabbits!"

"You! Stay in the cab," yelled one of the cits swinging round to face me and raising his spotlight.

A beam of light half knocked the door closed in my face. Or so it seemed. But I shut my eyes and kept yelling. "He's pure space junk and he's escaping. Look at him go, look at him go. A purity hazard! He'll pollute the desert with his alien seed! Strange things will grow!"

"Shut up," said the cit. But he swung the spot away from me and started probing the desert. The other cit opened up too. For a moment both beams swept about, turning the clumps of salt-bush into blazing ghosts. Then they found him, still running, still ducking and weaving. The two beams converged, nailing poor Tats. But he didn't stop running.

"Stop, we have you covered. Stop in the name of the law," a voice boomed out. One of the cits had a voice enhancer. His souped-up words radiated out into the desert like they'd keep going forever. But it was Tatters who kept going, getting smaller all the time.

"He's an alien, I tell you," I yelled. "He doesn't understand English. Chase the bastard!"

"You be quiet," shouted the cit without the enhancer.

"You'll lose him," I yelled.

The cits didn't say anything. Just looked at each other and nodded. Then they were running for the cruiser, slamming doors, turning on more lights. I could hear the whine of the compressor working the hydraulics. The cruiser turned, the suspension was still raising the body to off-road height as they hit the desert. I watched for a minute: it was a sight worth seeing, the cruiser bucking and rolling, flattening saltbushes, careering about. Headlights illuminating the sky one moment, peering down wombat holes the next. I could even hear the cits whooping and hollering—they love a good desert chase, the cits. I couldn't see Tats. Maybe he was lying low behind a bush. He'd be lucky if the cruiser didn't squelch him. I turned my attention to Miss Daisy, twisting the key in the ignition, bunny hopping the whole assembly, finding the clutch, finding a gear of some sort and then another gear. I was rolling. The aliens in the container were drumming their feet. I looked for the head-light switch and turned on the windscreen wipers instead. Then I found the right switch, the road lit up. I was away outta here.

Em Talking

He does go on a bit. Bloody Ned. All that stuff about inter-breeding with cockroaches the size of dinosaurs. "The aliens don't inhabit planets, they infest them. The scum of the galaxy." For god's sake. Did he really believe all that? Maybe, maybe not. No one had ever told him otherwise. But I'll tell you what, reader dear. I reckon he had great fun writing it all down yesterday, in the full knowledge that I'd be reading it today. Well, I'll take my cue from him: I'll be pitiless in my depiction of the little twerp. No holds barred, as they used to say on Earth.

* * * * * * *

The steel box was awful. Someone had a light and switched it on for a bit, but most of the time we were in darkness. The box bounced and swayed. After a while things settled down and the box remained fairly stable. You could hear the hum of the wheels.

"At least we've got to a road," Harri muttered.

I was leaning against Harri's shoulder with my back against the ribbed steel sides, "I could have been riding in the cab," I said to my brother. "Comfy seats, nice scenery. But I've stayed with you, Harri boy."

"You'd have been raped," Harri said.

"Oh, thanks," I said.

"Then he'd have cut your throat and thrown your body into the desert."

"Charming," I said.

"Wild dogs would have eaten you." Harri said, radiating gloom in the darkness. "Then the dogs would have died of food poisoning."

"Do you mind?" I said.

"Vultures would have eaten the dogs," Harri said. "Then the vultures would have died on the wing. A rain of dead vultures."

"Wrong desert for vultures," I said. "If we're talking about vultures then we're talking about India. You know, that's the big one that points up. With Sri Lanka balanced on the top. Didn't you do your homework? "

"Homework sucks," Harri said.

"Excuse me," said a voice from the other side of the box. "Pessimistic talk is grossly dysfunctional. We are very close to our goal now. I think a bit of uplifting singing is called for."

"O no, not again, not uplifting singing," Harri said.

"I'm afraid so," said the voice, it was that of old Mrs. Wozlebut, company uplifter. "Perhaps," she said, "Mei Lim would care to accompany us."

Smith Mei Lim was the owner of a twangleodium. Through all the alarms and deprivations of our journey she'd kept her bloody twangleodium. When the pirates had stolen her daughter during the Castor orbit, Mei Lim had kept her twangleodium, she never let it out of her sight, she slept with it clasped to her bosom. She started to play it now. Twangle twangle. Mrs. Wozlebut cleared her throat and proceeded to lead the singing. Most of the others joined in.

> *I am a lonely traveler,*
> *lost in space and time.*
> *Although my way is paved with pain*
> *I seek what is but mine.*

> *Chorus: Homecoming, homecoming,*
> *coming coming home!*

> *Home is where the heart is,*
> *I never more will roam!*
> *I know the hills of Earth are green*
> *The rivers sparkle, full of bream*
> *My forebears roamed Earth's gladsome glades*
> *I seek that I might greet their shades.*

The twangleodium kept up its jolly twangling, the voices of our party rose and fell.

"Crap," Harri said. "Pure crap."

They were starting on the second chorus when the box suddenly decelerated, twisting at the same time. Everybody was thrown forward and sideways. I hit my head on the steel side, but not badly. The twangleodium twanged violently and was silent. The box came to a shuddering halt.

"The driver can't stand the singing, Mrs. Wozlebut. He's coming to murder you."

"Don't be ridiculous, young man."

Then we could hear footsteps walking along one side of the conveyance.

"Here he comes," said Harri.

"Mei Lim," said Mrs. Wozlebut, "give me middle-C."

Mei Lim twanged. Mrs. Wozlebut croaked into the third verse. One or two others joined in again, but you could tell their hearts weren't in it. There were some confusing sounds from outside. After a few minutes the conveyance jerked into motion again. And jerked and jerked. Eventually we were running smoothly. I was asleep when it next stopped—with the same violence as before. I woke up and wanted to pee like an over-filled wine cask.

"Do you think he's stopped for a toilet break?" I said to Harri.

"Doesn't sound like it," Harri said.

And, indeed, you could hear more shouting and yelling going on outside. Someone was yelling "He's an alien, he's an alien! He's come to breed like rabbits!" And then there was something I couldn't make out, followed by "Chase the bastard!" Is that all they did on Earth—yell and shout at each other? It was incredibly frustrating being locked up like silk worms in a box, not being able to see anything, not being able to hear properly, busting for a leak. I reckon half the others were in the same condition. You could hear them shifting about, trying to get comfortable, get a bit of weight off their bladders. Then suddenly the conveyance was rolling again, humming along the road.

Ned Talking

I was away outta there, all right. But where to? All I had was a dead straight highway. And I reckoned I didn't have much time. There was no way I was going to make it to the big smoke, to Jackson's Port, before the cits caught up with me. There were hundreds of kilometers of road between me and the coast, a few tinpot little towns along the way and the odd turnoff that might lead to god knows where. And the truth was, I'd never actually been as far as the coast. I was a desert boy, an oil rat. I'd be running out of my known universe pretty soon. If the cits had caught Tats, or even if they hadn't, they'd be on the shortwave, calling in their mates, bringing up reinforcements. Choppers might fly. I'd have to ditch the semi and ditch it soon. And I knew just the place.

About ten kilometers ahead there was a side track. It was just dirt, corrugated, washed out in parts. It ran to a salt pan about five k from the highway. We called it the Ice Field—except it was actually salt. A blazing white expanse of crystals. When I was a little kid it had been completely smooth, featureless. Then it became a favorite spot for the people smugglers. Easy to see in the moonlight, dead flat, they couldn't miss it. Many didn't. The rusting hulks of half a dozen clapped out alien craft were lying around half submerged in the salt. Monstrous, expendable one-way hulks. There's two types of smugglers—the professionals with big, souped up runabouts. They come blazing in from their hideouts in the asteroid belt, ditch their human cargo, and zoom off. Three minute turnaround, max. The other sort are the one way ticket brigade. Broken down old hulks that wouldn't get a space worthiness certificate from a blind dog. The aliens buy them cheap on the black market and have a go themselves. You've got to say this for them—they have a go. Poor drongos who've never been to space before in their lives, navigating across one galaxy after another with a do-it-yourself book. Some of the aliens don't even know which planet they've crashed on. *Excuse me mate, is this Io?* Well there's a few crashed hulks littering the Ice Field, I'll tell you. It's getting a bit crowded. But what I reckoned, was that the Ice Field would be a good place to ditch the semi, in among the hulks. Then I could sneak back to the highway and continue hitching towards the coast. The cits would still be looking for the truck, they wouldn't worry about a lone hitch hiker.

I had about a k to go to the turnoff when I saw the lights

coming up behind me. Still distant, but closing fast. Cruisers, cits. One will get you ten. I did what I had to do. I switched off all the semi's lights, slowed to a creep and then swung the wheel. I just took to the desert. With nothing but starlight to see by, I just lumbered off, and kept lumbering.

The desert isn't exactly smooth. It's mainly gravel and dust and rocks and saltbush. Miss Daisy rolled and bucked and the steering wheel seemed to have a life of its own. I was leaning forward, peering out at the night. I was starting to see a little better. I looked at the mirrors. Nothing following me, although I could see lights on the highway, moving fast on the tarmac. But no one had taken to the desert. Just to make sure, I stopped Miss Daisy, turned off the engine. I opened the cab door and listened. I could hear nothing except some sort of night bird—a hooting, hunting sort of sound, an owl maybe. But it wasn't hunting for me. Even the aliens had stopped their yowling. They could have been dead, the container was so silent. Then I noticed the light on the horizon, dead ahead. There was something coming at me, straight out of the desert. I was about to do a runner, there and then. But then I relaxed—no need to run from the moon. I closed the cab door and waited for ten minutes as the stars slowly faded in the growing moonlight and the saltbush clumps emerged from the blackness—dark against the lighter color of the desert floor. When I reckoned I'd be able to see the track if I crossed it, I fired up Miss Daisy and crept off. I'd only gone a hundred meters when I found it. I swung the semi hard right and made for the Ice Field. Not that the track was much of an improvement on the open desert, it was more potholes than hard surface. But I knew we were headed in the right direction.

And then, there it was in the moonlight, a ghost sea, dead ahead. And after the roughness of the track, the Ice Field was pure heaven. The semi rolled across the salt as if it was silk. Jeeze, it's a weird place at night, the Ice Field. I'd been there a few times recently with some of the hoons from school. In some kid's dad's ute. You've got to bring your own firewood, there's nothing to burn out on the salt pan. At night you could think you'd been transported back in time to some ruined medieval landscape. You know, the hulks rise up against the night sky like black castles. There are bats in them. The salt shimmers in the moonlight, glows. It can be scary until you get the fire going. But then the firelight does it's magic and if you've managed to knock off a bit of hooch, that does its magic too. You start to think you're some sort of knight on a quest or something. At least that's what I used to think, but I didn't bother telling anybody else. Just swigged the hooch and dared other hoons to jump over the fire.

I maneuvered the thing, sorry, Miss Daisy, into the moon shadow of a wrecked freighter. You forget how big the things are. This one was half buried in the salt, but it still towered over the semi. The broken centrifuge section looked like a canola tank toppled sideways. There was a snapped off landing probe sticking out like a drowning man's arm. Whoever had brought this monster in for a landing had been enthusiastic about getting down to Earth.

I cut the motor, opened the door and clambered down to the salt. It crunched under my boots. For a moment the night was as still as a photograph—then it wasn't. I dived under the hull of the wreck. A chopper was coming up fast from the south. I hadn't heard it with Miss Daisy's engine running—but I heard it now. I know these guys, they have all sorts of crap on board. Heat sensors, night vision goggles, thermal imaging, not to mention spotlights that practically incinerate anything they shine them at. They'd pick up the semi. The heat from the engine would glow on their screens like a beacon. Then they'd close in and pick up my body heat. The sensors were that sensitive, they'd get me even if I managed to find my way deep into one of the hulks—and that would be a risk. I had no torch. There weren't just bats in those babies—snakes, rats and god knows what made their homes. I lay on the salt thinking fast. The sound of the chopper multiplied. There wasn't just one of them—there were two, maybe three. It occurred to me that there was safety in numbers, not only for the cits, for me.

I jumped to my feet and shot round to the back of the semi. Quick as a flash I unlocked the doors of the container. I gave them a tug and sprinted back to the cover of the hulk. It was my only chance: with aliens scurrying all over the place, the cits would have their work cut out, I'd have a chance to sneak away. From where I was I could see the dark cavern of the container, but I couldn't see in. Hell, it was a risk, letting a mob of aliens loose. But at first the buggers didn't come pouring out. Maybe they were dead. The choppers were almost overhead. Then a figure jumped out of the back of the container. Then another. Soon there was a whole hoard. They didn't muck about, they scattered into the night. A couple of them came towards the place where I was lying, hard up against the cold bulk of the hull. They were muttering to themselves in alien. They were undoing their flies.

Oh what! Soon there was a whole line of them, standing on the salt, facing the rusty side of the hulk. The nearest one was only a couple of meters from me. A guy might as well kip down in a urinal. I was onto my feet and making a dash. The choppers were overhead. The sound was suddenly deafening. The spotlights blazed, the whole place lit up like an explosion. There were aliens all over the shop, some standing, some squatting. I raced for the cover of a smallish hulk about a hundred meters away. The thing was tilted like the leaning tower of Pisa, but its landing ramp was down, twisted into the salt. I made it into the airlock. It was busted—both doors were open. There was nothing to stop me going further in—except the snakes and rats and spiders. So I just flattened myself into a dark corner of the airlock and watched the scene. The choppers were coming down, descending like fireworks, their spots still probing, illuminating the alien horde.

Talk about typical alien behavior: these loonies reckon they're coming home to the sacred land of their ancestors, but what's the first thing they do when they set foot on the holy planet? Piss on it. And having pissed, do they have the wit to scatter into the night, do they give the cits a run for their money?

No way, José. They just do up their zips and stroll over to the choppers. Cool as cucumbers. *Evening, officer, nice night for a sacred homecoming.* Or words to that effect in fluent alien: jabber jabber jabber. With the choppers' rotors slowly spinning to a stop I was starting to hear some of the dialogue. The cits were out of the choppers and wandering around with hand-held spotlights and voice enhancers- "All right, all right, everybody over here please. One big group, please. Just stand beside the truck. Just take it easy now." And then another cit started to say stuff in alien. Her voice enhancer made her sound like the town drunk—jabber, jabber, jabber. Or you'd think she was reading out the results at a school sports day with the amplifier on the blink.

They could have their sports day. It was time for me to slip away into the darkness. I was about to slink out of the airlock and duck round behind the wreck. Then I'd be off across the salt, keeping the wreck between me and the action. But I heard a cit say, "There's heat over there, Captain. In the airlock of the tilted one." And a beam of light winkled me out, blinding me. I just waited. I was stuffed. I was a goner. The charge sheet would be as long as your arm: hijacking a semi, driving without a license, endangering life, people smuggling, arson, breaking my bond...and then some. The light came towards me, although the cit had the courtesy to point it at the ground, I just got the reflection from a million billion salt crystals, hurting my eyes. The cit stopped when she got to the foot of the twisted ramp. I stood in the airlock, framed by rusting, buckled metal.

"Don't do anything silly. Come on, down the ramp now. Nice and slow."

There was nothing for it. I walked down the ramp and stood on the salt. The cit ran the spotlight quickly over me. As far as I could tell in the moonlight, she was about thirty with her hair tied up in a pony tail. She didn't look half as agro as her colleagues in the cruiser. She spoke quite pleasant:

"Just go and stand over there with your mates."

I stood where I was, what mates were these? The cit made

elaborate shooing gestures, trying to herd me towards the aliens.

"Don't speak English, eh?" she said and then started to talk to me very slowly in alien. Did she think I could understand the crap? I don't think she could understand very much of it herself, she sounded like someone who'd learned to speak from a book. But I got the drift: she thought I was one of them. Me! Anybody would think I had two heads or something.

I was about to sort the poor girl out, but I gagged on my words. Suddenly the charge sheet as long as your arm started to look a bit theoretical. Best to be an alien for a while.

I walked across the salt with the cit walking beside me, still trying to talk to me in alien. When we were twenty meters from the group of aliens beside the semi she left me and strolled over to where the other cits were gathered beside one of the choppers having a conference of their own. I kept going towards the aliens, walking to my doom. What would happen if the cits left me completely alone with them? I approached the group and stood on the fringe, about a meter and a half from the nearest alien. Jeeze, I felt weird. I shivered and it wasn't only because the night was cold. No one said anything, least of all me. The cits now fanned out, busy with their spotlights, making a thorough search, probing the hulks, examining the semi, disturbing the bats, talking into their mikes. They were calling up reinforcements. A cit approached the group and started counting heads, mine included.

"You can sit down if you want to," he said. "It'll be an hour or two before the transports arrive."

No one sat down. The cit spoke very slowly, "You will all be taken by helicopter to the detention camp at Spearchucker. You will be processed there and your status established. Do you understand?"

A girl of about my age, maybe a bit older, emerged from the center of the group and stood a couple of meters away from me. She said to the cit "We are genuine refugees. Our own planet is doomed." She spoke very nicely, very clearly, although you could tell that English wasn't her native language.

"Everyone is always a genuine refugee, lady," the cit said. "In ten years of rounding up you people I've never met one who wasn't a genuine refugee. Genuine refugees are a dime a dozen."

"In our case it is true," said the girl.

"Not for me to decide," said the cit. "They'll sort you out at Spearchucker."

An old man spoke up: "Excuse me, Officer, but would it possible be for us to of some refreshments partake. My companions and I are famished."

"*Of some refreshments partake*," said the cit and laughed. "Who taught you blokes English?"

"We have a serious course of study undertaken," said the old guy. "It is our most heartfelt desire model citizens of Earth to be becoming. Our ancestors from here came."

"Every bastard's ancestors came from here," the cit said. "Earth is the ancestor capital of the universe."

"I'm afraid I don't understand," the old guy said.

"Don't worry about it," the cit said, "You mob just sit down and wait for the transports, they'll bring some soup with them. Go on, sit down."

"Good idea," said the girl and sat down. After a couple of seconds, a few other people did as well. Then suddenly I was the only one left standing. I felt a bit exposed, I sat down quickly as well. The cit ambled off to join his companions who were returning from their search empty handed. Nothing happened for a few minutes. Then slowly the aliens began to talk amongst themselves in their own lingo. Jabber yabber blabber. The moonlight was quite bright enough for me to see that they were all looking at me. They were talking about me. As well they might—they knew I wasn't one of them, even if the cits didn't.

Without standing up, the girl bumped herself over the salt until she was sitting close beside me. She had long reddish hair that shone in the moonlight. Her skin might have been a pale silver color and her lips might have been blue, but it was hard to tell. For a bit of space junk, she looked sort of OK.

"Where's the man with drawings on his face?" she said.

"Tats," I said. "Tats did a runner."

"You mean he ran away?"

"Just that."

"And who are you? And why are you sitting with us?"

"Err..I'm Ned."

"You don't look like a genuine refugee to me, Ned."

"Well...err...um," I said. "But I'm a fugitive from justice," I said, and rather liked the sound of the phrase.

"An outlaw?" said the girl.

"Too right," I said, sitting up a bit straighter.

"What crimes have you committed?"

"Umm...people smuggling," I said. "Helping you lot."

"And how have you helped us?"

"I brought you here," I said. "I took over the driving from Tats."

"Mr. Tats was meant to take us to Jackson's Port. It's a big city with a large Newharp population. We would have blended in. I don't think bringing us here, to this place, was really what you'd call help."

"Well," I said. "Well, you see it's like this...."

"Like what?" the girl said.

"Like, if you go to this Spearchucker place and they decide you are genuine refugees, then you'll be able to stay on Earth legally, they'll give you permits. If you just went to Jackson's Port and blended in, then you could be arrested at any time and deported. Stress," I said.

"Stress?" the girl said.

"There's a lot of stress involved in being a fugitive. You can die early of stress related cancer. I ought to know, I'm a fugitive myself."

"And how long have you been a fugitive?" the girl said.

"Err...," I said, "about three and a half hours."

The girl packed up, giggling. She had a very pretty giggle. Her teeth were very white in the moonlight. Her eyes sparkled.

"Sorry," said the girl. "My English is not very good. I thought you said you'd been a fugitive from justice for three and a half *hours.*"

"I did," I said.

"Forgive me," said the girl. "But am I right in thinking an hour is one twenty-fourth of an Earth day?"

"Something like that," I said.

"Some life of crime," the girl said. "Three and a half hours!"

"I'm not just a people-smuggler," I said. "I'm on a bond, you know, good behavior, but I've just gone and broken the bugger. It was for illegal use of a tractor. Me and Johnno and some of the yahoos from school—down the main street at midnight. Johnno had knocked off a jar of hooch, we were all a bit, you know, merry. And now the cits will try to pin the Mothers and Babies on me."

"Pin babies onto you?" said the girl. "Why?"

"It's just an...you know...an expression. They'll say it was me who burned the Mothers and Babies to the ground."

"You burned who?" said the girl, shocked.

"Not *who*," I said. "*It*. It's a building—The Mothers and Babies Institute."

"Why do you use the present tense?"

"Eh?"

"Why do you say 'It's a building?' If it is now burnt down, surely you must say 'It *was* a building.'"

"Yeah, yeah," I said. "Whatever."

"Anyway," said the girl, "You are an arse...."

"Look, what is this?" I said.

"I'm sure that's the word," said the girl. "Someone who deliberately burns down buildings is...."

"...an arsonist," I said. "The *-onist* bit is very important. And it wasn't me who done it. It was old Ma Harrison—one of her purification rituals. She was heaping hot coals on the place where sin had been. But things got out of hand."

"Forgive me," said the girl, "My English is...."

"Stop saying 'forgive me' all the time," I said. "Your English is real good."

"No it is not," said the girl. "For example, I would have said 'really good' not 'real good'".

"Yeah well," I said, "If you work hard, one day your English will be as real good as mine."

"I'm sure it will," she said.

Behind us someone stood up, walked across the salt and sat down again. It was a boy, maybe a year older than the girl, say seventeen or eighteen. He looked hard at me—he wasn't real friendly. Then he started talking quickly to the girl in their own lingo. The girl said something in reply—I guessed she wasn't all that impressed with what the older kid was saying. A bit of an argument started. I could sense the rest of the group listening. The girl turned to me and said, "This is my brother, Harri. He thinks you are going to rape me. But I've told him you are only an arsonist, you only burn mothers and babies. Please be introduced. Harri, this is Ned. Ned, this is Harri."

"G'day," I said.

Harri didn't say anything. I extended my hand. Harri didn't shake it.

"Well, anyway," said the girl. "My name is Em, pleased to met you."

Em and I shook hands.

"Does Harri speak English?" I said to Em.

"Not a lot," Em said.

But Harri started speaking very quickly again in their own language. He seemed really angry now. You should have seen the old Harri, waving his arms about. Half spitting his words at his sister. Gesticulating at me.

Behind us other people started joining in. Arguing amongst themselves, arguing with Harri and Em. It was all getting rather heated. Then a horrible twanging sound started up. One of the aliens had an instrument, one of those things that sounds like a vet having a go at a cat without anesthetic. I think the old girl was trying to calm everybody down with the music. Some of the aliens started singing along: howling and yowling with the instrument screeching and twanging. Em bent towards me, so that her mouth was a few inches from my ear. She steadied herself with a hand on my shoulder.

"I've told them you'd be useful," she said. "Some of them don't agree."

"What do you mean," I said, "useful?"

"I've told them it would be useful to have a friendly Earthling in our party. You can tell us what to say in this detention place. You can give us tips. Tell us the things that genuine refugees have to say. We'd have a better chance of getting permits."

It seemed a mad plan to me. I'd never pass for an alien in a million years. "Look," I said. "I'd have to pretend I'd come from outer space myself. They ask you questions in Spearchucker, lots of questions. Like the guy said, they assess your status. There's no way I can pass for an alien. I couldn't answer all their questions. I speak English too good. I can't talk alien. I don't look like an alien."

"What does an alien look like?" Em said.

"Like, like...you know, like weird."

"Like me? Weird?"

"No not you," I said, "But what about this mob of cater-wauling loonies, singing their halfwit songs? No one is going to mistake me for one of *them*."

"They will if you're dumb," Em said.

"Oh thanks," I said.

"I'm serious," Em said. "You can be my brother. And Harri's brother too. Only you can't speak. You're an idiot boy. And you can't understand much of what is said to you. Birth defect. Major brain damage. Nice kid, pity about his higher faculties."

"So I'm not only an alien," I said, "I'm a mental defective. A real lame brain. Pure space junk. Thanks a million."

"It's a pleasure," Em said.

Things were moving along—they were moving along a bit too fast for my liking. Still, it would be one way of avoiding the long arm of the law, hiding out with the aliens.

"Do you think you can drool?" Em said.

"Drool?" I said.

"That's the word," Em said. "I learned it in Advanced English

305. You've got to have a constant dribble coming out of the side of your mouth."

"Oh choice," I said.

"You've got no choice," Em said. "You want to avoid the law, you've got to become one of us. A speechless alien. A real drooling halfwit from outer space."

"Can I breed like rabbits?" I said.

"What you can do...." Em started to say, but her brother pulled her roughly away.

I looked at Harri, Harri looked at me. I didn't like what I saw. But I don't reckon Harri liked what he saw either. And I reckoned Harri's English was good enough to understand my crack about rabbits.

Em spoke sharply to him. I couldn't understand her, but I could guess. I reckoned she was telling Harri baby that he had no choice. If she wanted to adopt me as a brother, he could go jump. Harri might have been the older one, but I reckoned his little sister ran the show.

Harri shrugged.

Em said to me, "So? Are you coming along for the ride to this Spearchucker place?"

"I might as well," I said.

"You're shivering," Em said. "Harri will lend you a tunic." Then she said something to Harri in alien.

Harri said something back. You could tell he wasn't too keen on this tunic idea. I wasn't too keen myself. Some other bugger's alien clobber, it would be riddled with disease. Germs unknown to science. I was about to tell Em I didn't want the thing, thank you all the same. But she said something real sharp to friend Harri, who shrugged in a get-stuffed sort of way and tugged his backpack off. It wasn't a very big backpack—just school bag size—and there wasn't much in it. He hauled out something and held it out to me.

"Go on, take it," Em said. "It'll keep you warm and make you look like one of us."

She was right. If I was going to hide out with a mob of weirdarse mutants, I'd have to look like a weirdarse mutant myself. My skin crawled as I took the tunic thing from Harri's hands. It was slippery with disease. And it hardly weighed anything. It would be useless against the cold.

"Err...look...," I said.

"Get into it," said the girl. "Get into it, now."

I looked at the garment in the moonlight. There were no buttons or zips. I'd have to pull the thing over my head. I swallowed hard, clamped my mouth shut and quickly tugged the slimy cloth over my head. For a moment my face was smothered, trapped. The germs were against my skin. Then I was breathing the air again, trying not to throw up.

"Well done," Em said. "Feel warm?"

It took me a minute or two to realize it, but the tunic was as warm as toast. It could have been a huge, padded eiderdown.

"Thanks," I finally said.

"A pleasure," Em said.

Harri grunted.

Em Talking

I've got no complaints about the above. I'd have written the final scene on the Ice Field pretty much the way Ned has. I can't remember the bit about asking Ned if he was an arse- though. I reckon he just made that up. Ned swears he remembers the exchange perfectly well. Who knows what was really said, it was all so long ago.

* * * * * * *

They took us away in this rattling machine with great spinning knives slashing at the night sky. It was the most primitive thing I'd ever been in. Worse than the container. It's true we were sitting on benches along the walls. And there were little windows you could look out of. But there was an awful lot of noise. You couldn't talk. But you could sing and Smith Mei Lim led the singing, twanging at full volume.

Homecoming! Homecoming!
Coming, coming home!

Everybody except Harri and me sang at the tops of their lungs. They'd just got to the *gladsome glades of Earth* bit when the idiot boy started howling. He stuck his nose up in the air like a dog and he howled. He howled like a banshee, he howled like a fiend from hell. One of the citizenship police yelled "Pipe down!" Everybody looked at the idiot boy—he was sitting be-tween me and Harri. Harri was pretending he wasn't there. I was beginning to wonder if I'd done the right thing in bringing him along. It was up to me to shut him up. I put my mouth right next to his ear and said. "I think you'd better be quiet," but the idiot just howled louder. The chopper machine rattled, the twangleodium twanged, everybody sang. But the singing became ragged, no one could compete with the howling. The singing stopped. The battle was now between the idiot and the twangleodium itself. The idiot stopped howling long enough to take a huge breath. In the relative silence Smith Mei Lim twanged merrily, a look of triumph on her face. But then the idiot boy gave tongue. This time round he sounded like a dog being strangled by a boa constrictor. Even Smith Mei Lim looked startled. Her twanging faltered, but then she gave it everything she had. Two strings on the twangleodium snapped simultaneously. Mei Lim said something that might have been a curse—then she clapped her hand to her mouth. Mei Lim never curses, it's against her religion. She shot a look of pure hate at the idiot. But the idiot was now totally quiet. He was doing a good job of drooling, spit was leaking from the corner of his mouth. He rolled his eyes. Smith Mei Lim played a cracked chord on the remaining strings. Instantly the idiot howled again. The twangling stopped. The howling stopped. Everyone was silent. The machine rattled. I turned my head and looked out of one of the small windows. A couple of stars looked back. I thought they might have been the Dog Star and its friend, but it was hard to tell.

When we'd first arrived in the Earth's solar system, when we'd been in the smugglers' refuge in the asteroid belt waiting for the right moment to make the dash to Earth, I'd spent hours just staring at the stars. I'd given them more time than I'd ever given them on Newharp. I'd tried to locate our own galaxy and maybe I'd succeeded, but it all looked so confusing from this angle, and the plexidome the smugglers used wasn't very clean. There was no day or night on the asteroid. The Earthlings' sun was just a brightish blob, it didn't make much difference at that distance. I'd cleaned a section of the dome—breathing on it and rubbing it with a handkerchief—and looked and looked. I was sure I had located our own galaxy, in which poor, doomed Newharp was orbiting our suns, nearing oblivion. But then Harri had become all cynical and said that even if the galaxy I was looking at was our own, the light coming from it had left a million years before Newharp had even been settled, a million years before our ancestors had been taught the secret of ultra-c travel. At the time when the light I was seeing had left our galaxy our ancestors were still on Earth. But in those days our ancestors had been hairy, shambling creatures who had discovered how to sharpen stones by hitting them with other stones. Homo erectus they were called because they'd mastered the art of standing up. Sort of. Floating around in the plexidome, Harri had started on a long, gloomy lecture about homo erectus and their disgusting habits. I'd had to hit him to shut him up.

The chopper machine began to sway and descend. I looked down through the little window and there, in the blackness below us, was a lighted square. As we sank towards it, it became clear what it was: the perimeter of the detention camp—this Spearchucker place. There were two fences, running parallel all around the square. There were other lights, within the square, street lights, lights from the windows of rows of long low buildings. We sank down, bumped, and the rattling stopped and the whirling knives started to slow down. Someone wrenched the door of the chopper open from the outside. "Welcome to Camp Spearchucker," a cheery voice called out, "Please refrain from smoking until you are inside the reception center."

"How can we smoke?" I said to the idiot. "We're not on fire."

"Cigarettes," said the idiot. "The demon weed."

I didn't know what he was talking about.

Ned Talking

Em did all the talking. She talked for me, she talked for Harri, she talked for the whole damn tribe. They processed us pretty quick. Name, age, gender, planet of origin, got any diseases? Everyone came from some joint called Newharp and no one had any diseases. Pig's bum! Who ever heard of an alien without a disease or two? I would have claimed to have leprosy or something, just to make me authentic, but I wasn't allowed to speak. So Em told the clerk filling in the form that I was as fit as a fiddle physically, but mentally a bit light on. *Neuron deficient* were the actual words she used. The guy looked up from the form and said, "Yeah, the old neurons, eh? It helps to have a few. Where did he get the strides?"

"Strides?" Em said.

"His jeans. He appears to be wearing Earth jeans. And sneakers."

"We bought them second hand from a smuggler on the asteroid," Em said, smooth as butter. "Someone stole his proper clothes when he was in the shower."

"Confucius he say: a fool and his strides are soon parted," the clerk said, trying to sound Chinese. Then he looked down and wrote something on the form. Smartarse.

Half an hour later me and Harri and a few other guys were checking into Single Men's B. Single Men's B was a cross between a battery chook shed and a footy club's changing rooms. What a joint, what a place to call home. Me and Harri scored a double bunk. Harri took the top, I took the bottom. There were a pair of steel lockers beside the bunks. Harri stowed his backpack. I had nothing to stow. Harri wandered away; I got the impression he wasn't too keen for my company. Which suited me, I wasn't too keen for his. I went outside to have a looksee.

I looked and I saw. And I wasn't impressed. I started to wonder if I'd done the right thing. I mean, I was staying out of juvey hall by hiding in this Spearchucker place, but what was the difference? It was true that in this camp you could move around without some warder hassling you, but in every direction you moved, you came up bang against these two huge wire fences. Well, you came up bang against the inside fence. Between it and the outside fence was a mob of Rottweilers pacing up and down and crapping all over the place. The whole perimeter was lit up like a crime scene. There were these fierce white lights on poles—you didn't want to look up. They forced you to take in the ground level action, the pacing dogs, the illuminated turds. I wandered along parallel to the fence. A Rottweiler started to shadow me, keeping pace on the other side of the wire. What a day. I'd woken up in the morning in my own bed in my own house, I'd gone to school, I'd gone to work at the Mothers and Babies and then—bugger me—the whole world had gone apeshit. All because old ma Harrison had decided to heap a few coals on the place of sin. I mean, of course the yahoos who'd broken into the Mothers and Babies had sinned on the couch—where else would you expect them to sin? On the floor? So old girl Harrison has to dump her bucket full of hot coals straight onto the couch. Raving and ranting her words o' purity. Of course the thing went up in flames, what did she expect? Then she's yelling at me to put it out. Saying it was all my fault because I wasn't standing by with a bucket of water. Saying it was probably me that had done the sinning in the first place. And now here I was in the middle of the night imprisoned with a mob of aliens—an alien myself. Someone stuck a knife in the small of my back.

Ah what? I spun round to face my attacker, my new tunic ripped on the knife. It wasn't an attacker. It was three attackers and they all had knifes. They were hard guys, making hard demands—in alien. They might as well have talked African. They were a filthy looking mob in weirdo clothes, the sort of gear you might wear if you were pretending to be king of the sewers. As for their hair, you could use them as dunny brushes. They started jabbing with their knives, pointing at my pockets. A mugging, that's all it was, a simple, straightforward mugging. I put my hands in my pockets and pulled them inside out. One snot rag—dirty. One key to the Mothers and Babies—now useless. One detention slip from school—I'd never done it, I never would. And that was it. The sum total of my worldly wealth. The chief mugger swore and cursed in alien and grabbed me by the throat. Jeeze his breath stank—alien tucker. His face was right up against mine, breathing hard. The other two stuck their hands down the back pockets of my jeans. Nothing doing, fellers—who keeps anything in their back pockets? They cursed and swore some more in their own filthy lingo and then pushed me violently towards the fence. I bounced off the wire mesh. The Rottweiler went apeshit and sprang, but it bounced off its own side of the wire. And then I was picking myself up out of the dirt and the three scumbags were nowhere to be seen.

Fifteen seconds. If that. More like ten seconds. Jeeze you grow up fast in a detention center—you wouldn't find me walking beside the fence at night again. I was getting the measure of these alien scum all right. Everything the League o' Purity said about them was right. Send the arseholes back where they came from. Put them in a runabout and blast them into space. Don't worry about provisions. Don't worry about a star map. Let them find their own way home. Morons, bloody morons, bloody space junk. Can't even do a mugging properly. I reached down an ran my finger round my ankle, inside my sock. My worldly wealth all present and correct. I was no fool. I'd gone and stuck my supply of newbucks into my right sock back in Single Men's B. All of one point eight newbucks. I was rich, I could buy a hamburger. Assuming this Spearchucker alien paradise ran to a hamburger joint. I made my way back towards the lanes between huts, where there were a few people about. Safety in numbers. Except that the numbers were all alien bastards.

I was passing the door of Single Women's H when Em tapped me on the shoulder. She hadn't been mixing it up with muggers, she'd been having a shower, brushing her hair, changing her clothes. She looked real great—for an alien.

"Hello idiot boy," she said.

"I'm not an...."

"Don't talk," she said. "You're dumb, remember?"

"I'm not as dumb as...."

"What's up with you?" Em said. "You look all crazed, crazy. You're covered in dirt."

"Fucking aliens...."

"Have you been in a fight, Ned? Already? We've only been in this place an hour. But don't tell me. You mustn't talk. We'll find somewhere private later."

I howled.

"And don't howl either," she said. "Let's go and explore. They say the mess is closed, but there are private food stalls. We can get something to eat."

We started to walk towards the brighter lights at the end of the lane we were in. We had to dodge a mob of aliens coming the other way. For a few seconds I was in front of Em. She caught up and said, "There's blood on the back of your tunic, and it's ripped."

I didn't say anything. I was dumb. I just made stabbing motions with my hand, plunging in the imaginary knife.

"Oh god, idiot boy, a knife fight?"

I nodded my head.

"I don't know that bringing you along was such a good idea."

I held up two fingers and looked around for someone who hadn't arrived.

"What's that meant to mean?"

"Two late now," I whispered.

Em groaned. "Look, we'll get something to eat and then find somewhere where we can talk—but be quiet for now."

Em Talking

I had a bit of trouble getting the idiot boy to eat. We located the market part of the camp easily enough. It was a sort of village square outside the mess. Most of the stalls were closed or closing, but a couple were still open. The first one we looked at was disgusting—a great brute of a Kovalev was stirring a vile stew in a pot over an open flame. God knows what he'd put in it, the stench was enough to drive us away. The next stall had a sign in Newharp: *Aunty Mazower's Nine Spice Heaven.*

"Yum," I said to the idiot boy. "Nine spice rolls. You'll love these." But before we bought any I had a good yak with Aunty Mazower. She said she came from Blewbury. I said I'd been there once on a school excursion. It turned out we even knew a few people in common. I asked her how long she'd been in the camp. She said two and a half Earth years. My heart sank. What a fate: straight from Newharp to this Spearchucker place, and that's where she'd stayed. I asked how much a couple of nine spice rolls would cost. I had a collection of coins and credits left over from the asteroid, I pulled them out of my pocket. There must have been a dozen monetary systems represented. But Aunty Mazower just shook her head and said that none of that stuff was worth anything on Earth. I think she would have given us the rolls for nothing, but the idiot boy pulled some Earth money out of his sock and silently gave it to Aunty Mazower. She said it was 1.8 and that that would do.

We walked slowly round the market. It was now almost deserted and the lights were going out. I wolfed my nine spice down. It wasn't quite right, it wasn't authentic, but I supposed it was the best Aunty Mazower could do with nothing but Earth produce to work with. The idiot boy sniffed his. Then he prised the roll open and looked inside. Then he managed to get his teeth around the roll, but couldn't bring himself to bite. His adam's apple went up and down like a pump. He took the roll out of his mouth and held the it at arm's length. I thought he was going to be sick.

"Go on," I said. "It won't kill you."

"It's rat poison," he said.

I was going to tell him not to speak, but there was no one within earshot. The market was almost deserted. "It's a nine spice roll," I said. "Go on, eat it. You're starving."

"No, actually I'm not very hungry."

"Take one bite. Get one mouthful down your throat and I'll eat the rest."

He did it. And he kept it down. But it was a struggle. I didn't make him eat any more, I was keen for it myself.

The one source of noise and light was a small building behind a couple of scrawny trees. We wandered towards it. Standing in the semi darkness underneath the trees we could look through the open door. It was a gambling den. There was a jongma game in progress. People from half a dozen planets were sitting round a table, slamming down tiles, yelling out scores in half a dozen languages. I've never gambled myself. It's a mug's game. I looked sideways at the idiot boy—his eyes were ablaze. Oh god, a gambler. First he gets in a knife fight, then he wants to gamble. Then my own eyes opened wide. The stakes! There were more pellets being shoved around that table than I'd ever seen in my life.

"Look at the pellets," I said to Ned. "There's hundreds of them. You could buy a planet with them. You could *power* a planet with them for a thousand years."

"Alien beads," Ned said. "They're worthless."

"Worthless! Do you know what they are?"

"Sure, like you just said: in the old days you could buy planets with them. When your ancestors left Earth they'd land on a planet and buy it off the natives—*Here mate, have a handful of beads, a sack of flour, a couple of tomahawks and a blanket. Right, sign here. Thanks for the planet. Now piss off, this joint's legally ours.* They were complete bunnies, the natives. They fell for it every time."

"That's not quite how it happened," I said.

"Listen. I've done Interplanetary History. Year Four—I done

this project—Beads in Orbit."

"Those things are fusion pellets, Ned."

"They're just alien beads, Em. We had a collection in Reception at Tidy Consolidated. They're counters, chips. They're like match sticks, buttons off old shirts. They're good for playing games with."

"They're cold fusion pellets, Ned. They're pure energy."

"They're beads."

"Ned. You take one of those blue pellets, combine it with one of the white ones in a reactor and they'll give off enough electrons to power a major city for a year."

"You'd need a reactor."

"Everyone's got reactors."

"News to me."

"You're trying to tell me there are no cold fusion reactors on Earth?"

"None that I've bumped into."

"Those pellets," I said to the idiot boy, "are worth millions and billions of whatever currency you use here."

"Why?"

"Because they're the intergalactic *means of exchange*. They're what planets trade with, you dolt. They've got intrinsic value because they can be used as fuel. Most people just trade with them, but it's the fact that they *are* fuel that makes them worth something. Even if Earth has no reactors—which I don't believe—you can still trade with them."

"They're worth nothing here," Ned said. "We don't do interplanetary trading."

"You don't *do* interplanetary...."

"Nothing to sell," Ned said. "We practice rugged self-sufficiency."

"You sound like a politician."

"It's the League o' Purity's watchword: rugged self-sufficiency. Paul Lean says so."

"Who's Paul Lean?"

"He's the big boss of the League o' Purity. He used to run

a goldfish shop, but now he runs the League. He's standing for People's Deputy in the elections. There's posters all over Tidy—*Paul Lean keeps us Clean.*"

"What is this rubbish?"

"It's not rubbish. It's what everybody believes. Tidy Town is the heart of the heartland. We're one hundred percent behind Paul Lean. Fortress Earth for ever! Keep the bloodlines pure! Away with alien decadence! Fight disease! Old Ma Harrison is president of the local branch, she's Paul Lean's right hand woman."

"And who is this Mrs. Harrison?" I said.

"She's the reason I'm here. She burned down the Mothers and Babies."

"So you can't be feeling very well disposed to her," I said.

"Well, no. Not really."

"And she believes all this pure bloodlines stuff?"

"She certainly does that. You ought to hear her—she reckons Paul Lean is god. She's one hundred percent behind him."

"And you? Are you one hundred percent behind?"

"I dunno, Em. Stop getting at me."

"I'm not getting at you, Ned. I want to know what you believe."

"Maybe I don't believe anything."

"Nobody can believe *nothing,* Ned. It's an impossibility."

"Look," Ned said. "I believe what I can *see*—right?"

"What can you see?"

"I can see a mob of space junk aliens playing games with piles of worthless alien beads. All jabbering and jibbering. That's what I can see."

"Look at me, Ned. Go on, look at me."

"I'm looking."

"And what do you see?"

"You."

"And who am I? A piece of space junk?"

"Oh Jesus, Em. No. You're *you.*"

"A bit of space junk? Something the cat dragged in from the

cosmic cess pit?"

"Em, you're...you're...pretty."

"Oh, thanks," I said. "That's a real compliment. Pretty! What does that mean? I've got good teeth? My...what do you call them, Ned? My...." I quickly held my hands in front of me.

"Tits. I mean breasts."

"My breasts are the right size? Is that what 'pretty' means?"

"Oh, all right. You're beautiful."

"Get real, Ned. I'm a human being—a human being from outer space, but a...."

"What about the interbreeding?" Ned said.

"What interbreeding?"

"With the creatures on your planet. The...the...cockroaches like dinosaurs."

"The cockroaches like dinosaurs? What is this...?"

"Paul Lean says...."

"Forget Paul Lean. What do *you* say? Do I look like someone who's descended from cockroaches? Or dinosaurs?"

"You're different."

"Rubbish! I'm the same as everyone from Newharp—we're all descended from the Ancestors who came from Earth."

"And then interbred," Ned said. "Don't forget about the interbreeding."

"We didn't interbreed. The native animals on Newharp don't even use DNA. They're a sodium based life form. Their genes are binary encoded...."

"So how come you've got two heads?"

You've got to say this for the idiot boy: he knows how to deliver punch lines. He just stood there next to me, looking at me, not a muscle moving in his face. In the dim light under the tree, he was the picture of earnest sweet-reasonableness. He was looking at someone with two heads—he just wanted to know why.

I had a straight choice: I could bust him in the face, knock his teeth down the back of his throat—or I could burst out laughing. I clenched my fist and swung, but the laughter got in the way.

My fist went wide and I collapsed on his shoulder. I was almost hysterical. Ned put his arm round my waist.

"There, there," he said. "But how come your skin's all silver?"

"It's a fashion statement, you idiot, I had my melanin re-jigged. You can do that on civilized planets, you know."

Then I made myself think about the really serious stuff he'd just told me. "Look," I said. "About Earth doing no interplanetary trading?"

"We don't," Ned said. "That's why those beads aren't worth anything.... You can't buy anything with them."

"How do you think Harri and I paid for our trip here?" I said. "How do you think our parents paid the smugglers?"

"No idea."

"They paid in fusion pellets. I've...we've...I shouldn't tell you this. Ned can I trust you?"

"Sure."

"I've..I've...got half a dozen pellets sewn into my...what do you call it?" Again I quickly cupped my hands under my breasts.

"Bra," Ned said. "It can't be comfortable. Lumpy little beads sticking into...."

"When you're a refugee," I said, "comfort is only a minor consideration."

"Comfy or uncomfy," Ned said. "They're not worth anything. And where does Harri keep his? Are we talking bead-spangled Y-fronts here?"

"Sorry?" I said. "Why fronts?"

"Doesn't matter," Ned said. "If all you own is a handful of alien beads, you're skint."

"Skint?"

"You're broke."

"Broken? Nothing's broken."

"You have no money, Em. You can't buy anything. You can't trade with those beads. A blind dog wouldn't give you a lick for them."

"Oh god," I said, and I let myself understand what I'd been hiding from for the last five minutes. I felt as if I was suddenly naked, suddenly without protection in the world.

"Don't worry," Ned said. "That one point eight I just used for the rat poison was all the dough I had. I'm skint too now."

"Listen," I said, making a desperate attempt to give my pellets back their value, "If you haven't got cold fusion on this planet, what do things run on? What powered that chopper we came in? What makes all the electricity for this camp? You people used up your fossil fuels years ago. We did the Great Earth Fuel Fiasco in school. It triggered the Economic Ice Age—everyone knows that. It's the main reason this place is so backward."

"Gemco," Ned said. "Everything runs on gemco."

"What's that?"

"Genetically modified canola oil," Ned said. "It's geo friendly or something. They grow it in the irrigation areas. Like where I come from. Real pretty in a pukey sort of way, sort of yellow. You know, the flowers. Fields of them. We call them oil fields."

"We *cook* with that stuff," I said.

"Yeah, so do we," Ned said. "And use it as a medicine; use it to clear away pimples and blackheads; use it to give your hair a lustrous sheen with body and bounce; use it to polish sporting trophies; use it to oil the wheels of commerce; use it to summon up the dead. It's the oilerlife."

"The what?"

"The oilerlife. The...oil...of...life," Ned said very slowly.

"Some life," I said.

"Cures space-rot," Ned said. "The plague from beyond the stars."

"Oh, and how many people suffer from space-rot?"

"No one. Because every bugger and his dog gets stuck into the gemco. If your ute breaks-down in the desert, you can stay alive for weeks just drinking the gemco out of the fuel tank."

"Aw, yuk."

"Thousands and thousands of years ago they used something called petrol. That was a bummer of a fuel. Guys went mad drinking that stuff. They had to ban it."

"They just used it all up," I said. "Driving cars. The reserves ran out."

"Too much heavy drinking," Ned said.

"Ned, did you actually *do* any history at school?" I said.

"Not a lot," Ned said.

I was beginning to think I'd learned more Earth history on Newharp than Ned had learned on Earth. Then I saw the smile he was suppressing.

"You bastard," I said and punched him on the shoulder.

"You reckon I'm a real numbskull, don't you?" Ned said.

"I reckon you've got a warped sense of humor," I said. "But actually, Earth boy, I quite like you."

"You're not too bad," Ned said, "for a dirt-poor alien with two heads."

Ned Talking

She did say that: I quite like you. *I remember her saying it very well. It was one of the most delightful things anyone had ever said to me. Also I remember the bit about her asking me the English word for breasts. As if she didn't know. It was a nice intimate question, even if we were arguing at the time. It was something you'd ask a friend but not a stranger.*

* * * * * * *

We weren't the only ones watching the jongma game. From where Em and I were standing we could see people in the shadows around the table. They were just standing, or sitting on bunks, just watching the color and movement of the game. I reckoned they had nothing better to do. But one set of eyes in the shadows wasn't watching the game. It was watching us— me and Em. So I watched the eyes. It was a bit hard to see who they belonged to—seemed to be a guy, wearing the same sort of clothes as Harri. Must be from the same place—Newharp. Hell, I'd only been in the camp a few hours and already I was picking up the differences.

The eyes were moving. They were still watching me and Em, but the guy had dropped down from the upper bunk he'd been sitting on and was circling round the jongma game towards us. The light fell on him. I didn't much like what I saw: thin face, hair shiny with some sort of oil, weird alien earring, mean looking mouth. Walked like a cat, very light on his feet. I reckoned he was about twenty, maybe twenty two. He looked like a guy who'd carry a concealed weapon—if not a knife, then worse. I'd trust this hombre about as much as I'd trust the scumbags who mugged me.

"Who's this guy?" I said to Em as he slipped out of the open door and came towards us.

"Don't talk," Em said quickly. "I know him from home."

Condemned to silence again. Not that I was complaining, the guy wasn't a chat show host. He came up to Em and said something, some sort of greeting. He smiled, but it was a cold smile. Em said something in return and smiled as well—her warm, open smile. I wasn't too keen for this. Then the pair of them did what aliens do, I'd seen it a couple of times already. They didn't shake hands, they didn't kiss, they rubbed their cheeks together—first one cheek, then the other. And the bloke hadn't shaved. Even with all the noise from the game, I could hear the bristles scraping along Em's face. The poor girl. And then they were both turning to me and Em was introducing us in her own lingo. And then suddenly the guy was holding me by the shoulders and pulling me towards him. I pulled backwards, but he was too strong. He was sandpapering my face with his bristles. One alien greeting another. Bugger me, I was being hugged and sandpapered by an alien. I got a whiff of sweat and hair oil. I nearly chundered, it was worse than the rat poison. But the guy let go of me and then looked at me hard for a couple of seconds and turned back to Em. It's a good job he did. It took me another couple of seconds to get my wits back. You'd think they'd know not to touch you. But I suppose this guy didn't—he thought I was an alien just like him. Or did he? I hadn't liked the way he'd looked at me for those couple of seconds. His face had only been half a meter away from mine, and his eyes had been hard and black, and he'd looked like a man who wasn't easily fooled.

The guy and Em were jabbering. I hadn't a clue what they were on about although I reckoned I could recognize the words for *yes* and *no*, just from the way Em said them in answer to the guy's questions. Except I didn't know which word was *yes* and which word was *no*. So I just looked at Em, trying to read her face, trying to understand her gestures. I didn't look at the guy much—the sound of his voice was enough. It was the sound of someone you wouldn't trust an inch: all reasonable on the surface, cold and menacing underneath. I knew the type, knew it only too well. And Em was being so open, she was like a kid at a party, she even laughed at something he said, she looked happy. The poor girl hadn't a clue—even I could see that. Then the guy said something that sounded like "see you around" only in alien. He turned to me and touched me on the shoulder and said something that might have been, "take care," in alien. And then he was gone back through the door, into the gambling den.

"Who was that?" I whispered.

"Let's get away from here," Em said. "Where we can talk."

We found a couple of seats and a little table next to a closed up stall on the other side of the market area.

"So, who was he?" I said.

"Cicero d'Pettitt. Choice bit of work, eh?"

"You seemed happy enough to see him."

"It doesn't pay to look truculent with Cicero," Em said. "And anyway, I *am* happy to see him. I was in love with him once. Before they put him in Re-Ed."

"Oh yeah," I said. "And what's truculent mean?"

"Don't you know? It's your language."

"Yeah," I said, "and you learned my language by swallowing a dictionary."

"It means...surly, reluctant to do what he says."

"So what did he tell you to do?"

"Not a lot. He just offered me money. Real Earth money, not beads."

"To do what?"

"Nothing."

"Oh come on Em, for pete's sake. A guy like that doesn't offer you money for nothing. What's he want?"

"In the camp? Nothing."

I got it, I got it in one. I'm not stupid. I said to Em, "But when you get out of the camp, you have to work for the bastard in an alien sweatshop for peanuts—right? For years and years—right?"

"Right. And he offered you a job as well. But because you're a dumbo you'll only get half as many peanuts."

"And work for twice as many years?"

"I'm afraid so."

"Well I reckon friend Cicero is one employer we could do without."

"He's not the employer. He's just recruiting for Newharp businesses in Jackson's Port—he's got contacts on the outside. They supply the cash. The guards bring it in, for a cut."

"Well, anyway. We're well out of it."

"Listen, Ned, Cicero says there are only five ways to make money in this camp. You can steal it. You can win it gambling. You can sell your possessions—if you've got any possessions. You can sell sex. And you can sell your labor—your future labor. So which option do you prefer?"

"That's easy," I said. "Steal it."

"And get caught. And get a knife in your gizzards?"

"Guts," I said. "A knife in your *guts*. Gizzards is another of your dictionary words."

"You can call them what you like," Em said. "You don't want a knife in them."

"True fact," I said. "So what did you tell him?"

"I told him we'd think about it. We'd discuss the matter with Harri."

"Good old Harri."

"Do try to get on with Harri," Em said. "He's my brother."

"In this camp," I said. "So am I."

"I just told Cicero you were my second cousin once removed. He knows the only brother I've got is Harri."

"Oh great.... So now he can dob me in to the authorities."

"I don't think he's an informer," Em said. "He's a hard man, but he's not a parrot."

"Parrot?"

"It's what we call informers on Newharp—*talking like a parrot.*"

"Canary," I said. "*Singing like a canary.*"

"Same meaning."

"But he might be a blackmailer," I said. "He could threaten to tell the authorities—as a way of blackmailing me into some sweatshop."

"Yeah, he might try that," Em said. "He might just try that."

"And then if I said, 'No thanks, not to day, Cicero old mate,' he'd *have* to go and tell the authorities, so as not to be a wimp."

"Could happen," Em said. "I don't know how long we are going to be able to keep up the pretense anyway. You haven't really got the Newharp touch."

"Thanks," I said. But I don't think Em had meant it as a compliment.

"Now tell me," Em said. "What happened to you earlier on? You looked really wild when I bumped into you."

"Some mongrel alien bastards mugged me. Down by the fence."

"I'm a mongrel alien bastard myself," Em said.

"I know, I know," I said. "Now ask me if we ever have muggings on Earth. Go on. *Do Earth people ever pull knives on each other?* Go on, Em, ask me."

"All right, idiot boy, do you ever have muggings on Earth?"

"Yes we do," I said. "So I can't complain about mongrel alien bastards from outer space, can I?"

"No you can't," Em said.

"Then we're agreed," I said.

"I think we ought to get some sleep," Em said. "It's been a long day."

When I got back to Single Men's B, the air was alive with snores and farts from around the galaxies. I found my bunk, kicked off my shoes and piled in fully clothed, I felt safer that way. Harri shifted in the top bunk.

"Hey, Harri," I whispered. "Em says I've got to make an effort. I've got to try and like you."

But if Harri had heard, he didn't say anything.

Em Talking

I lay on my bed in Single Women's H. My first night on Earth. I didn't know what to think about the planet of my ancestors. Everything was too confused. I was too tired. But I knew one thing: I was glad I'd picked up the idiot boy. As I'd told him to his face, in a bizarre sort of way I quite liked him.

Ned Talking

The above must be one of the greatest chapters ever written. I'm staggered that Em could compose the whole thing in a mere week.

* * * * * * *

After we'd been in the camp for about a month they started doing the interviews. These were the fair dinkum interviews, the ones that decided if you were a genuine refugee or not. They did them in family groups. The whole family got the same result: in or out. Em and Harri didn't have much of a family, their olds were back on Newharp, having a hard time of it. The mob that Em and Harri had traveled with—old man Sam Yang Rhee and his happy twanglers—were some sort of band of religious nutters. Half the twangling that went on was hymns and crazy demands on their gods. The twanglers had taken Em and Harri along with them as an act of charity. Harri hadn't been exactly grateful, although Em had always been friendly and polite. But as for family, they were down to themselves. Except now they'd gone and adopted me. So the three of us—two brothers and a sister—rocked up to the interview in the main Administration building.

"Don't howl too much," Em whispered to me as we loitered in the corridor outside the interview room.

"Just a little howl," I said. "Now and then."

"I think it would be better for us all if you didn't howl at all," Em said.

The door opened. A guy with a silly beard said, "Do come in, won't you?"

Em, Harri and I sat in a line on a line of chairs that could have held a dozen. There was a meter or two of floor space in front of us and then a long table. Behind the table was the interviewing panel: three women and the bearded individual. The woman in the center seemed to be in command. She was wearing ordinary clothes. One of the other women was in some sort of uniform. Her uniform looked odd, I didn't think she was a soldier. Maybe a salvo. The middle woman cleared her throat.

"Now, we should introduce ourselves. I am Ms. Amelia Ashmore, the camp commandant. This is Captain Shoehorn from the Alien Affairs Department." The uniformed old girl nodded to us. "This is Dr Wilkinson, also from the Department," the bearded loony nodded. "And this is Ms. Harrison, our translator. She speaks four inter-galactic languages including Newharp."

I nearly died. Sue-Ellen. I hadn't recognized her. She'd gone and got herself a job jabbering away in alien. For a moment our eyes met. Sue-Ellen looked as if she was going to say something but checked herself. Just in time—she could have blown the whole scam.

"...but," the Ashmore woman was saying, looking down at the papers in front of her, "perhaps we will not need Ms. Harrison's services. I understand that you two have learnt English, although your brother here has difficulties."

"He's mentally defective," Em said.

"Yes, well, that might be a problem," Ashmore said. "Refugee status is not normally granted to chronic welfare recipients."

"He's a willing worker," Em said. "Just give him simple tasks—morning, noon and night. He never stops."

"Well," said Ashmore, looking thoughtful, "We can discuss that aspect later. Now I have to formally establish your identities."

She looked down at some papers in front of her and said, "You are Emceesquared Gonzales-della-Harpenden, Harri Gonzales-della-Harpenden and Edward brackets Ned close brackets Gonzales-della-Harpenden?" I nearly choked. What sort of surname was Gonzales-della-Harpenden? And no one had told me Em's name was Emceesquared.

Em said, "We are genuine refugees. Our planet is in the hands of monsters."

"Let's just get the formalities over with first, shall we?" said the woman smoothly. "You are Emcee...."

"Yes, yes," Em said. "You've got all our details correct."

"And you three are siblings? You all have the same parents?"

"So we have been told," said Em with dignity. "It is a wise child that knows...."

"Quite," said the woman. "And your parents, where are they?"

"In the hands of monsters."

"Err...monsters?" said the woman.

"Monsters," said Em.

"These monsters. Can you describe them to me?"

"They are loathsome to behold."

"I'm afraid I will need a better description than that," said the woman. "To qualify as genuine refugees you will have to show that you have reasonable grounds for believing that your life would be at risk were you to be returned to your planet of origin. Do you understand?"

"Newharp is doomed," Em said. "Even the monsters are

doomed."

"Why is that?" said the woman.

"The rock."

"You are worried about a rock?"

"Of course we are," Em said with a slightly hard edge to her voice. "I'm sure this has been explained to you a thousand times already. We are hardly the first refugees from Newharp you have interviewed."

"We have to assess each case on its own merits," the Ashmore woman said. "Please tell us, in your own words about this rock."

"There is a rogue comet. It is due to collide with Newharp in two Earth years' time. Total annihilation is inevitable."

The woman leaned back in her chair and looked first to the man on her right and then to the woman on her left. She looked at her fingernails and then said, "Dr Wilkinson, perhaps you had better explain."

The man leaned forward and spoke like a robot. He'd clearly said everything he was saying a thousand times before. He said, "The technology for destroying or deflecting potential impact bodies is quite simple. It consists of judiciously placed explosive devices which are detonated well before the incoming body approaches anywhere near the threatened planet. We even have such technology available to us here on Earth. We have this technology even though our own civilization has not, in recent years, advanced quite as quickly as yours has."

"It certainly hasn't," Em said with feeling.

"The Economic Ice Age was a regrettable but natural phenomenon, young lady, but...."

"The Economic Ice Age was caused by man-made wars," Em said. "And ecological irresponsibility combined with pollution, global warming, famine and plague. Not to mention destruction of the ozone layer, depletion of the top-soil and over-population. It was not a natural phenomenon. You people breed like rabbits...."

"Yes, quite, young lady," said the man, annoyed. "You seem to understand our problems only too well. But we also understand yours. If your planet has the technology to send endless streams of so-called refugees across one and a half galaxies, then it certainly has the technology necessary to deflect a rogue comet. Rogue comets have not been allowed as a legitimate reason for granting refugee status for the last eighty nine years."

"One," Em said, holding up a finger, "The precise size of the comet's corona has yet to be measured. It may be the size of a small moon. It may be far too big to deflect with a few bombs. Two," she said, holding up another finger, "the monsters won't permit it."

"Won't permit what?" the man said.

"Won't permit the deployment of anti-comet devices."

"Oh for God's sake," the uniformed woman said. "That dreary old excuse. Surely you can dream up something better than that. If you think this Will of God party nonsense is going...."

"Captain Shoehorn!" the Ashmore woman said, and the uniformed woman fell silent. "I think we should allow Ms. Gonzales-della-Harpenden to tell us in her own words what she thinks the problem is. Unless, of course, one of her brothers wishes to say something?" The woman looked at Harri.

"My sister can speak for us all," Harri said.

"And you, young man?" the woman said, looking at me.

"Ned only howls," Em said.

"Ah yes, of course, the howler," the woman said, perking up, looking at me with interest, "We've heard about the howler. You have quite a reputation in the camp, young man."

I looked blankly at the woman. I didn't howl. The woman seemed a bit disappointed. At last she returned her gaze to Em. "Now," she said, "about these 'monsters' as you call them. You say they've taken over your planet?"

"They infest the place."

"Who exactly are they? Are they humanoid?"

"They're worse than animals. They're the Willergod Party. They used to be a small sub-group, but they multiplied."

"I told you so," said Shoehorn with satisfaction. "The old persecuted minority trick. Ninety-five percent of their planet is a persecuted minority."

Ashmore looked hard at Shoehorn, but didn't say anything. Then she said to Em, "And this political party, this Will of God Party, what do they believe?"

"They believe the rock is being sent by god. They believe that when it destroys our planet everyone with a spotless soul will go straight to their rotten heaven. To deflect the rock would be contrary to their god's will."

"So they don't allow...."

"They don't allow anything. They run the place like a prison."

"Do you not have democratic means for installing a more congenial government?"

"We used to. The Willergods have suspended all political activity. The whole place is now run directly by their god. The Willergods are endlessly telling everyone else what their god thinks, they're the only ones who have access to the putrid, loathsome thing."

"We try to encourage religious tolerance here on Earth, Ms. Gonzales della Harpenden, we try not to refer to other peoples' gods as putrid, loathsome things."

"But it's the truth," Em said.

"This is getting nowhere," the man Wilkinson said. "If we are to give your application for refugee status serious consideration we need to assess the reality of your perceived threat. How are these Will of God people threatening you personally, apart from their general policies in regard to comet deflection?"

"You have to start the school day singing, *All Hail to the Harpist,*" Em said.

Harri laughed and said, "And if they think you are pronouncing it Harp Pest they put you in jail for a month."

"Surely not," Ashmore said.

"Surely it is so," Harri said. "Although the joke is better in Newharp."

"Our parents are now members of a guerrilla band," Em said. "They are in the mountains fighting to overthrow the Willergods. If we were returned to Newharp we would be used as hostages. Our lives would be in danger from the moment we landed. There is also reason to believe that the Willergods wish to eliminate everyone without a spotless soul before the rock arrives. They want only true believers on the planet by day zero."

"We've heard that one before, too," said Shoehorn.

The interview looked set to go on for hours. I studied Sue-Ellen; I was still getting over the shock of her being in the camp. She's seven years older than me. She'd been in Year Twelve at Tidy Consolidated when I was in Year Five. A big, spotty girl, chewing gum, smoking in the toilets—and not always tobacco—endlessly telling everybody to rack off. The principal couldn't stand her—used to keep out of her way. Her mum, old girl Harrison, used to try to get her to lose weight by putting rocks in her lunch box. There we'd be, on the benches under the trees at lunchtime with everyone chomping on their sandwiches and pizza and then there'd be this great stream of f-words from Sue Ellen and she'd be emptying these rocks out of her lunch box and picking them up and throwing them. Broke a window in the sports shed once. Took out a little Year Four kid another time. But now here she was looking great—running away with an alien had done wonders for her complexion. Or maybe it was motherhood. Or just the passing of time. She'd slimmed down something remarkable too. Maybe the alien tucker wasn't so fattening. Whatever. Here was this reborn, slim, elegant Sue-Ellen in poncy clothes with a classy gold name tag above her right tit. *Sue-Ellen Harrison—Interpreter* followed by a whole lot of crap in alien. Jeeze I wanted to hear her sprout some alien—I reckoned it would be the funniest thing since Johnno drove his old man's ute into the irrigation ditch. But there wasn't much chance—Em's English was too good. So Sue-Ellen just sat there looking cool and calm and professional but saying nothing.

"Now...um...about your brother, young Ned here," the Ashmore woman looked at me and then returned her attention to Em.

"As I said, mentally defective," Em said. "But harmless."

"Can he understand English?"

"He is an idiot savant," Em said. "He has strange powers."

"But as far as language goes?"

"Sign language," Em said. "I can communicate with him by signing with my hands."

"Well, if you would," said the Ashmore woman. "Please ask Ned if he fears being sent back to Newharp?"

Em half turned to face me. Then she twisted and waved her hands in front of herself in a rapid, complicated way—you'd think she was trying to shake off an army of ants. When she'd finished, I waved my own hands around like a mad swine and made cutting gestures at my throat. I rolled my eyes and howled.

"Ned says that if he is returned to Newharp the Willergod monsters will cut his throat," Em said. "They don't take kindly to idiots."

"Yes, well, I think we all got the gist of that," said the woman. You could tell she was pleased with her own powers of interpretation. "Now then," she said to Em, "please ask Ned if he is prepared to work for his keep if he is granted refugee status."

Em made a few more gestures. I gestured in return. Em said, "Ned says he is keen to work at any job the authorities wish to give him. He is especially interested in flower arranging and threading beads on strings."

"Yes, well I'm not sure if there are any openings in those fields," Ashmore said. "Ask Ned if he would be interested in lunar mining."

Lunar mining! The old girl had to be joking. They weren't sending me off to the Moon to work in one of their hell holes— grubbing platinum and crap out of the rock miles below the surface. Living in a plexidome bubble full of old farts, clunking around in a spacesuit, cold as a witch's tit.... But Em was already gesticulating away. There was nothing I could say, I just waved my hands about in return.

"Ned says he is keen to be a lunar miner."

"Splendid!" Ashmore said. "No living off welfare for our

young howler, eh? Now, if we could return to the question of these Will of God people. I take it that they are, in fact, your fellow citizens. They are merely genocidally inclined?"

"Sorry, I don't understand," Em said.

"They wish to ethnically cleanse...."

"Cleanse?" Em said, "They're filth. Everything they touch becomes dirty. How...?"

Suddenly Sue-Ellen sat forward. "If I may interpret here," she said. And then she said a lot more. In fluent alien. It was amazing to hear. She went at it like a freight train. Yabber, yabber, yabber. No humming and hawing and looking for the right word—the mad babbling sound just came pouring out of her lips. I sat there stunned. It was like watching someone you've know all your life suddenly turn into a pet cockatoo, screeching and hooting on its perch. Except a cockatoo would make more sense, might even ask for a cracker. But what Sue-Ellen was saying was making sense to Em. Em started to join in, she was grinning. The pair of them were having a right little chinwag. I looked at Harri boy—he could understand too, although he didn't say anything. I looked at Ashmore and the other two—you could tell they couldn't understand a thing, although Ashmore was trying to *look* as if she was understanding every word. She had this expression of know-it-all appreciation on her dial. Poser. Then Sue-Ellen sat back and said something to Ashmore about Em having trouble with extension—or something. I was too gobsmacked to take in the next minute or two of the interview.

When I started paying attention again Em was going on about how the Willergods had been rounding up people and re-educating them in huge camps. She said many people just disappeared, never to be seen again. Or, if they were seen again, they'd been tortured. It all sounded pretty grim to me. A good place to be out of. I looked at Ashmore and her mates. They were now sitting back, nodding. You could tell that they were taking Em seriously. Perhaps Shoehorn's little outburst about lame excuses had just been to test Em, to see if she was genuine. Finally Ashmore said, "Well, Ms. Gonzales della Harpenden...."

"Please, Em...."

"Well then, Em. We can't make a decision now, of course. I need to put your case to the Board of Review in Jackson's Port. But I think that we have heard enough to conclude that your fears about returning to Newharp are well grounded. We will let you know the Board's decision in due course."

Ashmore stood up, as a sort of signal that the interview was over. Shoehorn and Wilkinson stood up too. Sue-Ellen stayed seated—gathering papers together. The three of us got to our feet and made for the door. As we did so, Ashmore became quite friendly. She said in a conversational way, "Was your journey to Earth a long one?"

"One and a half Earth years," Em said. "Only some of it at hyper-c. And then there's nothing to look at. You are going faster than light. It's just black."

"I don't envy you," Ashmore said with a sigh. "I suppose the rest period on the asteroid must have seemed like heaven—the night sky, the beauty of ordinary space and time. New people to talk to, room to walk around in the plexi dome. Float even, I suppose those rocks can't have much gravity...."

Em let out a gasp and started to shake. I looked at her in alarm. So did Harri. Em muttered something in alien. Her eyes looked real wild, crazed. Harri and I caught her as she fell. We lowered her onto the floor and Harri loosened the buttons at her throat. I nearly said, Christ, get a doctor. I stopped myself just in time. But Ashmore was already hard at it, yelling into the intercom on the table for a medic.

"My sister has...how do you say?" Harri said, and then he started to yabber in alien.

"Fainted," said Sue-Ellen.

"Yes, fainted," said Harri. "It is wrong to talk about the asteroid. She had...bad experiences. She was...the smugglers. The men. They weren't nice. Not nice at all."

Sue-Ellen came round to our side of the table and squatted down beside Em. She took hold of her wrist. "Pulse is O.K.," she said. Then she said a few words to Harri in alien. Harri replied in alien and Sue-Ellen looked up at Ashmore. "The usual story," she said. "The smugglers think they own people, pretty young girls especially. Harri tried to prevent it. He half killed the rapist. They were lucky to get off the asteroid alive."

Just then the doctor arrived: a harassed young man with a stethoscope. But Em was already opening her eyes and trying to sit up. The doctor squatted beside her and tried to push her back down to the floor again. "Take it easy," he said. "You've had a nasty shock."

But Em pushed him aside and stood up, still shaking a bit. "It's all right," she said. "The shock was a few months ago—on the asteroid. This is just...a delayed reaction...is that the right expression?"

"Yeah that's right," said Sue-Ellen but I'm not sure if anybody heard her because everybody started talking at once. Harri and Em were talking in alien. Ashmore and her mates went into a huddle with the doctor and Sue-Ellen whispered to me out of the side of her mouth, "Do a bit of howling, Neddy-boy. This is one time when your howling is called for."

It didn't look like a good howling opportunity to me. But I couldn't risk telling Sue-Ellen that. I either had to keep my mouth shut or howl. Sue-Ellen jabbed me in the ribs with a ballpoint pen. I howled. Everyone looked at me. Em, who was recovering rapidly, put an arm around my shoulders and led me howling out into the corridor. Harri followed.

As soon as we were out into the main camp. Walking between the rows of huts, Em and Harri started to laugh, started to say excited things to each other in alien. Talk about weird behavior. One minute the girl's fainted dead away on the floor, the next minute she's as high as a kite and hooting with laughter.

"What's so funny?" I whispered.

"Learn to speak Newharp," Em said. "Your schoolmate did."

"How do you know Sue-Ellen was at school?"

"Like I said," Em said, "learn Newharp. You might start to understand what's going on."

Em Talking

There are things you try not to think about. But, of course, you think about them all the time. Or, if you can avoid thinking of them during the day, they come to haunt you at night. This camp, this Spearchucker place, was full of dreams and memories and mad, lost fantasies. Even in the daytime you could see it in people's eyes, in the blankness. You could see they were lost inside their own heads, walking the streets of towns and villages a galaxy and a half away. They were sitting in cafes, they were eating meals, they were going to work, they were playing sport, they were holding conversations with people they would never see again, whose fate they would never know. I was the same of course. At night, awake in my bunk, I cried sometimes. I cried for the distant happiness of my childhood, cried for my parents, cried for my friends, cried for my poor, beautiful, doomed planet. I sniveled into the pillow, as lonely and self-pitying as a girl can be. I didn't fight it—there was little to do except let the misery run its course, knowing that in the daylight I would put on the brave face that was needed to survive. I lived on the surface of things in the daylight, I even laughed, smiled, was happy after a fashion. In the daytime I'd allow myself to believe that maybe Newharp wasn't doomed at all. Maybe our parents had been over-protective, over cautious, bundling me and Harri off with Mr. Sam's band of twanglers. Perhaps, even as I was languishing here in this godforsaken place, the Willergoders were being overthrown in a glorious revolution, the anti-comet crews were going into action, flying their intercept missions, knocking the thing off course with their detonations. Our parents had said they'd send for us if everything turned out all right. But that would take years and years. The news itself would take years and years. And then there would be the pirates and the tedium and the whole awful trip to go through again, even if our parents could afford it, could arrange it.

The night after the interview with Ms. Ashmore and her team I'd hardly slept. The interview had stirred things up, unsettled me, left me even more vulnerable than normal. Although that Ms. Harrison woman had been a bit of a surprise, a bit of a shock. As the dawn approached I replayed her words in my mind. She'd been sitting there all through the interview like a statue, saying nothing, and then suddenly she was leaning forward and speaking fluent Newharp. She was good at it too— she still had a bit of an Earth accent and some of her slang was ancient, but the way she was going on, you'd think she'd been born on Newharp. And what she said was totally unexpected.

"You tell young Neddy boy here that there are about half a dozen arrest warrants out for him. Arson; illegal use; people smuggling; breaking his good behavior bond and a few other things besides. Every cit cruiser and chopper operating in a five hundred kilometer radius has his mug shot taped to the dashboard. If the Alien Affairs mob offer him a job on the Moon, tell him he'd better take it. Tell him to lie low up there for a few years. And for pete's sake, sister, tell him to stop howling—he's only drawing attention to himself. As for you and Harri—listen carefully to me—they can't send you back to Newharp, they simply haven't got the technology. But every time they grab a smuggler's runabout, they try to send as many refugees as possible back to the asteroid belt. Place of previous residence, got it? They send back the original mob but they also cram in as many more as they can ram through the door. Pack em in like sardines. So all these questions about Newharp are just a red herring as we say in English."

"A red fish?" I said.

"No, no," Ms. Harrison said. "A smoke screen, a way of lulling you into a sense of false security. You spend an hour or two telling them what a dangerous place Newharp is and then they just ask you a casual question about the asteroid belt. And you tell them it wasn't too bad. Bang! They've got you. So what you've got to do is convince them that you'd be in real danger from the local smugglers if you went back there. Tell them your lives would be in total danger on the asteroid belt. Got that? Never mind about Newharp. Now, say something to me—anything—this has got to sound like a dialogue—they think we're discussing grammar."

I said, "How do you know Ned?"

"I was at school with the little lout. God, what a yobbo. Giving cheek to the teachers, putting dead rabbits in the principal's pigeon hole. Dead pigeons in the deputy principal's exhaust pipe. Come home time and the old girl piles into her Dogstar, guns the motor and there's this gawdalmighty bang and a dead bird is sticking beak-first into the school letter box. Bulls-eye. Then there was the time when he...but I won't go on, it would take all day. Say something again."

Suddenly I couldn't think of anything to say. "Err...umm.... My forebears roamed Earth's gladsome glades. I seek that I might greet their shades."

"Bloody brilliant. Now about ethnic cleansing. It's a filthy phrase. It means mass murder."

Then Ms. Harrison sat back and said to Ms. Ashmore in English, "I think Emceesquared understands now—there was just a bit of vocab mix up—and some trouble with declension."

"Ah, yes," said Ms. Ashmore, "I thought as much. Declension. That can be tricky—declension."

"Too right it can," Ms. Harrison said and didn't say anything for the rest of the interview.

Ned Talking

God. Bloody Sue-Ellen. The way she went on about me being a regular delinquent at school, you'd think she'd been some sort of teachers' pet. Don't believe it, reader, don't you bloody believe it.

* * * * * * *

We'd found this spot, me and Harri and Em. It was down near the perimeter fence. There were a couple of ratshit little trees and a few smooth boulders. You could sit on the boulders in the shade of the trees and look at the desert. It was a pity that there were the two huge fences between you and the desert, but you can't have everything. We reckoned it was safe enough during daylight hours. We never went there at night. We took to talking to each other, there wasn't much else to do. And because I spent so long being silent, playing the dumbo, things used to build up inside me. When I was alone with Em, sitting on the boulders, stuff used to come pouring out, stuff I'd never talked about before. Even Harri, Mr. Doom n" Gloom himself, talked—occasionally.

One day, when just me and Em were sitting on the larger boulder, she said. "Tell me about your home town, this Tidy place. Why is it called that?"

"Because it's a shit-heap," I said.

"I don't understand."

"In the old days," I said, "before the Economic Ice Age, there was this Tidy Towns competition. These judges used to come round and look at your town and if it was real neat and had flowers planted outside the Mothers and Babies, then maybe you won the prize and got to put up a sign."

"What sort of sign?"

"Well, you know, a sign that said, *Welcome to Hixsville— winner of the Tidy Town Award for 2128,* Something like that. Then tourists would stop their cars and buy milk shakes. The local economy boomed."

"And your town won?"

"No," I said, "It never bloody won. Year after year someone would ram a few geraniums into the dirt outside the Mothers and Babies. And some other citizen would organize a working bee to clean the windows in the Main Street. And they'd slap a bit of paint around—that sort of thing. But it was a complete waste of time. The judges would rock in, sneer at the geraniums and go around picking up bits of paper and ice-cream sticks and putting them in the bin for all to see. Click! Some reporter took a photo. The local paper ran a pic of the judges cleaning up the town. (That's the local paper of some rival town, you understand). Then the judges would piss off. A few weeks later you'd read in your own local paper that some burg called Whoop Whoop had won the competition. You know: some miserable joint full of tight-arsed litter-pickeruppers. Or maybe it was full of bribers. The people in my town got jack of the whole thing. So they changed the name."

"They changed the town's name to Tidy Town?"

"They changed it to *Winner of This Year's Tidy Town Award* and whacked up a huge sign. Tourists stopped by the wagon load. Brilliant!"

"But what happened when the tourists saw what a mess the place really was?"

"Too late. Some kid had let the air out of their tires. So old man Tourist had to buy hamburgers and chips for the whole family while McLoggin's Auto Service took their time fixing the 'punctures.' Talk about prosperity! Civic pride, Em. Motivation. Service with a smile. Tidy Town had the lot. Those were the Golden Years of Tidy Town—I done a project on the Golden Years when I was in Year Four."

"They taught you this in school?"

"My oath they did. I got a gold star for my project."

"I'd love to visit your town, Ned. Even if it is a shit heap."

"Well," I said, "it's gone down hill since the Golden Years. We will not see their like again. And that's a fact."

"Why not?" Em said.

"Word got out."

"So no one was fooled by the sign anymore?"

"No. Word got out to all the other no-hoper towns around the place. They all changed their names. There were fifty or sixty Tidy Towns scattered around the desert. Scarcity-value went down the tubes. I done that in my project. You've gotta be unique to be a winner. Stand out from the herd."

"Have you got parents, Ned?"

"Eh?" I said.

"Have you got parents," Em said. "It's a simple question."

"Yeah, sure," I said. "I've got parents. Everybody's got

parents."

"You never talk about them," Em said.

"What is there to say?" I said.

"I don't know," Em said. "There must be something."

I was quiet for a while. I thought perhaps Em would start to talk about her own parents or something. But Em was as quiet as I was. The silence went on and on. Finally I said, "My dad's a pisspot and my Mum's the town bike. All right?"

"Forgive me...."

"Yeah, I forgive you," I said. "But did you understood what I just said?"

"I can guess," Em said. "Your father drinks a lot of hooch. Your mother drives a pedicab."

"A what?"

"They are an improvement on rickshaws," Em said. "More humane. And they go faster too. You're not the only one who's done projects at school—I did one on The Conveyances of Earth."

"What on earth are you talking about?" I said.

"Pedicabs."

"Sounds like pederast," I said.

"What's that?" Em said.

"Don't ask," I said.

"No. I'm asking," Em said.

"If you must," I said.

"What is it, Ned? What's a pederast? That's not a word they taught me in Advanced."

"It's...it's...a bloke...called...Mr. Robinson."

"Robinson?"

"Yeah. He took an interest...."

"In?"

"Me."

"Tell me, Ned. Tell me now. Go on, before you freeze up. I bet you've never told anyone else...."

"Nothing to tell."

"Pigshit."

"Your English is improving...."

"Bugger the English. Tell me, Ned."

"You...you...you...said it."

"Said what?"

"Bugger."

"It's a word I learned from you," Em said. "They didn't teach that in Advanced either. I don't know what it means."

"It means.... It's just a word. We use it all the time."

"I know you use it all the time. What's it *mean*, Ned?"

"Two guys. Together."

"Anal intercourse?"

"Yeah."

"So who was he? This Robinson?"

"Ran the club. Ran the church. Ran the Junior Purists. The Reverend Mr. Robinson. Call me Rob. Only when we're together, you understand."

"Did you? Did you call him Rob?"

"Never called him anything. Not when we were together."

"So he...buggered you? Is that how you say it?"

"Yeah. That's how we say it."

"Did your parents know?"

"No."

"So every week they sent you off to this club? This church...."

"No. I went to spite them."

"Spite who?"

"Spite my parents. They hated the church. Not hated it exactly. Reckoned it was full of wankers. Holy rollers, they called them. So I went to the club to spite them...."

"What did they say?"

"Didn't say much. My dad was too drunk. And my mum was earning a quid."

"She kept the family going?"

"Sort of."

"Driving the pedicab?"

"What fuckin pedicab? She was the town bike! I've told you, Em. She was the town bike."

"I don't understand, Ned. My English."

"Yeah. Sorry. Your English...it's better than my alien."

"What's the town bike, Ned?"

"My mum rooted blokes for money. Get it?"

"Rooted is slang for fucked?"

"You got it."

"Oh, Ned, mate."

"Oh, Em, mate."

"But this Robinson...he raped you?"

"Sort of. I didn't resist. He used the oilerlife."

"Gemco?"

"Yeah. That's one of its uses. Sexual lubricant."

"How often?"

"Dunno. Didn't count. It went on for about a year. Friday nights. After the Junior Purists."

"There are fifty-two weeks in an Earth year."

"That would be about right."

"But you kept going back to the club?"

"Yeah, that's the funny thing, isn't it? I hated it, but I kept going back."

"For fifty-two times?"

"Give or take."

"It's a lot more than Harri...."

"What?" I said. "What's a lot more than Harri?"

"What I'm saying, Ned, is that it happened a lot more to you than it happened to Harri."

"Harri?"

"Why do you think Harri goes on about protecting me from rape all the time. Sort of makes a sick joke of it?"

"Dunno."

"He can't talk about himself. Sort of...of...oh Christ, Ned. I wish you spoke Newharp. I can express myself properly in Newharp."

"Sorry."

"What I'm saying is that Harri can't talk about what happened when the pirates boarded the transport. It was when we were in orbit around Castor. Harri is...*displacing*...is that a word? He is displacing his feelings. It's not me he should be worried about. It's himself."

"They came on board? These pirates?"

"Yeah, the people smugglers let them. Afterwards the smugglers said they'd had no choice. The pirates would have blasted us otherwise. You know, punctured the skin. Let all the air out. So the smugglers just let them in—operated the airlocks for them. The pirates looted the luggage, took as many cold fusion pellets as they could find, raped a few people, killed one old guy who kicked up a fuss and left. They took a couple of girls with them. Smith Mei Lim's daughter, Tiger Lilly, and a girl called Jasmine. The smugglers just shrugged. They'd seen it all before. Maybe they really did have no choice. Or maybe they were in league with the pirates, were getting their percentage of the loot. Who knows? Maybe the chief pirate was the chief smuggler's brother. Maybe not."

"And you? You were all right?"

"Yeah. I hid. Harri wasn't so lucky."

"Jesus, Em."

"Jesus, Ned."

I looked at the wire and the desert beyond. On the horizon were some low hills. At dusk they went all purple and soft, but now they were just desert outcrops, hard and bleak. Summer would come soon, the heat would make them shimmer. There would be times when the heat haze would wipe them out completely. Closer to us, say five kilometers away, was some sort of bridge. I'd no idea what it was doing there. It was just a bridge in the middle of a dry landscape, ridged with dunes.

I said to Em, "So, tell me about Cicero d'Pettitt. How come you knew him on Newharp?"

"He worked in the local nonhydronic."

"The what?"

"Nonhydronic cleaning shop. They clean clothes without water, just chemicals."

"Dry cleaners. You're telling me that guy was a dry cleaner?"

"The shop was a front, Ned. What do you reckon?"

"Drugs?"

"That sort of thing. Half the bottles of dry cleaning fluid were full of controlled substances."

"So how did you get to know him?"

"I had this rather snappy little pants-suit. I spilt purple juice all over it. I took it to the nonhydronic."

"And Cicero offered you a sniff of one of his bottles?"

"He asked me out."

"You didn't?"

"This was a few years ago. We were both younger. Although he was about...let me work it out...four Earth years older than me. I thought he was rather glamorous. And he was, in those days. He was just a bit wild. He wasn't hard. He was just—you know—a bit like you."

"Me?"

"Well, you're no angel, Ned."

"And you went out together?"

"Sort of. My parents wouldn't have let me. Me being...these sums drive me mad...about fourteen and him being about eighteen. So I had to pretend I was going somewhere with Harri— but we just bumped into Cicero and his sister. And we sort of split up—Harri and Miranda went one way and Cicero and I went the other."

I didn't want to hear about this. It was the last thing I wanted to hear. But I asked anyway. "So what happened?"

"Not a lot. He only tried to get—you know—*serious* the third time we went out. But then the next week they took him away. And that was that."

"Who took him away?"

"Correction and Control. Cicero got a bit confused in the nonhydronic—the dry cleaners. He cleaned a lady's jumper with the wrong fluid. The lady went home, took the jumper out of the plastic bag and pulled it over her head. It was saturated with the stuff. She was zonked for six hours. Rolling around on the floor with her head in the jumper, seeing lions with two tails and no heads, seeing time running backwards, hearing the voices of the Ancestors prophesying doom. When she came to her senses she started screaming for Correction and Control. They went round to the nonhydronic and had a field day. They carted Cicero away and put him in Re-Education for a year or so. When he came out he was harder—you know—wiser. He'd learned stuff in Re-Ed, but not what they were trying to teach him."

"Re-Ed's a jail?"

"It's not a Sunday school."

"So he must feel right at home here."

"He says this place is the softest institution he's ever been in. He says it's a holiday camp."

"Well, I'm keen to get out of it," I said.

"Me too," Em said, "but unless we get refugee status we'll need money to bribe our way out."

"And money-bags d'Pettitt will provide?"

"Maybe."

I didn't say anything. But I reckoned there must be better ways of getting out of the place than selling your soul to Cicero d'Pettitt. I started looking at the fence in earnest, watching the dogs.

Em Talking

That was a bit traumatic, a bit heavy. Yesterday Ned brought the text round to my place himself, (normally we just bat the stuff to and fro in the ether). He was looking a bit haunted. He said he hadn't slept at all, he said he'd spent the night suffering flashbacks. We sat in the minor sunlight in my courtyard and drank coffee laced with silverberry. It was a bit early for the silverberry, normally we don't drink the stuff until the major sun has risen, but Ned insisted. He was showing his age—grey hair suits him, but suddenly I looked at my friend and thought, hell, the guy is old, he's going to die soon. And so am I. I told Ned to write something happy next time, but he said we'd just do the memoir as it came to us, in the proper chronological order. But he said he was looking forward to the bit about destroying the runabouts.

"I'm doing the runabouts, Em. I bags it."

"OK," I said. "I'll do some more Cicero."

"You're welcome to him. More than welcome."

* * * * * * *

Cicero d'Pettitt was lounging around up the back of my class. Now that the weather was turning hot and hotter he'd taken to wearing an Earth t-shirt with *Souvenir of Jackson's Port* printed on it; almost as if he had already been there. The sinews and muscles of his arms rippled when he stretched and stifled a yawn.

Me, teaching English to Cicero. It was a strange feeling. All my feelings about Cicero were strange. I wondered if he really wanted to learn English, or if he was in my class for other reasons. His presence wasn't making my job any easier. The last thing I wanted to do was make a fool of myself in front of Cicero. I had no idea how to teach English. All the language acquisition I'd done on Newharp had been with instant response didact machines. I'd grown quite fond of my English teacher in Advanced. Just to tease it, I had occasionally called it Towser, pretending it was a dog. It had been well programmed—at first it created a terrible fuss, going on about incorrect nomenclature and category mistakes. Then some playful sub-routine kicked in and it took to calling me Tabby or Tabbither and enquiring about fleas.

But there was none of that in Camp Spearchucker. It was all pretty basic. They'd given me a thing called a white board and a crude pen with a felt nib. And that was it. I was meant to teach English by writing by hand on this white board thing, and by talking directly to my "students". They were all older than me and most of them spoke no Newharp and little or no English. I was reduced to pointing at things: *this is a table, say*

"table". That's right, now this is a chair, all together, "chair".
I was surprised that Cicero joined in, it was so childish, but he did, he said "table" and "chair" along with all the rest. Halfway through the lesson I asked him a direct question.

"Cicero, how many fingers am I holding up?"

"Three, Miss."

"Don't call me Miss and use a complete sentence."

"What is 'complete?'"

"Full, proper, whole."

"You three fingers are holding up, Em."

"Not quite—You are holding up three fingers."

"No I am not. You are the holder finger girl."

"I'm talking about word order. Now someone else—you, Mr. umm de la Haye, how many fingers am I holding up?"

But poor old Mr. de la Haye was a bit out of it. He looked at me blankly for a few seconds and then said "four" in Kovalev.

"Wrong language," I said. "See if you can do it in English."

But he couldn't. So I spent ten minutes making sure every-body could count to ten.

"O.K." I finally said in English. "I'll see you all tomorrow. Same time, same place."

Three or four of the students pushed their chairs back and started to stand up. They'd understood me. As for the rest, I could have been telling them to bang their heads together—but they quickly took their cue from the first three and stood up too. I started to clean my white board with a foul smelling liquid I'd been told to use. When I turned round, one of my students was still sitting there. I'd half suspected he might be.

"You're a good teacher, Em," Cicero said.

"It's funny," I said. "Me being younger than everyone else."

"You were enjoying yourself—you were enjoying the power."

"It passes the time, Cicero. We've got a lot of time on our hands here."

"Here?" Cicero said. "We've always had time on our hands—here is nothing new."

"At home I was never still," I said. "There was never enough time in the day."

"Do you miss it—home?"

"What do you reckon?"

"We go back a long way—you and I," Cicero said.

"I only knew you for a couple of weeks before they shoved you into Re-Ed," I said.

"Those couple of weeks were a long time ago, a long way back."

"What are you getting at?"

"We understand each other, Em."

"I wouldn't be so sure," I said.

"The time will come when we get out of here."

"I hope so," I said.

"We could make it big in Jackson's Port."

"We? In a sweatshop?"

"Oh come on, Em. You're not sweatshop material. You know that."

"So what do you suggest I do?"

"I'll need a partner," Cicero said.

I looked at him and I felt the same tug, the same weakness at the knees, that I'd felt when I'd first met him in the nonhydronic. I could feel my heart. To give myself a bit of time to breath, I turned round and wrote the word *partner* on the white board. First in Newharp, then in English.

"It doesn't matter which language you use," Cicero said.

"The word is ambiguous in both languages," I said. "There are partners and partners."

"Sure," said Cicero.

"What sort had you in mind?" I said.

"Any sort you want," Cicero said. "All sorts."

"Cicero, I didn't come all this way to be a gangster's moll."

"I'm a businessman," Cicero said. "In Jackson's I'll need a business associate. I'll also need a wife."

"I'm only sixteen or seventeen or something."

"That's the trouble with Earth years," Cicero said, "They make you sound too old. Past it."

"It wouldn't work," I said. "We both know that."

"It could work very well."

"I'm not saying I'm not tempted...."

"Don't say anything at all," Cicero said. "Think about it." And then he changed the subject abruptly. "Why did you collect that little Earthling?"

"What Earthling?"

"The one you claim is your brother or cousin or whatever. I'm told you picked him up in the desert."

"You shouldn't listen to rumors."

"That twangling woman, Smith Mei Lim, says you argued that he would be useful for getting refugee status, that he'd know all the right answers. What would that little runt know about anything?"

"He looked lost," I said. "He was shivering. And he was in some sort of trouble."

"He'll be in a lot more trouble if he goes into the fermentation business," Cicero said.

"What are you talking about?"

"The Earth-boy and your brother—your real brother—have been knocking off canola oil and sugar from the kitchens."

"They're both on washing up duty," I said.

"They're both walking out of the kitchens every day with half a litre of oil and a packet of sugar stuffed under their tunics."

"They must have their reasons."

"There's only one reason, Em. Domestic gemco and sugar are the raw materials of all the hooch brewed in this camp. Listen to me, Em, the moonshine scene is heavy. It's run by very heavy dudes who aren't partial to competition. You tell those two idiots to pack it in, before someone else decides to use a bit of persuasion."

I was suddenly very angry. If Harri and Ned had hatched some halfwit scheme to make hooch, they'd no right to do it without telling me. I looked at Cicero. He was just sitting there, leaning back in his chair, all dark and hard and menacing and desirable and knowing exactly what he'd just done: he'd put me in his debt by telling me about this hooch business.

"Well thanks for telling me," I said.

"Pleasure," Cicero said standing up. "I've got to talk to a man about a dog. Take care, Em. Think about what I said." And then he put his hand on my shoulder and kissed me like the Earth people do, straight on the lips. "When on Earth...," he said and left the room.

I sat in the classroom for five minutes, trying to get calm. Then I went in search of Ned and Harri. I found them coming out of the kitchens. "What's all this about hooch?" I said to Harri in Newharp.

"What's what about hooch?" he said.

"I'm told you two are pilfering gemco and sugar."

"Not so loud, Em."

"This is really dumb," I said.

"Everybody pilfers," Harri said. "A bit here a bit there."

"Everybody doesn't try to muscle in on the moonshine trade."

"We're not muscling...."

"We are *borrowing*," Ned said in Newharp.

"Oh very good, Earth-boy," I said. "What else can you say?"

"The rivers sparkle, full of bream."

"Brilliant! Now, you listen to me. I don't know where you've got your still, but if you're caught brewing up hooch, or selling the stuff, the heavy boys will cut your toes off."

"We're not fermenting it," Harri said. "We are just collecting it, storing it."

"For what purpose?"

The two boys exchanged glances. Then Ned said in Newharp, "Insurance."

"Insurance against what?" I said.

"Insurance against...against...."

"Speak English if you have to," I said.

"The cold," Ned said in his own language.

"The gemco burns," Harri said. "And the sugar helps it along."

"Of course it burns," I said. "It's oil."

"Well, there you are then," Harri said.

"Look," I said. "Just promise me you are not moving into the hooch trade."

"We're not," they both said together.

I left them to it. I suppose I had to be grateful that they'd finally made friends with each other. What did they think they were going to do with their mixture of oil and sugar when the cold came round again? Rub it all over their bodies? The place was so hot at the moment I could hardly imagine the winter ever coming again. But it would. The Earth goes hurtling round its sun every three hundred and sixty five days. It makes you giddy just to think of it. The seasons flash past like the blades of a windmill. I suppose you get more birthdays that way—I'd be seventeen or eighteen soon. God, what a life.

Ned Talking

Harri and I were sitting on the rocks under the trees, saying nothing to each other. On the other side of the double fence, the desert extended to the far hills, shimmering slightly in the afternoon light. The desert was endlessly ribbed with dunes, but it had one other feature. About five kilometers away stood the bridge. It was just there, in the middle of the sand for no good reason, looking a bit fragile in the haze. The ground appeared to swell up on either side, like ramps. Then there was the bridge in the middle. You could see straight under it, straight to the shimmering hills beyond.

"Stupid place to build a bridge," I said.

"It's not a bridge," Harri said. He was just stating a fact.

"Looks like a bridge to me," I said.

There was silence for a minute or so. I watched some ants on the ground. They were moving grains of sand around. They seemed to know what they were doing. Then Harri said, "Yeah, it's a bridge. Of sorts."

"Stupid place to build it," I said again.

"I'm being poetic," Harri said. He spoke like he was

explaining the bleeding obvious to a moron.

"You reckon it's a poetic bridge?" I said.

Harri was silent for another minute, then he said, "It's an old launch pad. This place used to be a rocket facility, remember? It's a bridge into space."

I looked at the thing for a while. It looked so unreal in the shimmering haze. You'd think twice about walking across it. "How do you know its a launch pad?" I said.

"That's what they used to look like. We did old Earth history at school, it was full of stuff like *The Departure*. The Ancestors probably blasted off from this very place. They did that in those days: blasted off. The ships ran on hydrogen and oxygen—a mad way to make things move. They just put the two gasses together and ignited them under the craft. Bang, whoosh, zoom, away the thing went. Up and up. But even the oxygen and hydrogen weren't enough, they had solid boosters as well. Just strapped onto the side. You know, giant fireworks—things you'd let off on Ancestor Day only bigger. This whole place would have shuddered, Ned, it would have shook like an earthquake when those things took off. Flames, smoke, more noise than a volcano—all to get a pissfarting little rocket into space. And the poor people inside, the Ancestors, praying and shuddering, yelling at their gods to keep them alive."

I'd never heard Harri talk so much. This was the longest speech he'd ever made in English. Even in Newharp he didn't talk much. This was amazing. I said, "But they got all the way to Newharp in those things—those mad machines."

"God, no," Harri said. "They'd still be traveling. Those old crates didn't exactly shift. The planet they were aiming for, the first one they knew to have proper conditions—you know, breathable atmosphere, not too hot, not too cold, plenty of water—that planet, when they got there, was already inhabited."

"Bummer."

"But the inhabitants were friendly. They sat the Ancestors down, educated them for a couple of generations, gave them a proper ship with hyper-c, a stella map, and sent them on their way."

"Good of them," I said.

"Oh everybody is really friendly, really charitable. The whole universe is full of friendly, charitable life forms."

You wouldn't have known it—not from the gloomy way Harri was speaking. But I said, "It restores your faith in human nature."

"Most of them aren't human," Harri said. "And it's in their nature to send refugees to some other planet. Any other planet. That's what charity is: finding someone else to deal with the problem. Even if it takes a couple of generations."

We slumped back into silence. When you're just sitting around in a detention center with nothing to do all day long, you get real tolerant of silence. I studied the ants some more. They were big buggers. The grains of sand they were shifting weren't really sand, were more like gravel. An alien in a Kovalev head scarf sat down beside us. She'd just appeared out of nowhere. She wore the scarf like a hood, you couldn't see much of her face. I wondered what she wanted. I knew Harri couldn't speak any Kovalev. This old girl would have to talk English or Newharp or we were stuffed. For a moment she said nothing, just looked across the desert to the launch pad, her face shielded by the cloth. Then she spoke in good Newharp, although her accent was a bit rough. You'd think she had a cold.

"A pleasant afternoon, gentlemen," she said. "Although a trifle warm."

"Rain wanted," I said in Newharp.

The woman spoke some more, but this time I couldn't understand her. I looked at Harri, but Harri wasn't speaking.

"Jesus, Ned," the woman said in English, "You're a slow learner. All I said was, 'The rain in Spain falls mainly on the plain.' Put in a bit more effort, why don't you?"

"Sue-Ellen!"

"Not so loud."

"What are you doing here?"

"Having an illegal conversation with a couple of aliens—I'm

not meant to fraternize."

"Why not?"

"Because I might start rumors. I might spill the beans. I might get into compromising situations, that sort of thing. They don't exactly trust me—I am married to a Newharpian after all."

"And how is Prince Charming?" I said.

"To the best of my knowledge he's fine. He lives in Jackson's Port. And his name is Astolphe Scott-Wok."

"God," said Harri speaking for the first time, "*that* family."

"A pillar of Newharp society," Sue Ellen said.

"That's one way of putting it," Harri said.

"Have you and Prince Charming split up?" I said.

"We spend time apart," Sue-Ellen said.

"So where's your baby?" I said.

"With me, in the staff quarters."

"You're a single mum really, aren't you Sue-Ellen? With an alien baby. Just like your mum said you'd be."

"The old bitch."

"Actually she thinks you're dead," I said. "She thinks the aliens ate you."

"I know," Sue-Ellen said. "I sent her an anonymous email to that effect. I said how tasty I'd been. Yum yum."

"Really, Ms. Harrison," Harri said. "Starting those sorts of rumors...."

"I know, I know," Sue-Ellen said. "I shouldn't have done it. It just fans the flames of prejudice etcetera etcetera. But I wasn't feeling very stable at the time. Mother-daughter relations are tricky things." Then she turned to me and said, "And how is Tidy, by the way. The same old dump?"

"Pretty much," I said, and we started to gossip.

Sue-Ellen and I were in agreement on one thing: neither of us wanted to go back to Tidy—ever. We were well out of the place, even if we were stuck in an aliens' detention center. But then we spent an awful lot of time yarning about the old town, talking about mates from school, wild nights at the Ice Field. I'd never hung out with Sue-Ellen's mob, the age difference was too great.

But I knew what they'd been up to since she ran off with the alien. And I told Sue-Ellen about the time Johnny Wannamarra and I had stumbled on a hooch still and just had to sample the brew. Harri started to yawn. Suddenly Sue-Ellen noticed the length of the trees' shadows and said, "Look, I didn't come here to gossip."

"Oh really?" Harri said.

"No, I came here to spread rumors. I've got to go."

"So, what's the rumor?" Harri said.

"The cits have captured no less than five runabouts. They all came in at once. And the cits were waiting, hiding in the misery busses. They went storming onboard like rats up a drainpipe."

"The smugglers must be pissed off," I said.

"The smugglers have done a deal—they always do."

"And the deal is...."

"The deal is that the cits hang on to two of the runabouts as insurance while the smugglers use the other three to empty the camps."

"Camps?" I said.

"This isn't the only one, you know."

"What do you mean by *empty?*"

"I mean empty. They run a shuttle service. They ship everyone back to the asteroid belt. Everyone. No one gets refugee status. If the smugglers do a good job, they get the other two ships back."

"But we told the interview panel," I said. "We told that Ashmore woman. Em fell down on the floor. We can't...I mean Harri and Em can't...."

"They'll just say they are shipping you back to a different asteroid," Sue-Ellen said. "It's a big place by all accounts, the belt. Millions of asteroids."

"Is this actually true?" Harri said. "About the five smugglers' craft?"

"Look, I was there when the deal was made," Sue-Ellen said. "I'm an interpreter, remember,"

"So it's not just a rumor," Harri said.

"It's gospel," Sue-Ellen said.

"Listen," I said. "We want out. Me and Harri and Em—we want out of this joint. And we want out to Jackson's Port, not out to some rock in the sky."

"Then you'd better start a riot. Make a bit of noise. Assert yourselves. Stop sitting around on your bums all day doing nothing."

"Have you got a car?" I said. "How do you get back to Jackson's Port when you go on leave?"

"Now you listen, Neddy-boy. If I'm caught with aliens onboard, I get done for people smuggling. And there's no way I could do a deal—I couldn't ship anybody back to the asteroid belt in my car. I'd be looking at two years hard. Minimum."

"But you do have a car?"

"I don't usually walk to Jackson's."

"What sort?"

"It's got wheels and an engine—it goes."

"What sort, Sue-Ellen?"

"It's a Gamma Crux."

I nearly fell off the ground. A Gamma Crux, a G-cross! Sue-Ellen hadn't bought that on her interpreter's pay. I said, "A present from Prince Charming?"

"Astolphe doesn't want me and Helen broken down in the desert in some old crock, does he?"

"Who's Helen?"

"My daughter."

"The alien baby?"

"That's right, Neddy-boy. The alien baby."

"Jeeze," I said. "In a G-cross we won't need roads. We'll just blaze away straight through the desert...."

"It's not on, Ned...."

"...That way we'll avoid the roadblocks."

"That way we'd be a sitting duck for every chopper in the skies, numbskull."

"They'll be concentrating on the riot. All the choppers will be swarming around here."

"When I said you ought to start a riot," Sue-Ellen said, "I meant you should start a strong protest, something designed to reach a peaceful, political resolution to the crisis."

"Jeeze, Sue-Ellen, remember that Year Four kid you took out with a rock? Protesting about your mum's idea of lunch?"

"I've grown up since then. You ought to grow up too, Ned. Now, I've got to go."

And Sue-Ellen was gone, wrapping the Kovalev headgear around her. Slinking away like any refugee.

"We're not going back to the asteroid," Harri said, flat as a tack but meaning every word.

"Too right we're not," I said.

"You can't go back, Ned. You've never been there."

"And I'm going to keep it that way," I said.

We both looked at the desert behind the fences. There was a Rottweiler in the gap, just standing looking at us. After a couple of minutes, Harri said, "Ms. Harrison's right. You should put in a bit more effort."

"At Newharp?"

"I'll teach you. We'll do an hour a day. Translate this: the big black dog was rotten and viler."

"Give over, Harri."

"Do it, Ned."

It wasn't very hard. The only word I didn't already know in Newharp was *viler*. By tea time I knew that and a whole lot more.

"Enough for today," Harri said. "We've got to go and start a rumor."

But, of course, I had no part in starting the rumor. I was officially dumb. Harri and Em did all the work. They told one or two people and away it went. They say rumor spreads like wildfire. Rubbish—wild fires are orderly things, we get them sometimes in the canola stubble, they spread in the direction of the wind. Not this little rumor. It was all over the place in seconds—an explosion. Chow-down was something else again. Every table was buzzing, that's the word, buzzing. The normal jabber jabber jabber was replaced by buzz. But it was an anxious, angry buzz. People flitted from table to table, whispering in ears. Cicero d'Pettitt was in on the act. He was whispering two bob to the dozen. Light on his feet, appearing at one shoulder and whispering, gesticulating with a nod of his head, slipping away to whisper over the shoulder of another anxious looking alien. God knows what he was saying, but his dark eyes were alight. I reckon he reckoned there was a newbuck or two in it for him.

By the end of the meal a delegation had been formed—about a dozen aliens from half a dozen planets. They were mainly oldsters. Cicero wasn't part of the delegation, but then he didn't strike me as the delegate type—more your back room wheeler and dealer. But the oldsters needed somebody to speak for them, so old boy Sam Yang Rhee came over to our table and started talking very seriously to Em. I even understood a word or two—more than that, I understood whole sentences: they wanted the best English speaker in the camp to come with them. It was a privilege. Em just nodded, the nod of somebody who knew her time had come. And then off the whole mob trooped to confront Ashmore and her mates, a weird looking bunch in all sorts of clobber. The mess hall went a bit quiet—there was no point in whispering now, all anybody could do was wait for the return of the delegation. In the silence Smith Mei Lim started to twangle. And no one kicked up a fuss. The hall went even quieter—people were listening to the stuff as if it held some sort of answer. There was a bit of absent minded foot tapping. Normally when Mei Lim tried twangling in the mess hall there were howls and cat calls, usually from the Kovalevs, always from me. The Kovalevs reckoned Newharp music sounded like gurgling drains. They weren't far wrong. You could build up a bit of sympathy for the Kovalevs—until you heard their own music. Live dogs played like bagpipes. Well, maybe not quite, I never enquired too closely. You'd see them up there on the stage, you wouldn't want to go and investigate. We waited.

Em Talking

As we were walking across the camp to the administration block Mr. Sam Yang Rhee said to me, "This is a heavy responsibility that has been placed on your shoulders, Em. Your linguistic skills have given you a role not normally allotted to a girl of your years."

I knew what the old boy was getting at: my job at this meeting was to faithfully translate the sayings of my elders and betters. I wasn't to engage in direct negotiation myself. I thought it best to reassure him.

"Ms. Harrison is very fluent in Newharp," I said. It might not be necessary for me to say anything at all."

"That might be best," Mr. Sam Yang Rhee said. "But please make a mental note of everything that the authorities say to each other in English, you can tell us afterwards."

"Will do," I said. Obedient little girl that I was.

We were shown into the interview room—the same one in which I'd thrown my fit. There were seven or eight Camp staff on one side of the table. I recognized Ms. Harrison, Ms. Ashmore and the chap called Dr Wilkinson, the man who had lectured us on the ways of dealing with rogue comets. Some of our party sat on the other side of the table. The rest of us stood behind them. Someone tried to offer a seat to Mr. Sam Yang Rhee, but he said he preferred to stand. I could see his point. If he sat down, he wouldn't be able to see me. As it was he stood next to me, shoulder to shoulder. On the other side of the table Ms. Ashmore appeared to be in command. She welcomed us in English and Ms. Harrison translated the welcome into the four main languages used in the camp. I shifted my weight from one foot to the other. If everything had to be said five times over, we were in for a long day. Ms. Ashmore said she understood that some unfortunate rumors had been flying around the camp—she would let Ms. Harrison explain to us how baseless these rumors were. She sat back and nodded to Ms. Harrison. Oh good, I thought, we are down to a mere four languages.

I'll say this for Ms. Harrison, she's a cool customer, very cool indeed. Sometimes she spoke in Newharp, sometimes in reasonable Kovalevese, sometimes she spoke in simple Hydralinga, sometimes in a slow version of Skyroan. And all the time she was preaching reassurance, pouring oil on troubled waters, calming fears. No, there was no truth in the rumors. No, it was not the case that five smugglers' runabouts had been captured. Five? she said smiling. You people know the smugglers better than I do—would they be so stupid as to land five craft at once? Put all their eggs in one basket? No, it wasn't the case that anybody was scheduled to be deported to the asteroid belt. Here on Earth, she said, we believe in due process. Does anybody know what due process is? No? Look, let me explain. And explain she did. At length in all the languages she knew. Look, she told us, all your appeals for refugee status were being considered by the proper authorities in Jackson's Port—it would be quite improper for anything to happen until the judgments have been handed down. And then, of course, there was always the appeal process. Those of you who have been here longer than most, you know about the appeal process, don't you? Some of you may, even at this moment, be appealing against the appeal process. Appeals go on and on. It's all called due process. The very foundations of Earth's many legal systems are built deep into the rock of due process. It is the basis of all we believe in. The suggestion of a mass deportation to the asteroid belt strikes at the very bedrock of civilized values—it could not happen.

That's right, I thought, it could not happen without due process. But who decides what due process is?

"So how come there are all these rumors?" I asked in English.

People turned to look at me, and then looked back at Ms. Harrison. But the interpreter didn't reply, she looked sideways at Ms. Ashmore who leaned forward and spoke instead. "You must realize, Ms. Gonzales della Harpenden, that a camp such as this is a breeding ground for...."

"...rabbits," I said.

"I'm sorry?" Ms. Ashmore said.

"You want to tell us that rumors breed like rabbits?"

"No...well...in a sense...yes."

"What is she saying?" Mr. Sam Yang Rhee said to me in Newharp. "Why this discussion of rabbits? Please just translate, Em. Let your elders do the talking."

"She's saying yes and no," I said in Newharp.

"Yes, I understood that much," Mr. Sam Yang Rhee said in Newharp. "Even I know the English for yes and no. Also the word for rabbit. But it is hardly helpful to talk about rabbits."

"Mr. Sam Yang Rhee says that this talk of rabbits is hardly helpful," I said to Ms. Ashmore.

"We are doing the best we can," Ms. Ashmore said. "And it was you, Ms. Gonzales della Harpenden, who started to talk about...."

"The point I am making," I said, "is that even rabbits don't just appear from nowhere. They don't just pop out of the ground."

"Do you actually *have* rabbits on Newharp, Ms. Gonzales della...."

"Certainly, the Ancestors brought a large selection of Earth fauna and flora with them. We have rabbits, but no elephants."

"Then you'll know that rabbits *do* just pop out of the ground. They do it all the time. One minute the field is empty, the next minute it is full of rabbits. Rumors are the same. They just appear from nowhere, nowhere at all."

"Someone must have started the rumor," I said. "Just like some rabbit in a hole has to have a mother and a father."

"Well, I assure you that no one from the Camp authorities is responsible. You should enquire amongst your own...."

"What is this crap?" said a Kovalev in his own language. At least, I think that's what he said.

Ms. Ashmore looked sideways at Ms. Harrison.

"The gentleman wishes to know the precise nature of our discourse," said Ms. Harrison.

"Tell him we are discussing the possible source of this most unfortunate and most untrue rumor. Tell him he has nothing to worry about."

Ms. Harrison spoke in Kovalev for a minute or so. I could only understand every second word, so I stopped trying. Instead I just looked at this Sue-Ellen Harrison woman, watched her gestures, watched her eyes, listened to the tone of her voice. She almost convinced me: she was so earnest, so reasonable, so open and honest. If Harri and Ned hadn't told me the source of the rumor, I would have believed everything she was saying—even though I couldn't understand Kovalev very well. It was funny to think that she and Ned had been at school together, even though Ned had been in some junior form when Ms. Harrison had been in the top form. Compared to the idiot boy, this woman was so well dressed, so mature, and she spoke Newharp so well. I wondered what her husband was like. Harri had said he was a Scott-Wok.

When Ms. Harrison had finished speaking I said in Newharp, "On behalf of my people, I must formally inform you that we don't trust a word you say, Ms. Harrison." Then I turned to Ms. Ashmore and said in English, "We have been told—that is to say, we have heard a rumor, that a deal has been struck with the people smugglers. The rumor says that Ms. Harrison here was the interpreter when the deal was made."

Ms. Ashmore threw up her hands and smiled. "Well that's rumor for you. In point of fact, Ms. Harrison hasn't been out of this camp since her last leave—over a month ago. I can vouch for that. And anyway, the Earth authorities never, ever make deals with people-smugglers."

"The people-smugglers could have been brought here," I said. "There is no reason why Ms. Harrison would have had to leave the camp."

"No the people smugglers could not have been brought here. If we catch smugglers we don't place them in detention centers like this one. We put them in proper jails—people smuggling is a criminal offence. But, I assure you, no smugglers have been arrested recently."

"If a deal was struck, they could have been released. You could have struck the deal and then sent the smugglers back to their crafts. To the *three* craft they have been allowed to keep."

"Could. Could. Could," said Ms. Ashmore, smiling. "All sorts of things could happen. The moon could be made of green cheese, but it isn't."

"What's this about cheese?" Mr. Sam Yang Rhee said to me. "Cheese is solid milk. Please *translate,* Em. That's why you are here, not to formally inform."

I spoke in Newharp to Mr. Sam: "Ms. Ashmore says the moon is not made of green cheese."

"But why are we talking about cheese? First rabbits, now cheese."

I spoke in English to Ms. Ashmore: "Mr. Sam Yang Rhee wants to know why are we talking about cheese."

"Ms. Gonzalez della Harpenden," Ms. Ashmore said, the smile gone, a look of weary seriousness on her face, "one could be forgiven for thinking that you are deliberately using your excellent command of the English language to confuse people."

"She thinks I am confusing you," I said to Mr. Sam Yang Rhee.

"You are," Mr. Sam Yang Rhee said.

"I am." I said to Ms. Ashmore.

"Well don't."

* * * * * * *

It took a fortnight for the rumor to die. But it did. There were no attempts to ship people back to the asteroid belt, no runabouts suddenly appeared in the desert outside the fence. Life in the camp returned to its old rhythms. Perhaps our delegation had been a success—perhaps we had shown the authorities that we would not go quietly and they'd thought better of it. Perhaps Ms. Harrison had made a mistake—although she had told Harri and Ned she'd been the interpreter when the deal was made. I supposed it was always possible that Ms. Harrison had started a false rumor for her own purposes. Maybe it had been a political stunt, something dreamed up by her husband. Starting rumors for political or commercial gain was an old Scott-Wok tradition. On Newharp the Scott-Woks are a very close knit family with a vast empire of interlocking businesses—some of which were quite respectable. There was always some Scott-Wok or other running for Mayor, or being forced to leave office because of a scandal.

"What do you reckon about Ms. Harrison's husband," I said to Harri in Newharp one evening when the three of us were sitting under the miserable little trees.

"She says he's a Scott-Wok," Harri said.

Ned said in English, "Stir-fried haggis?"

"What?" I said.

"It's what they eat," Ned said. "the Scots. It's worse than alien tuck."

"What are you on about?" I said. Very deliberately, I chose to speak in Newharp. I wanted to know how much the idiot boy could understand. Harri had said he'd been teaching him some simple phrases.

"I'm on about haggis," Ned said in English.

"What's haggis?" I said.

"They get these sheep," he said. "And they rip out their guts. And they fill the guts with barley and that sort of crap."

"Why?" Harri said.

"To eat."

"Oh yuk!" Harri said. He's got a weak stomach, my brother.

"Every culture has its own cuisine," I said, still talking in Newharp.

"I don't know what *cuisine* is," Ned said in English. "But I know what alien tucker is—especially when some halfwit plonks it down on my plate."

"You were hoeing in last night in the mess," I said. "You were heaping more on your plate."

"Yeah, but that was crispy fried nine-spice rolls," Ned said. "With tomato sauce."

"Alien tuck," I said.

"Tomato sauce!" Ned said. "My country was founded on

tomato sauce. It's heritage, it's our life blood. So what do you mean, alien tuck?"

"I'm talking about the crispy fried nine-spice...."

"Couldn't taste it," Ned said. "That's the beauty of tomato sauce. It smothers all taste. With enough tomato sauce you could eat roast dog."

"Yum," Harri said.

"Shut up, Harri," I said.

"Can't I ever express an opinion?" Harri said.

"No," I said.

"Just because you talk English better than anyone else, you think you're the queen of the universe," Harri said. "Mr. Sam Yang Rhee says you've got an exaggerated sense of your own importance. You are riding for a fall."

"Mr. Sam could learn proper English himself if he tried."

"It's not that easy," Harri said.

"Any fool can learn," I said. "Take Ned."

"Ned speaks English anyway," Harri said. "He was born here."

"Hey, Ned?" I said.

"Yeah?" he said.

"If I'm talking in Newharp all the time, why don't you reply to me in Newharp? Go on, talk to me in my own language."

"You don't talk to me in Newharp, Em."

"I haven't said a word in English for the last five minutes," I said.

"Well, bugger me," Ned said.

Ned Talking

If you ask me, dawn was the worst time of the day in the camp. All the color and movement of the night were gone. The day, any day, every day, dawned grim. If you wanted to look at something, your own feet were your best bet. If you looked around you just saw queues of bleary-eyed aliens stinking of sour alien BO waiting at the ablution blocks. Those guys who'd been on the hooch the night before were paying for it now. Hangover city. The rising sun sneered at the empty day ahead. Nothing to do. Not a lot to look at. Freedom and the joys of civilization never seemed further away. For me most of all. I needed out. I began to make serious plans.

Then, early one morning about six weeks after Sue-Ellen had started the rumor—which everyone had now forgotten—the place felt different. I noticed it the moment I stumbled out of Single Men's B. The queues of aliens were tense. People were speaking in whispers or not at all. And everyone was casting glances towards the rising sun. Squinting.

Bloody cits. The stupid bunnies had snuck the runabouts in at night, quiet as mice, but they'd gone and parked them just where the sun would make them into silhouettes the moment it came up. The runabouts were as plain as cardboard cutouts against a window. They were sitting there in the desert about two kilometers away—squat beasts with probes and disks sticking out—they could have been insects, or fat arse spiders sitting there, ready to pounce. And what's more, they weren't the only things lurking in the dunes, the authorities had brought in a heap of troops. Perhaps I was the only one to realize it. The army boys and girls were trying to keep a low profile, but the dunes weren't tall enough. You could see the flat tops of the troop carriers, see the aerials. Those babies weren't the sort of things the cits got around in—I knew who was skulking inside: real army guys with real guns and steel helmets and all sorts of military crap. I watched the scene for a while and then made my way to the ablutions block. There were half a dozen guys shaving at the open-air sinks outside the showers. I stood around, waiting my turn in the showers, listening to the mutterings between razor scrapes. Most of it was in Newharp, but there was a Hydrian present and a bit of the grunted conversation went on in lousy English. And it was lousy, I could understand more of the Newharp. But in both languages the message was the same. These guys would rather die than get back on board the runabouts. I reckoned we were in for a riot. Which suited me, suited me just fine.

Breakfast was tense. Em and Harri said next to nothing. I looked up from my alien hash and Cicero d'Pettitt was sitting opposite me. I hadn't heard him arrive, but there he was. He leaned across the table and said, "Listen, Earth-boy, I'm told you can drive."

I looked at him blankly.

"The time's coming when you'll have to learn to talk," Cicero said. "It's coming real soon."

"My cousin is a dumb mute," Em said. "I've told you that. He's brain damaged."

"He might have the brain of a worm," Cicero said, cold and pleasant, "but you picked him up in the desert, and he can talk perfectly well. I've heard you and him talking. In English."

"Take it easy, Cicero," Em said.

"He speaks English, and he understands Newharp," Cicero said to Em. And then he turned to me, "Don't you, Earth-boy?"

I still looked at him blankly.

"Don't you, Earth boy?" Cicero said again.

There seemed no point in playing dumb any more. And anyway, I suddenly realized I had a bargaining chip. Cicero's remark about being able to drive wasn't just idle chatter. Harri had told me about the sort of crates they drove on Newharp. They sounded wicked, but the controls were all different. There was nothing to do with your feet, Harri said, no clutch, no accelerator, no brake. You could put your feet up on the dash if you wanted to. And there wasn't much to do with your hands either. You basically drove the things by talking to them—computers and crap did the rest. So, blow me down, here I was surrounded by all these hard guys from outer space, and none of the poor saps could drive. Wouldn't have a clue. If poor old Cicero piled into a hot wired vehicle in the middle of a riot he'd have no chance. You wouldn't want to stamp on the accelerator if you were going for the brake, would you? You wouldn't want to slam the cogs into reverse if you had the horizon in your sights.

"If I drive the getaway car," I said to Cicero in a mixture of Newharp and English, "What's in it for us?"

"Us?"

"Me and Harri and Em?"

"You get out of here," Cicero said, "that's what's in it for you. And you get gainful employment in Jackson's Port."

"In a sweatshop?"

"In a sweatshop, Earth boy."

"I was sort of thinking of a managerial position," I said.

"Then you might be thinking about the asteroid belt," Cicero said. "You could be the manager of the sludge converters in a smuggler's plexidome."

"And what have you got to offer?" I said. "How are you going to pay for your ticket in the getaway car?"

"With newbucks," Cicero said.

"Are you sure you've got enough newbucks?" I said. "I charge top-dollar for my driving services."

"You charge nothing for your lousy under-age driving," Cicero said. "All I'm using my newbucks for is bribing the guards. No one gets out of the staff carpark in a borrowed Gamma Crux without paying for a few blind eyes. And you three have got no cash." He looked hard at each of us in turn, and then said, smooth and friendly, "But don't let that worry you, you can pay me back in Jackson's Port. I'll extend you credit."

"Are we talking variable rates of interest," Em said.

"We're talking market forces," Cicero said.

"Seems we've got no choice," Harri said.

Cicero leaned back in his seat and smiled. "Oh, you've got a choice all right, Harri," he said. "You've got a choice between deportation to the asteroid belt and the pleasures of Jackson's Port."

And with that, Cicero d'Pettitt was gone on his cat feet.

"Imagine sharing a car ride with that guy," I said. "The world's greatest traveling companion."

"He's got the newbucks," Em said. "It's as simple as that."

I looked at Em. She'd spoken as if Cicero d'Pettitt was some sort of harmless uncle offering us a free afternoon at the circus. Every time I saw Em and Cicero together I got a tight knot in my guts. Cicero gave me the creeps—but the fact that Em still liked the guy was something I couldn't hack. Period.

"I'm not hot wiring Sue-Ellen's G-cross," I said. "We'll take something else."

At which point we were joined by Mr. Sam Yang Rhee who sat down in the same seat from which Cicero had just removed his arse.

"Good news," old man Sam said. And he smiled, a tight, stressed-out smile.

"I'm glad to hear it," Em said.

"We are all going to Portland Head."

"Where's that?" Em said.

"By the sea, in the North West Quarter," poor old Sambo said. "I'm afraid it is still a detention center, Em, but it has a far better climate and many more amenities. There are palm trees and a beach."

"This is the line, is it?" Em said.

"I'm sorry," Sam said, "What do you mean, line?"

"This is the nonsense the authorities are coming out with—they're telling you that those runabouts are just going to be used to transport us all a few hundred kilometers across the face of planet Earth?"

"That is, indeed, the case. I have just come from a meeting with Ms. Ashmore. She has given her assurances."

"Oh, Mr. Sam," Em said. "Why didn't you take me to this bloody meeting? I'd have got the truth out of her."

"Ms. Harrison was there. She translated very competently."

"Look, Mr. Sam," Em said, "Those runabouts are capable of going to the asteroid belt. If you've got any sense you won't go on board. You won't let wild horses drag you on board. If the authorities reckon all they want to do is cart you about Earth, demand ordinary old choppers for the trip to this Portland Head place. Tell them you'll go overland in a bus. Don't get into anything that's capable of leaving the planet."

"We would only jeopardize our chances of a favorable ruling if we were to refuse a lawful order."

"I know, Mr. Sam, I know," Em said. She looked suddenly tired, you'd think it was late at night, not breakfast. "Look, you do what you think is right, Mr. Sam," she said. "O.K.?"

"I will do what is right for all of us, Em. And now I must talk to the others."

Mr. Sam Yang Rhee stood up and made his way to another table. He looked old and a bit doddery, but he was soon yarning away with old girl Wozlebut, making his pitch, trying to convince her, trying to convince himself. Jeeze he looked earnest. You'd think the bloke was selling encyclopedias door to door.

"There's nothing we can do," Em said. "We'll just have to let the poor old bastards go. At least they'll only be taken to the asteroids. They'll get another chance. Some smuggler will dump them back on Earth soon enough."

"Assuming they can pay," Harri said.

"Oh, let's give them our beads," Em said. "The damn things are worth nothing here and I'm sick of them sticking into my tits."

"Sure," Harri said, distracted. "But how are we going break out of this place? *Before* we are herded on board the runabouts with all the others?"

"Torch the joint," I said.

Em Talking

I didn't think Ned's plan had much merit. Our job was to get ourselves outside the perimeter fence and into the staff car park—I couldn't see how setting fire to the barracks inside the fence would do any good. Ned said it would create the necessary diversion. I said a fire would certainly cause a bit of interest, but the two fences would still be intact and the Rottweilers would still be prowling around between them.

"Prowling?" said Ned. "The smoke will drive them crazy, they'll go ape."

"Well that's just great," I said. "Apeweilers. Just what we need."

"I don't reckon they'll put up much resistance," Ned said.

"I don't reckon we will either," I said. "They'll go straight for our throats and that will be that."

"Have faith, Em," Ned said. Then he turned to Harri and started talking about the drum of accelerant that they just happened to have hidden away in the roof of their quarters.

"What's this accelerant?" I said.

"It's made from gemco and sugar," Ned said.

I was beginning to wonder about Ned. He claimed he wasn't an arsonist, he claimed that the Mothers and Babies place had been set on fire by Ms. Harrison's mother. But why had Ned been running away from the fire when he hijacked the misery bus? I watched him whispering to Harri—there was a real light of glee in his eyes. He could see the flames and smell the smoke already. And Harri wasn't much better, he was quite animated, I hadn't seen him so alive since we'd left Newharp. The truth was: they were arsonists, the pair of them, they just wanted this fire for the fun and games of it. I thought they were both mad. But I didn't know the half of it. If I'd known how Ned was proposing to get through the perimeter fence I'd have gone to the authorities. Well, maybe I wouldn't. But I wouldn't have had any part of it, I'd have thrown in my lot with Mr. Sam Yang Rhee and his model citizens brigade. Suddenly Cicero d'Pettitt was by my shoulder.

"Come outside, Em. I've got a job for you."

"Oh yeah?"

"Yeah."

And he turned and slid out through the mess hut door, not looking back, just totally confident that I would follow him. And I did, feeling angry with myself for doing so. I told myself I owed Cicero nothing, nothing at all. But I had a vision of him back on Newharp behind the counter of the nonhydronic, dark and beautiful with a gold earring, taking my juice-stained pants suit, holding it up, smiling at me and saying how pretty I'd look in it once he'd cleaned it. He had been beautiful then, and we'd laughed together at the same jokes, walked together along the esplanade at Santa Gertrudis and felt happy together—before the controlled substances had got to his own brain, before the Re-Ed had taught him stuff no one ought to know, before he became hard and cold and impossible to touch. But, whatever he was now, Cicero was a link to my past. As he said, himself—we went back a long way. He was part of me. I was angry that this was so, but I went outside and listened to him.

"You've got to get the money to the man," Cicero said. "They suspect me."

"What money, to what man?"

"There's a guy called Waldron, Clem Waldron. Short, fat, mustache like a horseshoe. Works in the main office. Go there, say you've brought the translated documents he wants. Give him this."

Cicero stuck his hand under his shirt and produced a large brown envelope. I took it from him. It was fat with something.

"This is full of newbucks?" I said.

"Don't ask. Just take it to Waldron. Tell him we'll use the suspected food poisoning option."

"What are we arranging, Cicero?"

"We're arranging safe passage out of here. But it costs. Now take the stuff to Waldren. No one will suspect you, they know you do translations."

Cicero turned and walked away—he didn't look back. He just knew I'd do what he asked. And I did. I walked through the camp, noticing the tension in people's faces, noticing the way everyone glanced towards the east, towards the three squat, ugly runabouts in the desert, and then just as quickly looked away. Nobody stood and stared, nobody wanted to acknowledge their presence. I reached the front door of the main administration building. It was beside the main gate—the only gate. The whole building straddled the perimeter fences. You could enter by the front door in the camp and leave by the back door into the staff carpark. That's assuming you could get past the locked doors and the armed guards. A guard on the front door asked me what I wanted. I said I had some translations to give to Mr. Waldren. He said he'd deliver the envelope himself. I said I needed to discuss some of the terms I'd used. I was allowed inside and escorted to an office with a long counter dividing the room. Behind the counter half a dozen people were working at desks. I'd never been in this bit of the building before, but I could sense that there was just as much tension in the office as there was outside. None of the office workers seemed to be concentrating on what they were doing. They all looked up at me and the guard, as if we were the bringers of news.

"The girl wants to see you, Clem," the guard said.

One of the office workers got up from his desk and came over to the counter. Cicero had described him correctly: short, fat, drooping mustache. He also looked about as trustworthy as a month old nine spice roll. If we were relying on this man to get us out of the camp, we were taking an unholy gamble. He looked at me as if I might be some sort of ice cream, something to lick and slobber over. I felt a bit sick. All the other office workers were watching, the guard beside me was watching. This was going to be a very public exchange.

"So, what can I do for you, young lady," he said.

"I'm Emceesquared Gonzales della Harpenden," I said. "I've been doing some translations. I've brought them over myself because there are some things that need explaining."

"I can't remember asking for any translations recently," Waldren said. "I think they must be for someone else." He spoke like someone keen to avoid extra work. He made no move to pick up the envelope on the counter.

"It's stuff to do with the d'Pettitt committee," I said. I was sweating. For a minute Waldren made no response, then he got the message.

"Oh yes, *that* committee," he said, picking up the envelope as if it held a winning lottery ticket. Which I suppose it did. "I'll deal with the material ASAP, no worries." And he turned to go back to his desk without another word to me.

"The thing is," I said to Waldren's retreating back, "There's a bit in the original document that I've translated as 'suspected food poisoning' but the original phrase is really untranslatable. The condition doesn't only occur due to food, the poisoning can be, you know, psychological, it's optional." I really was sweating now. I was trying to sound like a pedant, somebody obsessed with language.

"I'm sure you've translated everything perfectly, Miss err Gonzo de...." The man said, sitting down at his desk and sliding the envelope into a drawer.

The guard and I walked back to the main entrance in silence. As I was about to leave the building he said, "You could have given those newbucks to Clem in a clear plastic bag, Miss. Everyone knows the bastard's bent. Half the illegal hooch in the place is courtesy of Waldren Enterprises."

"I'm just the messenger," I said.

"Nobody's going to shoot you," the guard said.

When I got back to the mess hut, Harri and Ned were nowhere to be seen. I went to the lavatory and locked myself in a cubical and half undressed. Then I went to work on my bra with my penknife.

I found Mr. Sam Yang Rhee with a group of PentaNostras under a tree. Smith Mei Lim was quietly twangling, Mrs. Wozlebut appeared to be praying and Mr. Sam was talking earnestly to some of the others. He was assuring them that the authorities would do nothing that wasn't covered by due process. I skulked on the outskirts of the group for a few minutes but soon lost concentration. Mr. Sam's voice faded into the background, he could have been an insect, a cicada or something so familiar that it is impossible to listen to the sound for more than ten seconds without your mind wandering. Suddenly I felt grief, real grief. I almost choked. I knew with all my heart that we were at a parting of the ways. I had no idea how this day was going to end, anything could happen. But I knew this: I would never again be a part of this group of loopy PentaNostras. I would never hear the twangle of Mei Lim's instrument, never listen to the crappy words of the Homecoming Song ever again. I was unutterably sad—it was a bizarre, loony thing to feel, but

I felt it. When Harri and I had first found ourselves bundled onto an illegal galactic cruiser without our parents, in the last crazy, hectic days on Newharp, we'd cursed when we found out who our traveling companions were going to be. Cursed and sworn and privately mocked them. Not so privately on some occasions. Harri's refusals to join in their praying and singing were as dramatic as they were offensive. He'd been angry and hurt and confused and all these emotions had been focused on our fellow travelers—especially on their singing. But they'd prayed and sung and gently chided us. They hadn't rejected us as we had rejected them. And now, when we were going to part, I felt bereft. There was a lull in Mr. Sam's entreaties. I walked over to him and said, "Can you do something for me, Mr. Sam?"

"Certainly, Em. What do you want of me?"

"Please look after these," I said and scooped the cold fusion beads out of my pocket and handed them to him. Mr. Sam looked down at the beads nestling in the palm of his wrinkled old man's hand.

"Alas, Em," he said, "as we all know, these pellets are worth next to nothing on Earth."

"I know," I said. "But please keep them. If you ever need to use them, use them."

Then I turned and walked quickly away before anybody could say anything. At least my bra feels half civilized, I muttered to myself. But before I could mutter anything else I was half knocked off my feet by a group of Kovalevs running in the direction of the single men's quarters. Fire! they were shouting to each other.

* * * * * * *

All right Neddy boy, here's your chance, now you can do the destruction of the runabouts.

Ned Talking

And I will. But first the fire.

* * * * * *

Talk about whoosh! You should have seen the gemco go. The sugar had given it a bit of high octane all right, high as a kite. Harri and I had laid the trail from one end of Single Men's B to the other. Right down the central corridor. Then we'd lit the end of a bit of tightly twisted paper and laid it carefully down with the other end touching the gemco. We'd scarpered over to Single Men's A and started to do the same thing. We were half way through laying the trail when we heard B go up. "Keep going," Harri said. "Let's get this done." We finished the job to the sound of people rushing about outside. We could hear the inferno crackling like a chook. We were out of A and standing in the laneway watching B go up when behind our backs there was a whoosh of flame from one end of A to the other. Like everybody else we high tailed it out of the laneway. With both buildings blazing, the lane was going to become a bit warm. Bells started ringing. People rushed about. Smoke billowed out of windows. The roof of B suddenly ignited in the middle and the fire blazed up to the heavens. The air was full of burning bits of ash and sparks.

"Pity it's not night," Harri said. "It would look better at night."

"You can't have everything," I said.

"We need to get Em," Harri said. But as he spoke she appeared beside us.

"This your work?" she said.

"What do you reckon?" I said.

She shrugged. "What now," she said.

"We see if it spreads," I said.

And spread it did. Maybe it was burning embers from A and B that did the trick. Maybe a few of the hotter headed aliens helped things along. Who knows? But soon half the buildings in the camp were going up. People were being pushed back by the heat, back to the perimeter fence. I'd been right about the Rottweilers—they went ape. They were beside themselves. There was a wail of sirens. The camp's two fire trucks had come storming in through the main gate. They were crewed by camp authority staff who'd pulled red overalls over their normal gear. This mob weren't particularly professional. They got too close to one burning hut. The backed off and rammed a hole in another. The guys on the back sprayed foam like kids pissing on a wall, but not all of it went on the burning buildings. A group of Hydrians got covered. They screamed and cursed, shaking the foam off themselves like dogs after a swim. The army suddenly appeared in their troop carriers, roaring around the outside of the perimeter fences, making for the main gate. The place started to fill up with soldiers, who ordered everybody about, but didn't seem to know how to control the fire.

"Time to move," I said to Harri. "Come on, Em."

Harri took hold of his sister's hand and began to run with me towards the nearest fire truck.

"What's going on?" Em gasped. "Let go, Harri."

But Harri didn't let go and we all arrived at the fire truck a few seconds later. The heat was intense. The driver was trying to back the thing away from the flames. The guy on the back with the big foam gun was crouching down, trying to keep out of the way of the heat. A burning ember landed on my shirt sleeve, but I brushed it off before it burnt my skin.

"OK," I said, "Into the truck."

I took a flying leap at the passenger side of the cab and wrenched the door open. I was in. Harri followed. Em followed.

"Let go of my bloody wrist," she yelled at Harri.

Harri let go, but Em didn't scarper. She slammed the door shut, cursing. "Who do you think I am?" she yelled at her brother.

The driver, yelled, "Get out, get out the lot of you! Only trained fire crew allowed." The driver was that Dr Wilkinson bloke.

"No, you get out," I said and dived across his lap, knocking his hands off the steering wheel. I had the door flapping open in a second. Harri gave the pair of us a godalmighty shove. I took a flying dive out of the truck on the driver's side—Wilkinson came along for the ride. I landed on top of the guy, stunning him. I was onto my feet and back into the truck. It was just like old times. You can't keep an old hijacker down.

Except that instead of Tatters hanging on to the mirror struts, we now had a couple of guys on the back manning the foam guns. To bad. We were out of the joint, and they were coming too. I selected some sort of gear and swung the truck round to face the perimeter fences. I flattened the pedal. Harri found a switch marked "siren" and flicked it. A radio speaker at the back of the cabin babbled and jibbered—I thought I recognized Ashmore's voice but the siren drowned her out. People scattered in front of us. The first perimeter fence approached. We all ducked as we hit the wire. The windscreen shattered, the cab was a snow storm of fractured safety glass, but the truck kept going. There were screams from the back of the truck. Great arcs of foam sprayed wildly though the sky. Harri looked out of the rear window.

"One of the guys is stuck on the top of the fence," he said.

"He'd better stay there," I said. Already maddened Rottweilers were leaping at the truck, barking like guns, their great snouts snapping. The second fence approached. We ducked, the truck crashed through, dragging half a kilometer of fence with it. The truck slowed, its wheels spinning in the sand. The leaping Rottweilers started aiming for the place where the windscreen had been, but there was mesh fence draped over the hole.

"Back up," Em yelled. "Get us out of this fence."

Easier said than done. I'd no idea where reverse gear was. I tried a couple, the truck almost stalled. And then I had it. We were roaring backwards, back towards the blazing camp. But the fence fell away and then, when I slammed the truck into a forward gear, we went hurtling forward, over the remains of the fence and out into the desert. We were free! After a fashion.

"What now?" Em shouted. "We're not going to drive this thing all the way to Jackson's."

"Why not?" I said, laughing and hooting at the sheer joy of being alive, the sheer joy of being at the controls of a mighty fire truck bucking and rolling as it hurtled through the desert. "We just point this little baby in the right direction," I shouted, "and away we go."

"Can't hear you" Em shouted. "Turn the bloody siren off."

Harri flicked the switch.

"That's better," Em yelled. "But you haven't thought this through, have you?"

"Relax, Em. We're going round in a big arc. We'll end up in the staff car park. We'll knock off a proper car."

"I'd already arranged that," Em yelled. "This is completely unnecessary."

"Arranged? How?"

"I bribed one of the office workers."

"Using what? Beads?"

"Newbucks—thousands of them."

"Oh god," I groaned, "Not Cicero. You didn't...."

"It was a better plan than this...."

"Nothing with Cicero in it is a better...."

"Watch out!"

The truck hit some sort of burrow. There was a violent jolt. It jumped. The three of us nearly went through the space where the windscreen had been. The steering wheel slammed into my ribs. I couldn't speak, but I kept control of the truck, sort of. There was a violent hammering on the roof. The remaining guy on the back was making his presence felt. Harri bunched his fist up and hammered back, cheery like.

"What's that?" Em yelled, pointing to the left. A blotched oblong was surging though the desert.

"Troop carrier," I gasped. "We'll drag it off."

The troop carrier was churning along in fine style, its half-tracks grinding up the desert, sending up a huge plume of dust. It was matching us for speed, but closing on us sideways. It would be bumping us within a minute.

And then I saw them. Slightly off to our right—the runabouts, they were bigger than they'd looked. If we were going to play chasey with a troop carrier, what better playground than a landing field? I aimed at the middle runabout. There was a low sand dune in the way. We went over it, the truck growling as it surged up the side, all wheels spinning, leaping from the crest, front wheels clear of the dirt, thump and a burst of acceleration as we shot down the other side. The carrier was racing parallel, a few meters to our right. The runabouts loomed, they must have been twenty meters tall and sixty meters wide. Each one was sitting on three giant retractable legs. Their underbellies were well off the sand, perhaps you could race a fire truck straight under them. Perhaps you couldn't. Two of them had their boarding ramps down, drawbridges to hell. There was a bump as the carrier, nudged us from the side. I aimed for the middle runabout. It was like going under a low bridge—except there was no sign telling you what the clearance was. We went under with a rush and a violent screech of twisting steel as the top of the cab was ripped away by the runabout's underbelly. Jeeze, I hoped the guy in the back had hit the deck. I planted the foot. The underbelly raced over our heads, scoured by the remains of the cab. We were out the other side, the blue sky above our heads. The romance of the coupé. A sports truck! Every young man's dream. The carrier bumped us again from the side. I swung the wheel and threw the truck into a screaming paisley. The sand and the gravel went everywhere, it was raining saltbush. I straightened the wheel and we roared back towards the runabout.

At which point Father Christmas crashed in through the nonexistent roof. The old goat landed in the seats behind us, cursing and swearing. I turned my head to get a good squizz. The truck went out of control, sideswiping the carrier which had spun on its half-tracks like a silver newbuck and was getting its share of the action. But you should have seen the old coot in the backseat: bright red suit, black wellies, dazzling white beard.

Although, admittedly, the beard appeared to be made of fire-retardant foam. Actually it covered most of his face, but never mind, Father Christmas was raving, he was off the planet, he was away with the fairies.

"You mongrels, you stupid fuckin mob of mongrel alien bastards from outerfuckinspace. Wadderyer think yer playing at, you young arseholes...."

"Hello, Mr. Waldren," Em yelled at him. "Nice of you to drop in."

*　*　*　*　*　*　*

Guess what, Em, I'm going to let you finish the destruction of the runabouts. I believe you can be more objective, cool, dispassionate. I don't want to boast.

Em Talking

You wouldn't believe how calm I was. I was in the most ludicrous situation I'd ever been in. I should have been cowering under the dashboard, crouched down low amongst the broken glass, pleading with Ned to stop. Pleading with him to give up before we all died. But I wasn't. I was sitting back, enjoying the ride. I was beyond panic, beyond caring. Nothing was real. But I was living, for the first time in months I was living. It didn't matter that Ned was a deranged juvenile delinquent, it didn't matter that Harri was no better. It didn't matter that our chances of making a clean getaway to Jackson's Port were finished, over, kaput. It didn't matter that sooner or later Ned would roll the truck and kill us all. It didn't matter that the troop carrier thing was probably full of guys with guns. Nothing mattered. The day was warm, the sky was blue, the truck was alive, we were alive, we'd ripped the underbelly of a runabout, and Ned was swinging the truck round to bingle the lot of us into another runabout. I gave up, I sat back, I breathed the desert air, I commended my soul to god, or to the devil, or to chance, or to whoever wanted it.

And then the man who'd been using the foam gun on the back of the truck paid us a visit, tumbled over the edge of the ripped metal and landed with a thump and a curse in the back seats. I didn't recognize the man, he was wearing a fireman's suit and was half covered in foam, but I recognized his voice. An hour ago I'd been bribing him. Now he was screaming abuse at us, ordering Ned to stop the truck. I told him it was nice of him to drop in. But he just screamed and shouted.

"Stay calm, Mr. Waldren," I said.

"Stop, stop the godamned truck you mutant scumbag," Mr. Waldren yelled at Ned. He leaned forward over the back of the driver's seat and tried to wrench Ned away from the controls, grabbing him round the neck. The truck wobbled violently as Ned swung the steering wheel this way and that but we didn't slow down. Ned just made the truck go faster. Harri punched Mr. Waldren in the face. Ned bit his wrist. Mr. Waldren fell back into the rear seat. Then Harri slithered over into the back bit as well. I thought he was going to continue the fight. But he just put one foot on the backrest and hoisted himself up and over the ripped metal. Tearing his tunic as he went. He disappeared from sight. I'd no idea what he was up to.

There was a yelling sound from the troop carrier. A hatch had opened in the roof and a soldier with a voice enhancer was shouting at us.

"Stop. Stop or we fire. This is an order."

I looked at the carrier, it didn't appear to have any guns. Maybe the soldiers inside had guns, but there weren't any windows for them to poke them out. There were just some mean little glass windows at the front for the driver, but they were all closed. It was an empty threat. Ned was taking no notice. He was lining the truck up for another charge at the runabouts. This time at the one on the right. I just sat back in my seat, I let it all happen. It was a dream, it wasn't real. The soldier shouted some more stuff about stopping. I waved to him, I hope he thought it was a cheery, friendly wave. He didn't wave back. The black mass of the runabout was dead ahead between us and the horizon, although we could see clear under it. Its three legs were holding it a bit higher off the desert floor than the previous one. This time we'd just roar straight under it, its underbelly was safe.

On the troop carrier, the soldier pulled his head in and closed the hatch. The carrier suddenly accelerated, pulling in front of us. It was still off to the right, but it was fifty meters ahead. Dust and gravel started to sting our faces. But through the dust we could see the door at the rear opening. We were looking into the dark cave of the carrier's inside. Through the dust we could see soldiers. They had guns and they were pointing them in our direction. We were now almost at the runabout. If the soldiers wanted to stop us before we got there, they'd have to start shooting immediately. But Harri opened up before they had a chance. There was a noise like a rocket above our heads and the jet of foam shot straight and true through the carrier's open door. The carrier filled up in an instant, a mixture of foam and soldiers. Then we were under the runabout. The underbelly blocked out the sky, magnified the sound of the foam jet. The carrier veered wildly away. It slammed straight into one of the runabout's legs, snapping it off. For a moment everything was fixed, unmoving. The carrier, brought to a halt by it's crash just stopped. The huge, retractable leg, lay where the carrier had slammed it into the dirt. The underbelly was black above our heads, but unmoving. And then, as Ned steered straight for the white light of the horizon, above us the runabout began to tilt towards its missing leg. But we were out. We were away into the desert. We were free. I didn't turn round, I knew what I'd see—a two legged runabout, a sad, useless amputee of a craft.

"Shall we do the third?" Ned yelled.

I shrugged happily. I was easy. Ned swung the truck round in a large arc, facing the third runabout. But as we charged, it began to shimmer. It didn't move, but the legs retracted. The craft was hovering, held up by the force of its sotto-c drive. And then I suddenly wasn't so carefree, so blasé about my own fate.

I wanted to live.

"It's taking off," I yelled at Ned. "Get away from it!"

For a second Ned did nothing, just kept us on a course that would take us straight under the hovering craft. The idiot, idiot, idiot boy. He knew nothing of sotto-c, nothing at all.

"We'll be fried, Ned," I yelled. "Fried!"

I reached over and grabbed the steering wheel, turning it. The truck swerved. For a second Ned resisted, then he cooperated, taking the truck through the full 180-degree turn. We were racing away from the craft. But we still felt the wave of radiation as it took off for the sky—but it was just a taste of the heat that would have cooked the lot of us if we'd been under it.

"You'll pay for this you mongrel alien. You'll go to jail for ever and then they'll deport you back to the cosmic cess pit you come from, you...."

I turned round and said, "Hey, Mr. Waldren. There's going to be an investigation. A big-time government enquiry into today's events. Detectives. All over the place. Asking questions."

"You'll go to jail, the lot of...."

"So will you, Mr. Waldren," I shouted at him. "Taking bribes. Running the hooch trade. I'll have to give evidence. I'll have to say what happened. Under oath, Mr. Waldren."

"Vicious bitch," Mr. Waldren snarled. "They'd never believe you."

"Would you care to lay a small bet?" I said. "Even the guard knew I was giving you money this morning."

"Alien scum."

But he'd got my message: it would be a lot better for dear Mr. Waldren if the three of us just disappeared in the general direction of Jackson's Port. I could see recognition of this fact in the piggy little eyes looking out from his fat, foam covered face.

"Have you got a car, Mr. Waldren?" I shouted. "In the staff car park, is it?" Mr. Waldren didn't reply. "Go to the car park, Ned," I yelled. "Mr. Waldren is lending us his car."

Then I turned back to Mr. Waldren and held my hand out for the keys.

Ned Talking

I took the truck in a wide arc around the outside of the camp. We could see inside—it was a shambles, a total disaster area, although there wasn't a lot of action on the ground. The Rottweilers seemed to be running the show at that level. A few troop carriers were tearing around, but the troops couldn't get out for the dogs. There was a lone soldier up a tree who was taking potshots at the dogs, but he didn't look very well placed. The camp's other fire truck appeared to have run out of foam. Three or four more buildings were on fire and no one was doing anything about it. The real action was up on the roofs, people were ripping the place apart, hurling stuff down. I didn't have time to see any more, although I noticed a flight of choppers was coming up from the East.

There was a simple mesh gate into the staff car park and the command post next to it was unmanned. The truck flattened the gate in a second. We piled out of the truck. Father Christmas was a bit surly about showing us which car was his, but Em made a few sweet natured remarks about giving evidence under oath and the guy pointed to his Leo Minor. For a big time bribe-taker he sure drove a crappy little rust bucket. But it would have to do. I jumped into the driver's seat. Suddenly there was the sound of running feet, coming from the direction of the administration building. The passenger door was wrenched open and Cicero d'Pettitt dumped himself into the car. Oh great, just great. But there would be no getting rid of him. Em and Harri piled into back seat and I fired up the gemco.

At which point Sue-Ellen emerged from between two parked cars looking cool and collected and carrying a data cache. Em lowered her window and Sue-Ellen handed her the cache.

"When you get to Jackson's, get this cache to this address," she said. "If we don't get this riot onto the news, the whole thing will have been for nothing. And as for you, Neddy boy, just take it easy. Don't stack the crate. Now bugger off."

I needed no further encouragement.

We'd been rolling down the two lane road for half an hour in complete silence when Em said, "How long will it take to get to Jackson's Port?"

"Dunno," I said. "A few days."

"We'll need to stop," Em said. "We'll need to get fuel and food."

"Good job we've got Cicero on board," I said. "He's loaded."

"We're not driving this car all the way to Jackson's," Cicero said in a cold, pleasant, matter of fact sort of way.

"Oh no?" I said.

"No," said Cicero. "We'd be picked up. There will be warrants out for us. There will be road blocks."

"Got any better ideas?" I said.

"What I have, Earth boy, is a proper plan. Everything is arranged, and everything is paid for. You all owe me."

"Err...just what do we owe you for?" I said.

"We have a rendezvous with a local transporter just after midnight on the North-South highway."

"Local transporter?" I said.

"I believe the slang term is misery bus."

"Not me, buster," I said. "I'm not going in any damn misery bus."

"Suit yourself," Cicero said.

"What Cicero says makes sense," Em said from the back seat. "We'll all have a better chance with a professional. And if Cicero has already paid the bribes, it will be plain sailing. We'll get there."

For a second I was insanely angry, really pissed off. I gripped the steering wheel. My knuckles showed white. I was angry with Em for taking Cicero's side. Didn't she trust me? But at the back of my mind I knew she was right—we'd stand a much better chance of getting to Jackson's in a godamned misery bus, me included. After a few more minutes of silence, I said, "This professional transporter guy—who is he, does he have a name?"

"O'Grady," Cicero said. "A Mr. Jigger O'Grady."

I groaned. "Tats," I said. "It would just have to be Tats."

"I believe that is his nickname," Cicero said. "Are you acquainted with O'Grady, Earth boy?"

I said nothing for a while. Then I said, "Just look in the glove box, will you."

Cicero didn't move. After a second he said, "You feel the need for gloves?"

"Have you ever been in a car before?" I said.

"This is my first experience of a private Earth conveyance," Cicero said, sounding just slightly bored. "I must say I find it all a bit primitive."

"Yeah," I said. "Well see that handle in front of you. It opens a compartment called a glove box. Now do us all a favor and take a squizz inside. See if Father Christmas keeps a first aid kit on board."

Taking his time, Cicero opened the glove box. There was indeed a small first aid kit in it.

"Good," I said.

"Are you hurt," Em said from the back. She was really concerned. I wasn't angry with her any more. I half wished I did have a small injury for her to patch up.

"No," I said, "I'm fine. But by the time we meet up with Tats I think I'll have third degree burns all over my face. You can bandage me up."

By one o'clock in the morning we were all sitting in a container rattling down the North-South highway with a mob of Kovalevs (poor patsies, they were just off the runabout, they hadn't a clue). And me, I looked like an Egyptian mummy. The disguise had worked, Tats had even given me a hand up the step ladder. "Christ," he'd said. "Who are you, you poor freak? The curse of Tutankhamen?"

PART TWO
JACKSON'S PORT

Ned (aka Ishmael) Talking

I learned my trade in the wharflands—a rough area, but politically stable. There was no argument in the wharflands: the Tetrides ruled, OK? It said so in spray-paint on a hundred crumbling brick walls, tin fences, the burnt out wrecks of old canola rollers. Anybody who could read Newharp would understand. And if you didn't read Newharp, or at least speak it, the wharflands weren't really the place for you. They weren't nicknamed Little Newharp for nothing. And if you were gainfully employed in Little Newharp, you were working for the Tetrides. Or your boss was working for the Tetrides—or your boss's boss. And if you were working for the Tetride bosses in the wharflands nobody else tried to muscle in—it wasn't worth their while. The Scott-Woks ran the same sort of deal on the North Shore, over the other side of the harbor. I'd have been dead meat if I'd tried flogging brushes on the North Shore—but us wharf rats, we never crossed the harbor, never went over the water. The territory had been neatly parceled out. Scott-Woks to the north, Tetrides to the south. But then, way out to the west, there were the tracts, the new developments, the satellites. Virgin territory—full of Earthlings, not too many aliens out there. Cicero gave me the good news.

"Time to expand, Earth boy," he said.

"Expand what?" I said.

"Expand the territory. Grab market share."

"What are you on about, d'Pettitt?" I said.

"The bosses are sending you into the tracts, it's an honor, Earth boy. Everything west of Coburg is yours."

"Thanks," I said. "But I'm happy working the wharflands."

"Anyone can work the wharflands," Cicero said. "Look upon the tracts as a challenge. If we don't grab them, the Scott-Woks will."

There wasn't much point arguing. I was a crash hot brush salesman, one of the best the bosses had. I could do English, I could do Newharp, I wasn't too bad at Kovalev. But I was on the run from the law, the bosses could shop me any time, with-draw protection. I might have been a bit of a hero to the general Newharp population—destroyer of Spearchucker, vanquisher of runabouts. But I reckoned that cut no ice with the bosses—I was as useful as my ability to sell brushes and associated prod-ucts. I didn't have much to bargain with. I took the light rail to the tracts.

God they were bleak, the tracts. It made me long for the jumble of the wharflands, the higgledy piggledy shops and doss houses and lanes and alleys—the cafes, the gambling dens, the sweatshops. There was none of that in the tracts, but there wasn't the clean nothingness of the desert either. The tracts were neither jumble nor nothing—they stretched for miles, boxes under the sun. Windows with Paul Lean posters facing out into the street. *Paul Lean makes us Clean!* Guys fiddling under the bonnets of clapped out Dogstars, cutting grass with clattering two-stokes, the whiff of badly burnt gemco in the air, kids on bikes looking for something to vandalize. Guys with great suction pipes cleaning the gutters—cleaning what out of the gutters? It wasn't as if there were any trees pouring leaves down the spout. I walked around for a while and then selected a door at random and knocked on it. After all, that's what I did—knock on doors. I was a door to door salesman. I was selling brushes: hair brushes, clothes brushes, dunny brushes, tooth brushes, multi-purpose brushes, you name it. Except I wasn't only selling brushes. Brushes, you could say, were my cover, my disguise, my foot in the door.

The door opened. I put my foot in. "Morning, missus, a very nice morning if I say so myself, which I do."

"Wadderyer want?"

"Just a moment or two of your time, missus, no harm in that is there? No there isn't, if I say so myself."

"Piss off."

"You'd pay fifty newbucks in the shops, missus."

"I wouldn't pay...."

"Indeed you wouldn't. No self-respecting member of the

community would pay fifty newbs if they could get it for twenty-nine point nine nine. That's the beauty of it."

"Beauty of what?"

"The beauty of the Full-On Brush Leader incentive scheme."

"You're full of crap."

"Everyone's full of crap, missus. That's why we need Full On dunny brushes. One of life's essentials. If I say so myself."

"I'm not buying."

"I'm not selling."

"Well whadderyer doing then?"

"Enrolling you in the Full On Brush Leader incentive scheme. You pay nothing."

"You just said I'd be up for twenty nine point nine nine."

"No I didn't. That's what the ordinary member of the community pays. Brush Leaders pay nothing—they get their brushes free. They get them free, gratis and for nix. It's their status see—their status within the community. Where they go, others follow. And you, missus, you are Brush Leader material. Anyone can see that."

"Just how old are you, you little squirt?"

"Old enough to know a born Leader when I see one, missus. And I'm seeing one now."

"And these Brush Leaders? They get free brushes?"

"They do indeed."

"Well give me one. Go on, hand one over. Give us a free brush."

"Easy on there, missus, easy on. We're talking training sessions, we're talking brush handling and management, we're talking a nice little earner. Not only do you pay nothing. We pay you! Are you keen to capitalize? Keen to reap the rewards that your position in the community entitles you to? You are? Of course you are!"

"I never said...."

"You never said you weren't. You never said you were not keen to make megabucks by being a local Full On brush supremo. Check this little beauty. What a brush!"

"Looks like an alien's hair-do."

"It's our Sweep-Stakes Winner—have your hall carpet dust-mite free in ninety seconds, that's right, missus, ninety seconds flat. Let me demonstrate. Excuse me…."

"Hey, whadderyer think yer…get out of my house."

"Now then, observe the elegance of the action. I just take a swipe at this diseased and festering carpet and in a jiffy it's…."

"Go on, get out. Bugger off. I'll call the…."

"You'll call the shots all right. You'll call them good! When your neighbors see the dust free elegance of your hall carpet, they'll drool!"

"Piss off, you. This is home invasion…."

"Drool, I tell you! And who'll be the Full On Brush Leader in your street? You will! And when your friends and neighbors want to invest in a Sweep-Stakes Winner—the brush of champions—who'll be raking in the commissions? Who'll be rolling in the newbucks, who'll be totting up the winnings, who'll be skimming the cream, who'll be salting it away? You will, missus, you'll be the winner. No question of that. No question at all. If I say so myself. Which I do."

"Just who do you think you are?"

"Mind you, we'll have to do something about the old liver. The old liver is a problem. But it's a problem we can fix."

"What crap is this?"

"You've got a liverish complexion, missus. No offence meant and none taken, I trust. But we at Full On can't have our products promoted by the diseased. We've got an image to protect. If you don't do something about the old liver you'll be a goner before you're forty and that's a fact."

"I'm calling the…."

"The hospital? You're calling the hospital? When did the overworked, overburdened hospital system ever do anything for the battler? You go to hospital, you'll catch more plagues and poxes than a alien! And that's a fact. What you need is a little private arrangement."

"I've heard about people like you."

"You have indeed, and now you've met one. You have not only met the man who can make you Full On Brush Leader for the whole neighborhood, you've met the man who can get you a new liver. Pancreas too, if you like. Kidneys on the fritz? No worries, missus, we'll see you right. Lachrymal gland not too frisky? I've got just the thing, new or reconditioned it would make the angels weep. Listen, missus, about hubby's prostate, I can offer the old boy easy terms on a brand new one, beats tying a knot in it, whadder you reckon? We're running specials this week on replacement arteries. The first meter is free. That's right, the first meter is yours absolutely free! Hurry while stocks last. Hearts? Can we do hearts! Life time guarantee. Believe me, if your new ticker conks out before you do, we'll replace it absolutely free. No, no, nothing's written down. Our word is our bond. That's our spoken word, you understand. You trust us, we'll trust you. I assure you, missus—this is all genuine Earth stock. No aliens involved. Look, say your cousin, nephew or neighbor had a bad experience with a Kovalev intestine, well it doesn't surprise me, they should have come to us in the first place. We've got the guts."

"There's laws against people like you. Paul Lean is leading the charge, he's got your number. Trading in organs, that's what you're doing—trading in organs. It's illegal...."

"Now look, 'illegal' is not a word we like to hear. We prefer 'informal.' That's right, we're an informal organization of like minded citizens helping each other without bothering the authorities with paperwork and permits and committees. If the good citizens of Jackson's Port can't help each other when it comes to body parts—what hope is there? Now, about your replacement liver...."

"It's aliens who run the organ dens, everyone knows that, Paul Lean says so. You're an alien, that's what you are, same as the last bloke."

"Do I sound like an alien, missus, do I look like an alien? Have I got an alien demeanor? No I haven't. But I can do you a very good replacement liver. What about night-sweats?"

"Night sweats?"

"Yeah, you get them, don't you, missus? Wake up clammy and sweating like a horse. It's a sure sign, one of the surest. Blurred vision? Running for the dunny three four five times a night? A bit off color first thing in the morning? Tingling in the fingers? They're all signs missus, signs and portents. Ignore them at your peril."

"You're *worse* than the last guy."

"What last guy?"

"The last maniac who tried to sell me an organ."

"Some other guy's been here? What did he look like?"

"Alien."

"Yeah, well I trust you showed him the door, missus. God knows what would have happened to you...two heads probably. That or you wake up with a tail. It's lucky for you I came along. Now about your...."

* * * * * * *

I'm sure you get the picture, reader. I won't go on. Modesty forbids, but If I say so myself, I was a crash-hot salesman.

* * * * * * *

And selling door-to-door was a better bet than working in the sweatshop, tending the incubators, sweating over the gene pools. Poor Harri, he was hard at it night and day—earning peanuts in the spare parts factory. Way below ground level, down in the depths. I'd never been down to the factory myself—it was all need-to-know and top security down there—but Harri had described the place. It was a sort of reverse morgue—they started with sludge and produced bits of body, growing them from a single cell. It didn't sound like fun city. No daylight and starvation wages for the illegals who worked there. Me, I was on commission, I made a newb or two. Em worked in an ethnic eatery called the Dog and Harp—waitressing, washing up, cooking, scraping the crap out of the ovens—shit work. The Dog was built above Harri's spare parts factory—there was a steel door and secret stairs at the back of the eatery's wine cellar. Cicero kept hinting he could get Em better employment, but she wasn't keen.

We all lived in Aunty Nagoya's doss house. The house of louse. Flopsville. What a rabbit warren, what an anthill, what a fire-trap! What a place to call home. I did, I called it home, I loved the joint, it was Home Sweet Home to me. I took to Aunty Nagoya's like a bug to a bed. Em and Harri weren't so thrilled. They'd known better on Newharp, they'd lived a life of cultured ease in dwelling places full of light and space and clean, uncluttered floors. Elegant furniture. Labor saving devices. Hygiene—they'd known hygiene! As Em and Harri told it, to have lived on Newharp was to have known domestic paradise. It was a pity poor old Newharp was doomed. Me, I was a Tidy Town boy. I knew squalor. Aunty Nagoya's couldn't teach me anything in the sleaze curriculum. Been there, done that. But Aunty's was full of life—alien life to be sure, but life none the less. And the streets all around us, running down to the harbor, down to the water. Sparkling blue in the distance, full of dead rats and plastic bottles and the millions of colors of spilt gemco when you looked straight down off a wharf. And I was safe on these streets, more or less. You wouldn't exactly say that the wharflands were a no go area for the cits. That wouldn't do at all, it would be an admission that law and order had broken down. The cits cruised about, checked registrations, broke up the odd fight, arrested some poor sucker every now and then. But they did as they were told. They did what the Tetride bosses paid them to do. They didn't arrest the wrong poor sucker if they could help it. Which they could. And I had protection. I was a bit of a hero—I'd wrecked the runabouts, I'd saved a few aliens from deportation, I'd delivered Sue-Ellen's footage to the telly station. Raised the alien profile, caused a few questions to be asked in high places. Although, mind you, the footage was a mixed blessing. Some of the high placed questions were a bit on the negative side. People's Deputy Paul Lean—he asked a few questions, like, why weren't all the aliens shot when the authorities had the chance? You'd see him on the telly at Aunty Nagoya's, old Paul Lean—ranting and raving. He was moving right along—he was building a solid political base. He wasn't just a People's Deputy, he was leader of a minor political party, one that might hold the balance of power one day. But in the wharflands we didn't care—we yelled abuse at Paul Lean's image on the telly and went back to playing jongma or stuffing our faces with nine spice rolls. The Tetride bosses ruled in the wharflands, OK? And there weren't any League o' Purity posters on our derelict buildings, no sir.

I reckoned life was good. And as I was a good salesman, one of the best, the bosses were well pleased with my track record—they paid a reasonable commission. They paid the local cits a reasonable bribe on my account. Talk about looking the other way, if I saw a cit, I saw the back of the guy's head. And anyway, I didn't exactly look like the young hoon who'd wrecked the runabouts, the hoon who'd broken his bond, hijacked the misery bus. I had a new identity, certain subtle changes had been effected. It was only right and proper—I was flogging body parts, the least I could do was profit from the technology myself. My hair was black, my nose now tended to the aquiline. Em's word, she'd learned it in Advanced English on Newharp, found it in a dictionary she'd swallowed, she said it meant hawk-like. I said I didn't know that hawks actually had noses as such.

"Their beaks, you fool, their beaks," she said.

And I had a new name, a *nom de guerre*, (Em again). Call me Ishmael. Ish for short. Em chose that as well, she said there was nothing fishy about it, it was a good Newharp name. It would do. Although she still called me Ned when we were alone. Which I insisted upon. It was my name, my real name. A name to be used by my real friends—that is to say, by Em. And Harri. Harri and I were now the best of friends in a gloomy sort of way. We shared a room at Aunty's.

It was getting dark by the time I quit the tracts. To tell the truth, I was keen to be out of the place. I didn't fancy the tracts after dark. The people I'd talked to had told me about the opposition one time too many. The Scott-Wok boyos were out and about, no doubt about it. But I'd had a few nibbles from the punters though: two possible liver replacements and one old guy who wanted a new spleen—reckoned the old one was clapped out, he didn't feel angry enough any more. I'd told them all I'd be back in a few days for the first down payment. I'd also sold three Sweep Stakes Winners, four tooth brushes and a Slop-o-Mop. Not a bad day's work. I slumped in a corner seat of the light rail. The carriage smelt of piss and cheap hooch. I had a little nap. When I awoke, I was almost at the wharflands. It was quite dark beyond the windows, but that just made the patches of light stand out. A sudden pool of light and you were looking at a Kovalev tavern, mad dancing, singing and haggling. Another bright area and there was a lottery seller flogging lucky tickets under a gemco pressure-lamp.

When I got back to Aunty Nagoya's there was a jongma game in progress. That was nothing new, there was usually a jongma game in progress. Aunty's eating, singing, gambling, shouting, telly-watching room was next to her kitchen. You had a hard time finding a place to sit down sometimes. You ate your breakfast standing up because last night's jongma hadn't finished and it wasn't worth your while trying to shift the gamblers. This evening the youngest player was Quincy, about my age, born on Earth, Kovalev dad and a Newharp mother, not that she saw much of them. Her home life wasn't too snap apparently, she preferred to live at Aunty Nagoya's. She helped Aunty in the kitchen; sometimes you found her vacuuming the passageways, changing the sheets—but not often. Quincy wasn't as pretty as Em, but she had red hair and coal black eyes that saw straight into you. At least that's how I felt when she looked at me—like you couldn't tell her a lie. You couldn't sell Quincy a body organ she didn't need. Or even a brush. I'd have been worried about her addiction to jongma if it wasn't for the fact that she usually won. Won hands down, scooped the pool, slid the alien beads into her handbag with a clatter, tucked the newbucks into her bra with a sleight of hand. She looked up from the table, saw me, and quit the game. The other players looked relieved.

"Come on," she said. "We're meeting Em and Harri at the Dog." You can call the Dog an eatery—but you could call it a restaurant, call it a cafe, call it a boozer, call it a place of ill repute, call it a farting, belching, gambling and fighting snake pit, call it exploitation city, call it a cultural hub. Everyone knows there's an organ factory beneath their feet, but no one mentions it. The place has a certain charm, it sells excellent nine-spice rolls. And if Em's serving you might get an extra roll.

Quincy and I walked through the alleys towards the Dog. She was wearing a patchwork Skyroan smock of many colors. Most of the colors were black, but they each had a distinct sheen. In the lamplight she changed colors like a gemco slick on dirty water. Last time I'd seen the smock it was being worn by an old Skyroan cat burglar who boarded at Aunty's and kept his cats out the back in a disused aviary. Quincy must have won the smock off him in a game.

"How were the tracts?" she said.

"You wouldn't want to live there," I said.

"What were the people like?"

"Desperate for organs—I got three potentials in one day."

"Virgin territory."

"Not quite," I said. "The Scott-Wok boyos have been moving in. I kept hearing about them. I was treading in their footsteps."

"They'll hear about you soon enough. Be careful."

"I will."

"Carry a gat."

"I'd rather not."

"Well, a knife at least."

"I'm a man of peace, Quince."

"You'll be a man *in* pieces if the Scott-Woks decide to carve you up."

"Thanks for the advice."

"Stick around the wharflands, that's my advice."

"The bosses want to move into the tracts—I don't have much option."

"Hell," Quincy said suddenly, stopping dead. "Look at this guy. He's like a juggler."

We were passing the entrance to an alley even narrower than the one we were in. There were makeshift tenements on both sides—old deserted factories with extra windows punched out of the walls with sledge hammers and rickety balconies jerry-built onto the original walls. Long bamboo poles and wires stretched across the alley five, six, ten meters above the ground. Some hopeful residents hadn't taken in their washing, it still flapped up there above the street lights, blocking out the night sky. A cat burglar was at work.

Most cat burglars only carry one cat. They need both hands to fling the poor beast into the air and both hands to catch it when it comes crashing down with the washing. But this guy was an artist, this guy was a two cat man. And he had them both in the air at once. Up went one cat, clawing like a bastard at thin air, grabbing at a shirt, sending the pegs flying, plummeting down again like a doomed parachutist. But while the first cat was still in the air, up went the second, a mangy, yowling tabby. They guy scooped the first cat out of the air, grabbed the shirt and sent the cat hurtling up again. The mangy tab was now on the way down with a sock. Only one sock. Not to worry—the first cat was heading straight for the second sock. With a yowl it grabbed it. The peg pinged off into the night. A head suddenly appeared in a window, a great stream of Newharp abuse poured into the night. Oaths, blasphemies, curses, a theory about the cat burglar's mother. Other heads appeared. More lights went on. More heads, more abuse. Waving arms. People were hauling in the washing, which now presented a moving target. The cat burglar didn't stop. Up went the cats, down came the washing. Down came a brick. Then more bricks. The people in the tene-ments were well supplied. A cooking pot hit the deck at the burglar's feet. He jumped, scalded by the contents, but he still caught the last sheet and its cat. With the speed of a magician he stuffed both cats into his sack along with the washing and sprinted out of the alley. He brushed past me and Quincy and disappeared through the crowd, ducking and weaving, a stolen sheet round his neck, flapping out behind him like a gigantic scarf.

"You've gotta admire talent," Quincy said as we turned and started walking towards the Dog.

"What about the poor buggers who've lost their washing?" I said.

"They probably stole it in the first place," Quincy said.

"You're a cynic," I said.

"I've lived here longer than you," Quincy said.

"True," I said.

"Gee, you've grown up since you arrived, though," she said, turning to look straight at me.

"I wasn't exactly a babe-in-arms," I said.

"You were a hayseed. Two years ago, you got out of that container and just looked around with big wide eyes peering out from those ludicrous bandages, staring at everything. Like you'd never seen a city before."

"I hadn't. I was a desert rat. Dead cunning. I'd just wrecked two runabouts and sent the other packing. I was a hero."

"Yeah, that's right," she said. "Like most heroes you were a simple soul."

"And now?"

"Now you are a bit more complex, Ish. You're a complex soul."

We'd reached the Dog. We slid through the bead curtains and into the place. It was loud, but not packed. The actual dog, the restaurant's mascot, a moth-eaten beast called Fido-Fido, was asleep in the middle of the room. There were half a dozen chop bones lying on the floor beside him, all unchewed. It's pointless throwing chop bones to Fido-Fido—he only eats sweet biscuits. Quincy and I stepped over him. He didn't budge. I looked at the walls. They'd changed the views. The views were a bit of a joke if you ask me. They had some way of making the walls look like windows. You could look out onto nice civilized scenes from Newharp. Pleasant snow covered mountains. Pastures green with weird-arse native Newharp beasts peacefully grazing. Wide streets, elegant houses. Odd looking sailing boats on a lake so blue it looked like plastic. A night sky with two moons and strange stars. It was all meant to make the patrons feel at home. Em reckoned it was meant to make them pathetic with homesickness—so that they drank more, ordered more expensive ethnic dishes, called for the playing of sentimental Newharp songs, threw money at the broken down musicians when they obliged.

Harri was already there. He was sitting at a table in front of a view of a forest of impossible trees. The trees were so weedy and skinny they'd never stand up. They swayed in the breeze like drunks. Mad animals with staring eyes and badly made feet jumped slowly from branch to branch.

"That thing's rubbish," I said to Harri as Quincy and I sat down. "They've just invented that view. Trees like that would simply fall over."

"They're not trees," Harri said, not bothering to turn round and look at the view.

"Well what are they?" I said.

"Seaweed," Harri said. "That's an underwater view."

"And those animals?"

"Fish."

"Well what about that thing there," I said pointing. "That thing waving its arms about and burping out silver balloons. What's that?"

Slowly Harri turned round and looked at the view. Then he turned back to the table. "It's a windmill," he said.

"Underwater?" I said.

"It's an old Earth custom," Harri said. "You ought to know all about it, Ish. Its a custom the Ancestors brought with them to Newharp. It reminded them of Home. Now they've gone and recreated it in a view on Earth to remind people like me of

Newharp. That's irony for you, Ish."

"Windmills under the sea? Silver balloons?"

"They're bubbles," Harri said. "That's an aquarium."

"Bloody aliens," I said.

"Place your order, Idiot-boy," a voice said behind me.

I spun round, Em the waitress was standing there, note-pad in hand. "G'day, Em," I said. "Gee you look special, tonight."

"Piss off," Em said.

They make the waitresses wear "traditional" Newharp dress at the Dog. Em hates it. She says it's about as traditional as a grass skirt would be in Jackson's Port. Secretly I think she looks utterly sexy in it. But I only tease her about it. I don't suggest she should wear those sorts of clothes around Aunty Nagoya's—she wouldn't talk to me for days if I did. "When do you get off work?" I said.

"Ten minutes," she said. "I'll do your orders and that's it."

We ordered up big. I was hungry, there's nothing like a day out in the sticks flogging organs to give you an appetite.

Em Talking

So the obvious question is: was Ned really as obnoxious as he makes himself out to be? All that salesman spiel, getting his foot in the door, that sort of stuff—is that how he actually carried on when he was door knocking? I said earlier that I was going to be pitiless in my depiction of the little twerp. No holds barred, I said. But there's no need, really, is there? He's doing it very nicely himself. In truth, reader, I think Ned's playing it for laughs when he writes this stuff. In reality, all those years ago, I think he must have been far more friendly, more sympathetic, more human, than he is making out. Those poor tract dwellers were desperate for company, for a bit of a gossip, for companionship however fleeting. I believe Ned was a good salesman because he provided a bit of human warmth to those poor neurotic, house bound, punters.

It's funny though—have you noticed how he keeps sliding

into the present tense? "Em hates it," he says, not "Em hated it."
Anybody would think we were all still living at Aunty Nagoya's.
Maybe Ned secretly is when he's writing about Earth. It's his
aging mind, reader dear. You don't have to be at death's door
to regress, sluggish synapses will do it for you. Anyway, back
to the Dog.

* * * * * * *

I set the places, including one for myself, I dumped the food
on the table and told them to start without me. Then I went back
through the greasy, steaming kitchen to the staff room. Staff
cupboard, more like. I changed into my ordinary clothes and
looked in the cracked mirror. You could do worse, I told myself.
I grinned. Yeah, but you could do a lot better, I told myself. A
girl can take only so much of the Dog and I'd been slaving in it
for two years. The time had come to move on. Cicero had been
telling me that ever since I started at the Dog. Give it a miss,
Em. Earn serious newbucks, Em, I've got this little scheme, Em,
you and me Em, we can make that Astolphe Scott-Wok guy look
like a pauper. He'll come to us for handouts. He'll be knocking
on the door of our mansion—we'll tell the servants to send him
round to the back door. Em.

I never asked Cicero what his little schemes were. I didn't
need to. But I always told him no. Thanks but no thanks,
Cicero—the Dog will do me just fine. And it had, up till now.
But now I need out. Out without Cicero's help.

Back in the restaurant Ned was telling the tale of his day's
work. Bloody Ned, bloody Ishmael. What a con-artist. You had
to laugh at his spiel—but you still worried for the poor bunnies
he sold organs to. Or brushes for that matter. Things were primitive on Earth, but they weren't so primitive they didn't have
vacuum cleaners. The Earthlings had had them for hundreds
of years, ever since the Economic Ice Age ended. What sort of
bored housewife would buy a Sweepstakes Winner when she
could whip along the hall carpet with a Suck-o-mat? As I've

said, they probably just bought the damn brushes just because they wanted somebody to talk to. The same thing goes for new kidneys, new pituitary glands, a better class of tit. You get a bit of conversation with an engaging seventeen year old. It's bad enough in the wharflands—but everybody here expects everybody else to be a con artist. It goes with the territory. But these tract dwellers—they sound like prisoners in solitary suddenly offered a chinwag with a friendly warder.

* * * * * * *

Oh help, I'm doing it myself: sliding into the present tense. You'll just have to bear with us, reader, we're a couple of old has beens. And check the vocab, will you. I didn't even think like that when I came down the ramp and stood on the planet Earth for the first time. "A better class of tit." I wouldn't have said that, I wouldn't have thought it. "A more appealing breast shape," would have done the trick—in English or Newharp. I blame Ned. He was a bad influence, infectious. Ned. Ishmael. Ish. Idiot boy. What I thought about him at the time was:

* * * * * * *

He's in love with me.

I wish he wasn't.

I wish he'd fall for Quincy. Quincy's a dish. If I were a guy... if I were a dyke...I'd fall for Quincy. Maybe I half have. Why doesn't the idiot boy take Quince to bed? Why doesn't Quince take Ned to bed? I'd love that. I'd love to think of my friend Ned and my friend Quince asleep, wrapped round each other, shagged out, happy. They could be—Ned and Quincy, they could be truly happy. They're made to be happy, if they want to be. Me, I'll never know real happiness. I'm not made that way. I think too much. I analyze too much. I not built for happiness and there are no organs that can change that. *Hey, Ned mate, sell me a happiness organ will you? No can do, Em—not in the catalogue—but I can fix you up with a wizard lymph node. I got it off a wizard who node no better.*

"What are you laughing at?"

"Internal monologue, Ish. I just imagined you'd said something really funny."

"What did I say?"

"Forgotten."

"How can you forget?"

"I was dreaming, Ish. You can never remember your dreams, they fade like the morning dew."

"Very poetic."

"Good evening everybody."

"God! d'Pettitt. Where did you spring from?"

"I walked in the door, Earth-boy. The same as everybody else." Cicero slid into a spare seat. I offered him some of my pickled blueberry. But he waved a dismissive hand—he doesn't eat much, Cicero. "So how were the tracts?" he said to Ned.

Ned shrugged and said, "Uneventful." Then he went back to forking green chili darkfish into his mouth. If Cicero wanted to know more, he'd have to ask more questions.

But all Cicero said was, "Good."

We were witnessing a bit of a standoff.

Cicero is Ned's boss. But Ned is Cicero's best salesman, and Cicero's standing with his own bosses relies heavily on Ned's ability to bring in customers needing organ replacements. And Ned knows this. And Ned is also jealous of Cicero's friendship with me. I looked at Quincy, but she wasn't meeting my eye. She leaned back in her chair and looked around the restaurant. Then she suddenly giggled and leaned towards Ned, whispering something in his ear. Ned looked sideways and grinned.

"So what's the joke?" I said.

"It's a traveling salesman joke," Ned said.

"Well? Go on, tell it."

"It's going to tell itself in a minute."

I looked across the room. There was a guy with a sack hassling a table of regulars. It happens a lot in the Dog. People come in off the street and try to flog stuff: lottery tickets, flowers, controlled substances, uncontrolled substances, cooking utensils, computers, pirated software, pirated footage, pirated food, discounted life insurance, every damn thing. When I'm on duty I make them buy drinks, or I ease them towards the door. If they don't go I call Hugo-the-Bounce. He knows which of them have paid the management a retainer and which haven't. If they haven't been regular in their payments, Hugo shifts them. But I wasn't on duty any more, so I just watched. The guy had sat himself down at the table, he was opening the mouth of the sack, showing the regulars something, talking smoothly by the looks of things. There was a certain amount of argy bargy and then money and an item from the sack changed hands.

"What's he flogging?" I said to Quince.

"He's coming over to us now," Quincy said.

The guy sidled across the Dog and without any introduction or embarrassment slid into the one empty seat. He was a thin Kovalev, thin but fit, early twenties.

"Cold night out," he said pleasantly.

"Cold as charity," Ned said.

"Pleased to meet you," said the guy and extended his hand to Ned. Ned shook it. "Name's Frisco," said the guy.

"Codwallader," said Ned amicably.

Quincy stifled a laugh.

"Tell you what, Codwallader," said the guy. "It's on nights like these you need socks—good, woolen socks. Straight off the sheep's back. None of your plastic rubbish."

"I can't stand plastic rubbish," said Ned.

"A man after my own heart," said the guy.

"Yeah, how is your heart, by the way?"

"Sorry...."

"You will be when the ticker ticks its last," Ned said. "It's your irises that are the give away. You know what they say—crook ticker, irises flicker." Ned leaned forward and peered directly into the guy's eyes. The guy blinked. Ned peered harder. The Kovalev's eyes appeared to go into spasm. "Holy cow," Ned said, almost in wonder, "I've never seen it that bad. What about sulphur fumes?"

"Don't worry about...."

"Denial, mate," Ned said with authority. "You hear the phrase, 'Don't worry about...,' and you know you've got a case of terminal denial on your hands. You get them, don't you, Frisco? The sulphur fumes? You're standing there in the old urinal, just easing the old bladder, and suddenly bang! A great gust of sulphur hits you up the snout. Something's not right in the water works department. You're pissing sulphur. And there you are denying it, pretending it's not happening. Telling yourself that a fit, young fella m'lad like you—and anyone can see you're fit, Frisco, anyone can see that—telling yourself that someone as fit as you couldn't have a crook heart. Telling yourself that the sulphur is just something you drank, that it's not a symptom of coronary decay! Well at least you've got the compensation of knowing that the end will be swift, Frisco. Massive, terminal infarction. Faaaaaarct! You're dead just like that...."

"Now listen, Cod...Cod...."

"...wallader, mate. Codwallader."

"Yeah, well listen, Codwallader. Let's not worry about my heart. It's your toes we've got to consider. On a night like tonight, with the wind howling through the alleys, straight off the harbor. And with the mists and damps creeping into the bones, the toes are the first to feel the pinch. Unless you've got good woolen socks. But they're not that easy to come by, are they? When did you last see a really first rate, tickety boo, pair of sheep's wool socks? Not for a month of Sundays."

You had to admire them. They were both expert salesmen in their own ways. But as the duel dragged on you could see that Ned was winning. The sock salesman was starting to wonder about his heart, but Ned was only mildly interested in the possibility of a cheap pair of secondhand socks. And the interest was faked—he was just being polite. I looked at the other faces around the table. Cicero was pretending to be bored, but was secretly admiring Ned's professionalism. Harri, for once, was openly amused. And Quincy—Quincy was keeping her black eyes on the two contestants, but was quietly slipping a knife out from under her smock. The blade glinted for a split second as she palmed it. What the hell did she think she was up to? We don't take kindly to stilettos in the Dog. There have been a few carve ups, and they are not pretty. They put the patrons off their food. And it's poor mugs like me who get to clean up the blood. I looked hard at Quincy, she caught my expression, but just smiled. Slowly she leaned sideways. I couldn't see what she was doing with the knife—the table obscured my view. But suddenly I guessed: she was slitting open the sock salesman's sack. This was a bit down-market: knocking off some battler's stock, ruining his sack. This wasn't like Quince.

Fido-Fido growled, a low menacing growl. This wasn't like Fido either—he never growled. I looked to where the dog was lying in the middle of the floor. But he wasn't lying. The beast was on its feet—something that usually took it three minutes to achieve. Fido-Fido's hackles were raised. The hair on his back was standing up like one of Ned's brushes. And he was growling directly at Quincy. The animal was objecting to Quincy's knife work. No it wasn't. Two cats suddenly shot into view—arching and spitting at the dog. The dog lunged. Patrons cheered. Hugo-the-Bounce came running. A chair was knocked over. Then another chair. Fur flew. The great barrel of a dog cannoned into a table full of patrons. Cutlery, food, drink, a handbag—all tipped onto the floor. The cats yowled and were out of the place, disappearing through the bead curtain like ghosts. The sock salesman leapt from his chair and was after them, running like the wind. Ned and Quincy were collapsed on each other's shoulders laughing like drains. Hugo-the-Bounce shrugged and walked back to his chair in the corner. It was a quiet night at the Dog.

Ned insisted on returning the washing in the sack to the alley it had been stolen from. We all stood in the middle of the alley and yelled at one of the windows that still showed a light. A head finally appeared. The window rattled open.

"We've got your laundry back," Ned yelled.

"I'll have the cits on you!" yelled the woman at the window. "Thieving cat burglars."

"We've come to give it *back*. You pay nothing. That's right, missus, the clobber is being returned free-of-charge. It's a service, an act of good citizenship."

It took Ned a bit of time to convince the woman he was genuine. Even then she didn't come downstairs and open the door. She lowered a rope with a basket on the end. I reckon she did most of her shopping that way.

We strolled back to Aunty Nagoya's; Ned, Harri and Quincy walking three abreast in front, Cicero and me bringing up the rear.

"So what did Earth-boy tell you about the tracts?" Cicero said.

"Ask him yourself," I said.

"I did. You heard his answer. He said it was uneventful."

"Perhaps it was."

"Come on, Em. What did he say?"

"Look, Cicero," I said, "I can't be your go-between. Ned is your salesman, you've got to find some way of talking to him yourself."

"The tracts are disputed territory," Cicero said without emotion. "There is going to be an all out war there. It's in Earth-boy's best interests that you tell me what he said. Did he mention any signs of the opposition?"

I was quiet for a few steps. Then I said, "Yeah, the Scott-Wok mob have been active. People mentioned other organ peddlers to him."

"Do you think I can trust him?"

"Who?"

"Earth-boy. He was at school with Mrs. Scott-Wok. If push came to shove the Scott-Woks could always offer him better employment."

"You'd better increase his commission."

"I don't set the commissions, Em. The bosses do that."

"Speak to the bosses."

"I have to be careful what I say to them."

"I'm glad I'm only a waitress. All I deal with is shambling drunks."

"You can do better than waitressing, Em."

"Yeah, yeah," I said, like I didn't mean it. But I did.

Ned Talking

Three days a week for three weeks I took the light rail out to the tracts. A couple of the other sales staff joined in. We started to carve out the territory between us. The tracts still spooked me out, but they were a push over as far as sales went. I had punters joining the queue, putting down their down payments, signing up for multiple organ transplants, buying brushes, donating skin cells for reverse differentiation—I had them by the ton. The real problem was going to be getting them to visit the wharflands for the actual operation once their replacement organs had been cloned. There were old girls and boys in the tracts who'd been born there, lived all their lives there, never been anywhere else. Convincing them to come in for their operations was a bit like getting them to go to the Moon. They'd heard about the wharf-lands, they'd seen it on telly. They knew it was chock full of aliens who ate babies for breakfast, People's Deputy Paul Lean said so. I had to spruik like a bastard:

"No, no, mate. I live in the wharflands. Trust me. Some of my best mates are aliens. It's cool."

"They say the organ dens are run by aliens."

"Only in the most menial capacity, mate. They do the sweeping and the polishing. Some bugger's gotta do it."

"They say it's alien technology—organ cloning, all this reverse differentiation. They say the aliens grow organs like a proper person grows pot plants. Fertilizer and blood and bone."

"No way, mate, the organs are grown in bottles. Good things come in glass, mate. Trust me, I've had a complete internal make over myself—and I'm the better for it."

I told Cicero about the problem. I told him the bosses ought to get a mobile clinic together. A canola roller with a container on the back—they could fit it out with all the gear for transplants. There'd be a certain poetic justice to it, I said, taking a container to the native Earthlings out in the tracts. Seeing as how half the aliens in the wharflands had arrived by misery bus. I told Cicero we could park the thing in a side street and the tract dwellers could hop on board, have a quick transplant, a cup of tea and a lie-down in the recovery suite and be back home in time for the evening soap. Hard cases could be kept onboard over night. Cicero wasn't impressed.

"Just get them into the wharflands, Earth-boy. Use your powers of persuasion."

I was beginning to doubt Cicero's business sense. I wasn't surprised when I came across an old canola roller with a container parked for no good reason in a dead-end street next to a small park. As I watched, a door in the side opened and a ladder was put down to the ground. A guy jumped out, not bothering with the ladder, and then another guy climbed slowly down the ladder, helped by the guy on the ground. The two men shook hands and the second guy shuffled away, one hand gingerly holding his stomach. A satisfied organ-recipient if ever I saw one. The fit guy was up the ladder and into the container in a couple of seconds. In went the ladder, slam went the door. It looked like a smooth operation to me. I reckoned at this rate the Scott-Wok mob were going to grab the biggest market share. And the big fish eat the little fish. It's a law of nature.

The next time I was working the tracts, I called in to a house I'd had dealings with before. There was an old boy called George who needed a new appendix—he hadn't felt the same since the old one was removed forty-two years ago. He lived with his old mother who was as blind as a bat and in need of new eyes. It gave me a warm glow to organize the new eyes. This old girl, Mrs. Travis, actually *needed* new eyes. With any luck she'd be able to see again. On this visit all I had to do was collect the weekly installment and give them a progress report on the cloning procedure back at the lab under the Dog. But when George opened the door, he seemed strangely agitated.

"I reckon you better come in," he said.

"I won't take up any of your time," I said. "I'll just give you the latest word on the cloning and collect the subscription and I'll get out of your way."

"No...I reckon you'd better come in," George said. He looked a bit nervous. "Ah...have a cup of tea."

"Full as a goog, mate," I said. "I had thirty six cups of tea at the last place."

"Yeah...err...well...I reckon you'd better come inside anyway," said George. He was sweating like a pig, he was as nervous as hell. I was out of the joint.

I turned and ran. I ran for half a meter. Then I bumped into this huge wall of blubber. There were arms attached to the blubber. There were hands attached to the arms. They grabbed me round the biceps and marched me backwards through the front door and into the house.

"Help!" I screamed.

"Shut up," said the blubber in Newharp.

I dropped the case of brushes I always carried. The blubber tripped. The blubber toppled. Bad move on my part—I was a split second away from being crushed and smothered under a hundred tons of falling fat. But the pressure on my biceps eased and I hurled myself backwards. Just in time. I was out from under. The blubber hit the deck with a violent loss of breath. I staggered backwards into the living room.

"Ah, at last," said a voice behind me in Newharp. "The famous Mr. Ishmael Codwallader, aka Ned Gonzalez della Harpenden, aka Edward Malley."

"Who the hell are you?" I said, spinning round.

"Let's just say I'm a fellow practitioner."

I looked at the guy. He was sitting in an armchair with a gat in his hand. He was about thirty years old and dressed in a flash business suit. I played for time.

"Fellow practitioner?" I said.

"That's one way of looking at it."

"You sell brushes?" I said. "You're another Full-On...."

"Neddy, Neddy," said the guy. "Let's not bandy words. You have a second string to your bow. I have half a dozen strings to mine, but we both have an interest in the physical well being of the good people of the tracts."

"What are they saying?" yelled Mrs. Travis from the corner of the room. "What are they saying? Why can't they speak English? Who are these people, George? George!"

The blind old girl was sitting on a kitchen chair. She wasn't just sitting in the chair, she was tied to it.

"What have you done to Mrs. Travis?" I yelled at the guy. "She can't see! She's as old as the hills. What have you tied her up for?"

"Mrs. Travis is helping us with our inquiries," said the guy.

"What inquiries?" I said.

"Speak English," yelled Mrs. Travis.

"Sorry, Mrs. Travis," I said in English. "This has got nothing to do with me...."

"That you, Ish?"

"Yeah, it's me."

"These louts said they were your friends."

"Pig's bum. I've never seen them before in my life. Honest, Mrs. Travis."

"Where's George?"

"I'm here," said George behind me.

I spun round. There was George all right. He was held in the vice like grip of the blubber who was now back on his feet.

"Let George go," I said. "What's he done to you?"

"Your concern for these good people is admirable," said the guy with the gat. I think it would be a good thing if we left them to get on with their lives, don't you?"

"They're my clients," I said. "I'm fixing them up. New appendix, new eyes."

"Ah yes. Well I'm sure they will be admirably looked after

by their new provider."

"What new provider?"

"Come, come, Neddy. Don't be naive. I think it's time we took a little trip. Don't you? I do believe I hear our taxi at the door."

I heard it too. I knew it wasn't a taxi. It was the semi with the mobile clinic on the back.

From what I could see, they'd done the container up real flash. All the operating gear you could possibly want. They put me in the recovery section. I sat on one of the beds. Gat-boy sat on the other. The semi swayed and jerked. You could hear the traffic outside, but, of course, you couldn't see anything. We could have been going anywhere.

"Where are we going?" I asked Gat-boy.

"For a ride," Gat-boy said.

"Could you point that thing in some other direction," I said. "I'm hardly going to make a dash for it."

Gat-boy didn't say anything, but he slowly moved the gun so that it was pointing at the floor.

"And who do I have the honor of addressing?" I said.

"Cut the cackle," Gat-boy said.

I supposed I'd have to take his advice. I didn't say anything for the rest of the ride. We seemed to be lurching along in traffic for hours.

Em Talking

The idiot boy didn't come home. He went out to the tracts one morning and disappeared. After three days Cicero was in a blue funk. He tried not to show it—but I'm well attuned to Cicero, I knew what he was thinking. He'd gone and lost his best operative—the bosses were not going to be pleased. They were going to be even less pleased if they thought he'd gone over to the Scott-Woks. Personally I didn't think this very likely, but Cicero did. He showed up in the kitchen of the Dog one morning. It was a slack time, I was cleaning one of the stoves, scrubbing the grease out with some gunk that got up my nose. Cicero leaned against a fridge. He looked thinner, more tense, darker than usual.

"They must've offered Earth-boy more newbs," Cicero said. "A bigger commission."

"The Scott-Woks?" I said. "They'd be more likely to offer him a swim in the harbor with concrete flippers."

"Everybody has their price. And he was at school with Mrs. Scott-Wok."

"Sue-Ellen Harrison works for the Aliens Board. I don't think she has much to do with the organ game."

"No, but her husband does."

"She doesn't see much of her husband. And anyway," I said, "he's in love with me."

"Scott-Wok? Bloody Astolphe? What are you talking about, girl?"

"Get real, Cicero. *Ned* is in love with me. He wouldn't go over to the opposition because that would mean leaving me. Leaving Aunty Nagoya's. Leaving all the friends he's got in the wharflands. He likes it here. He's not that interested in money."

"So where is he, then?"

"I don't know."

"The other sales staff are freaking out. They're refusing to go out to the tracts. I had to kick arse this morning just to get them out of the door."

"It's a hard life, Cicero—being a slave driver."

"You've changed, Em."

"Of course I've changed. I'm not the little girl who brought her pants-suit into your nonhydronic all those years ago."

"It wasn't that long ago."

"It was a long way away—Newharp might as well be a thousand years ago."

For a minute Cicero said nothing. He was preoccupied, jumpy—it made me nervous just to look at him. I returned to scrubbing the stove. Behind my back Cicero said, "There's a new group arrived, straight from home. The first runabout landed last week."

"Rumors, Cicero. Everything is rumors."

We were both silent. I suppose every refugee community that ever existed works in the same way as ours. News from home. It's what people talk about, speculate about, sing mournful songs about, dream about: news from home. I was no different—I still cried myself to sleep occasionally, remembering my planet, my childhood, my parents. Any new arrivals in the wharflands were the object of my intense, burning interest, until all their news had been extracted, digested, made part of the doleful set of stories we all told each other. But I had learned to be cynical, to present a hard shell to the world. I said to Cicero, "The buggers probably left Newharp before we did."

And that was a distinct possibility. There were many routes from Newharp to Earth, they all involved jumps at greater than the speed of light and then some travel well below it. You could be in orbit around some desolate star for months, years, waiting for the right moment to make the next hyper-c leap. New arrivals—fresh off the runabouts—could easily be carrying news that was history when people like me were still in kindergarten back on Newharp.

"This lot have come direct, Em. Hyper-c in one bound to the belt, then straight into the runabout. And the cits didn't pick them up."

I'd heard this rumor before: the messengers from home who had struck it lucky, made the trip with no stopovers, no pirate infested orbits, no stay in a detention center, who had news that was so fresh it filled your senses like new baked bread.

"Oh yeah," I said.

"Yeah," Cicero said.

"So what's their news?"

"They've revised the estimate. The rock isn't as big as they thought—they might be able to deflect it."

"Wish fulfillment—all the bombs in the galaxy couldn't knock it off course. You know that, Cicero. These stories are just stories. And anyway, the monsters haven't the wit to...."

"Things are getting politically unstable. There have been coup attempts. Ulrike Lewis has united all the opposition forces...."

"Ulrike Lewis," I said. "The Planet's Poet? She may be very old and very famous. She's hardly a dynamic leader."

"She's a symbol, Em. People unite behind symbols. With a united opposition the balance of power will shift.

"So the rock smashes into a planet that's got a full scale civil war raging. Great. That'll stop the hostilities."

"Well, it's not our problem at the moment," Cicero said. "Our problem is Earth-boy."

"It's not *our* problem. It's your problem. My problem is a greasy stove."

"The tracts are critical. If we lose the tracts, we'll never dominate the market. I've told the bosses I can deliver the tracts."

"Then put in more sales staff," I said. "Saturate the joint."

"I've told you. They're scared."

"Cicero, I've got work to do."

"If he shows up. Let me know immediately."

"I'm sure Ned will come and see you when he gets back. He does work for you, after all."

"That's a matter of opinion."

"Bye, Cicero."

"Bye," he said and was gone.

I continued cleaning the stove. It wasn't a job that required mental effort. My mind was as free as bird. Except that I didn't know what to think. I was worried about Ned for obvious reasons. But I was also worried about Cicero. For the first time in his life he seemed vulnerable. Cicero the hard man—streetwise, cat-like—suddenly he was worried about the bosses, worried about his job. I wondered what the bosses would do to him if he stuffed up in the tracts. I'd never met the Tetride bosses, I didn't know who they were, or how many there were, or even where they came from. Some of them could have been Earthlings for all I knew. But, like everybody else, I knew they ultimately ran the wharflands. The profits I helped the Dog to earn, ended up in the bosses' coffers. The organ den in the basement paid its percentage. Even the cat-burglars out on the street probably coughed up a few newbucks a week, paid for their cat-burglar's license. It was a funny thing, but I suddenly felt protective, I wanted to help Cicero, I wanted to stroke his brow, hold him tight to me. I hadn't shown what I felt, of course. I'd told him to go away, I'd told him I had work to do. And I hadn't shown him what I felt about the rumors from home. Oh god, I wanted those rumors to be true! I wanted my planet to survive, my parents and relations and friends to live. But all I'd shown Cicero was my cynicism—and perhaps I was right to be cynical. Because, as I'd said, rumors are just rumors, they're what people want to believe, not what's true. I looked down at the surface of the stove. I'd polished it good and proper, my tears were falling on a gleaming surface. By midnight the cooks would have laid down a new coat of grease.

Ned Talking

You wouldn't believe the joint. You wouldn't believe the size of it, the poncy, gleaming, glinting, humming splendor of the fittings. It was some sort of left over palace. The floor was polished rock—marble maybe. (Don't ask me, we didn't have marble in Tidy Town). There were these rugs: all intricate and woven—peacocks and lions and flowers. And the furniture was made of real polished wood and gold handles and—I don't know, silk? (What does silk look like, feel like?). And antiques: crazy old clocks with round dials and metal arrows pointing at the funny old numbers. Great metal bommy knockers swinging from side to side behind glass. Pictures on the walls—mad old biblical dudes striking poses in huge gold frames. And the whole palace was huge, rooms leading off rooms leading off corridors with vast gardens on the other side of the windows. Statues, fountains, real live peacocks screeching like banshees.

"Nice place," I said to gat-boy.

"I see you appreciate the finer things," gat-boy said. "In here."

The room he pushed me into wasn't as big as the ones we'd been walking through. This one was a bit more intimate—homey, you might say, comfy. It was only about twice the size of Aunty Nagoya's eating and gambling room. There was a massive desk made of polished wood and leather, another table with half a dozen chairs around it, there were a number of very deep soft looking armchairs. There were a number of hard straight-back chairs on spindly wooden legs. A fire was blazing in a stone fireplace. The walls were covered with glass book cases. The books looked old and moth-eaten. The glass reflected the cheery warmth of the fire.

"Sit down," gat-boy said, waving his gun towards a spindly chair.

But I tossed myself into one of the deep armchairs instead. "Comfy," I said.

"Please don't get smart, Neddy," gat-boy said. He sat down himself on one of the straight-back chairs.

"What do we do now?" I said.

"Wait," he said. "We wait patiently."

"I reckon I'd be right in saying that this prime bit of real estate belongs to Astolphe Scott-Wok," I said.

"You are indeed the guest of Mr. Scott-Wok."

"Christ, he's done all right for himself, hasn't he?" I said. Gat-boy didn't reply. So I tried again, "How do you read that?" I said pointing to an antique clock with a swinging bommy knocker.

"In the normal way," gat-boy said. "It's a normal analogue clock. Of the grandfather variety."

"Never seen one before. What's it say?"

"Twenty-five past twelve."

"Close to lunchtime," I said.

"Are you hungry?" a voice said behind me.

I tried to look round, but the chair I was in was so deep and high that my view was obscured. I was forced to stand up. I noticed that gat-boy was standing up as well. The guy behind my chair was dressed in formal Newharp clobber. He was about thirty. Dark black hair, silly beard, too much jewelry, but the earrings were pretty flash. He seemed quite friendly.

"Where the hell did you spring from?" I said.

"Ah," he said, "I'm afraid it's a terrible cliché, but it's one I couldn't resist. I just had to have it built."

"What built?"

"Watch," he said and walked over to one of the bookcases. This bookcase wasn't covered in glass. You could just grab a book. The guy grabbed a book. I reckon the book triggered a switch. The bookcase slid silently to one side. There was a passage behind it. The guy replaced the book and the bookcase returned to its original position.

"As I'm sure you know, the Earthlings have this tradition: murder in the study; secret entrance behind the bookcase; the butler is always the prime suspect, but, in fact, he never does it."

"You Scott-Wok?" I said.

"That is my name."

"About lunch...."

"What would you like?"

"Steak and eggs and tomato-sauce."

"What a splendid suggestion. I'll have the same." Scott-Wok turned to gat-boy and said, "Snodgrass, if you'd like to arrange things. I'm sure Ned and I will be most comfortable dining here."

"Very good, sir," gat boy said and left the room by the normal door.

"Do sit down," Scott-Wok said. "Has Snodgrass been waving that gun thing around the whole time?"

"Yeah. And is that his real name, Snodgrass?"

"I'm afraid so."

"No wonder he wouldn't introduce himself."

"He is a bit sensitive," Scott-Wok said. "My wife speaks very highly of you."

"Sue-Ellen," I said. "Yeah, well, err...I speak very highly of her."

"Tell me a little about yourself."

"How about you tell me why I've been brought here."

"In the fullness of time, Ned. After lunch, perhaps. Let's just engage in idle chit-chat for the moment. Get to know one another."

"I am a simple brush salesman," I said.

"I'm told you once shoved a dead pigeon up the deputy principal's pipe."

"*Exhaust* pipe," I said. "Even that old girl wouldn't smoke a dead pigeon."

"You'd be surprised what people smoke," Scott-Wok said.

"I don't think so," I said. "I've been around a bit."

"I'm sure you have. The footage of your escapade with the fire truck is one of my favorite bits of telly. I play it often. I have had whole dinner parties cheering you on, spilling their brandy, demanding instant replay."

"Everybody's gotta have their fifteen minutes of fame," I said.

"And, having had your fifteen minutes, do you have no further ambition?"

"I'm happy doing what I do," I said.

There was a knock on the door. Scott-Wok said, "Come," and the door opened and lunch arrived on a sort of trolley pushed by a maid in full Newharp gear. She set two places on the table, unloaded the tucker and departed without saying a word. "Let's eat," said Scott-Wok, "I'm starving."

Me and Scott-Wok plonked ourselves down at the table and hoed in. The food was exactly what I'd ordered: steak and eggs and tomato sauce. As well, there were french fries and a chocolate thickshake. No vegetables—absolutely no vegetables. A great wave of homesickness swept over me—this was Tidy Town tuck, this was Friday night after the pictures. All we needed was a bit of hooch.

"All we need is a bit of hooch," I said.

"I believe there is a distressing prevalence of under-age drinking in the desert townships," Scott-Wok said.

"Sue-Ellen would be a bit of an expert on that problem," I said.

"I believe you both led wild lives in your youth."

"I was just an ordinary desert rat—nothing special."

"Tell me about my mother-in-law."

I nearly choked, it was such an unexpected request. I had to think for a few seconds to work out who he meant. "Old ma Harrison," I said. "I'd never really thought of old ma Harrison as being your mother-in-law."

"I am married to her daughter."

"Old ma Harrison reckons you *ate* her daughter—she thinks that's what aliens do: eat honest people's daughters."

"It is a lamentable prejudice...."

"The reason she thinks that is because Sue-Ellen herself sent her mum an anonymous email. The email claimed to be from someone who'd personally eaten Sue-Ellen. The email said she'd been very tasty."

"One of the things I had to learn when I first arrived on Earth," Scott-Wok said, "was to appreciate Earth humor. My wife was a great help in that respect. But tell me more about Mrs. Harrison."

"She burnt down the Mothers and Babies."

"This is the institute in which she worked?"

"That's right. She was heaping hot coals on the place where sin had been—purifying the joint."

"The...err...*joint* was in need of purification?"

"Old ma Harrison is very religious. Some layabouts had broken into the Mothers and Babies after the pub one night. She reckoned they'd done it."

"Done it?"

"The sin of fornication or something."

We had a real good old chinwag, me and Scott-Wok. He was a nice sort of a bloke. Charming, you could say—a fair dinkum prince charming. I could see why the young Sue-Ellen had fallen for him. I felt he was really interested in what I was saying. He wanted to know all about life in Tidy, he wanted to know as much as possible about the scene in which Sue-Ellen had grown up. It was a pity she was so much older than me, we hadn't really run with the same crowd. I'd just been a little squirt in short pants when she'd been scandalizing the town, staying out all night, hitching home in the morning because the ute had run out of gemco while they were tearing up the Ice Field. But I told Scott-Wok as much as I could.

"She's not at home at the moment?" I asked.

"No she's back at Spearchucker. It's a good job they never worked out who took that footage. Did you meet Helen?"

"Helen?"

"Our child."

"Oh, the little alien baby."

"Scott-Wok laughed easily. I hadn't offended him. He said, "Some of my more conservative Newharp friends call her the little Earth baby. You didn't meet her at Spearchucker?"

"No, she was in the staff quarters."

Scott-Wok leaned back in his chair and pressed a button on the desk behind him. He spoke into a hidden microphone, "Karlin, please bring Helen to the east lawn if she's not still asleep." Then he said to me, "She still has a nap in the afternoon, but then she's keen for play. Come on, let's get some fresh air."

Sue-Ellen's daughter was a pretty child in a frilly dress. She played a mean game of lawn slogball. Scott-Wok and I were run off our feet fielding her passes. The peacocks screamed—they weren't impressed, but what the hell. The statue we were using as a goal took a number of direct hits, but it was a sturdy beast with two heads.

"What's it meant to be?" I said to Scott-Wok.

"It's a rodopi—a native Newharp carnivore," he said.

"It's a dog-goat," Helen said. "It's called Jimbo."

"If you say so," said her dad.

"I do," Helen said.

"Ned was at school with Mummy," Scott-Wok said.

"Did you learn English at school," Helen said.

"Err...sort of," I said. "But we all spoke English anyway."

"I can speak English," Helen said. "I can sing a song." And then she sang in English: "Scott-Woks all let us rejoice, for we are young and free. We've wealth for toil and lots of oil, our home is Gert-by-Sea. It's Gert-by-Sea, well bugger me, our land is Gert-by-Sea!"

"Who taught you that?" I said.

"Mummy, she made it up."

"That figures," I said and passed her the ball.

"We've called our house *Santa Gertrudis Por Mar*, after the capital of Newharp," Scott-Wok said. "But Sue-Ellen insists on calling it Gert-by-sea."

Helen took a shot at the statue and bounced the ball off its left head. "Catch, Daddy," she yelled.

Scott-Wok took a flying leap and plucked the ball out of the air.

"Throw it to Ned."

Scott-Wok threw me the ball. I passed it back again. We played on for another ten minutes. Scott-Wok said, "What about hooch?"

"What about it?" I said.

"Want some?"

"Sure."

The three of us went back to the study. Helen sat on a pile of cushions at the big desk and drew with crayons on a roll of butcher's paper. She drank with a straw from a chunky glass of flavored milk. Scott-Wok and I sat on each side of the log fire and sipped hooch. Except it wasn't hooch—it was something Scott-Wok called silverberry. The finest Newharp liqueur there was, he assured me. This stuff had actually come from Newharp, all the way, dodging the pirates, dodging the cits. It was worth its weight in gold.

As far as the alcohol content went, it was worth its weight in hooch. It took most of the skin off the inside of my throat. I started to feel a bit sleepy.

Scott Wok said, "Do you see much of the bosses?"

"Like the bosses of the Tetrides?"

"Yes, those chaps."

"I'm just a small fish. I don't even know who the bosses are, I've never seen one."

"You wouldn't want to," Scott-Wok said. "They're an ugly bunch. No style."

"Umm. They pay a reasonable commission," I said, "I'm not complaining."

"Have you got ambitions, Ned?"

"Err...umm...never really thought about it," I said. I was no fool. I recognized what was happening. This was the serious part of the conversation. I decided not to drink any more of Scott-Wok's booze.

"Here, let me fill your glass," Scott-Wok said.

I didn't want to offend the guy. I held out my glass.

"What do you see yourself doing in five years time?" Scott-Wok said.

"Five years!" I said. "Who ever thinks that far ahead?"

"It pays to have a vision," Scott-Wok said. "Surely you don't see yourself still living in that ants' nest, still peddling organs door to door?"

"I rather like living at Aunty Nagoya's," I said. "And anyway, how do you know I live there?"

"Any childhood friend of Sue-Ellen's is a friend of mine. I take an interest...."

"Like I've said, we weren't really friends. She's a lot older than me."

"But there's the shared background. Growing up in Tidy Town...."

"Mummy says Tidy Town is a shit heap," Helen said from behind the desk. "Only mad dogs and blow flies live there."

"Darling, what Mummy says isn't always strictly true. She has a poetic streak."

"Is it true?" Helen asked me.

"Well, I suppose Tidy's a bit more primitive than this place," I said.

"This place is a gilded cage," Helen said. "Mummy says we live in it like parrots on a perch."

"And perhaps, Helen, you should stop parroting your mother all the time," Scott-Wok said.

I was a bit muddled by Scott-Wok's booze, but I caught the undercurrent. The slight edge of anger wasn't really directed at his daughter. It was Sue-Ellen and her opinions that old Scotters was a bit pissed off about. A complicated marriage.

"Just one more glass," Scott-Wok said to me, back to maximum charm.

I looked down at my glass. Christ, I'd drained the thing. I must have been sipping without realizing it. "Err...it's powerful stuff," I said.

"I'm sure you're man enough for a little silverberry," Scott-Wok said, pouring. "How old are you now, Ned?"

"Eighteen. Nearly."

"By the time you are twenty you could be living in the lap of luxury, driving a fast car, making more in a day than you now make in a year. And girls...well, let's leave that bit unsaid."

"What's the deal?" I said.

"Deal? Oh, I don't know that there is any deal involved. Those would just be the fruits of honest labor on your part. A bright lad like yourself could hardly miss."

"Honestly laboring for who?" I said.

"Well, I suppose it might be to your advantage not to linger too long in the employ of the Tetride bosses. Unimaginative employers, in my opinion."

"You're offering me a job?"

"At the moment, no."

"Then why," I said, yawning, "did you have me kidnapped and brought here?"

"Kidnapped is surely too strong a word. I was just keen to make your acquaintance."

"Well listen, Scott-Wok old mate, I reckon I'm happy living

where I live and doing what I do."

"Of course you are, but you could always diversify."

"Meaning?"

"Meaning, you could become a...let us say, a foreign corre-spondent as well as a salesman."

"Corresponding with who?"

"Well, I for one am always keen to know what is going on south of the harbor, or out in the tracts."

I looked at the fire. There seemed to be more flames than before. Maybe I was seeing double. So Scotters wanted a spy. He probably already had a few—someone had told him where I lived. But he wanted another one, and I wanted to get out of his gilded cage alive. There didn't seem much harm in agreeing. I didn't actually know anything, I never had contact with the bosses, I was low level and keen to stay that way.

"I'll think about it," I said.

"Splendid," Scott-Wok said. "You look as if you could do with a little nap. You will stay the night, of course? I'm afraid I won't be able to dine with you—I have to go out myself—a tedious function. Snodgrass will see to all your requirements. Won't you Snodgrass?"

I looked up. Snodgrass had entered the room, he was standing directly behind my chair. I hadn't heard him arrive. Helen was nowhere to be seen. I hadn't heard her leave.

"I'm sure Ned will feel perfectly at home, sir," Snodgrass said.

"I'm sure he will," Scott-Wok said. "Now if you'll excuse me...." And the bugger was gone, disappearing through his magic bookcase, like a ghost through a wall.

"This way," Snodgrass said, helping me to my feet with a wrench that half dislocated my shoulder. "Been on the silver-berry, have we, Neddy-boy? Some people get all the breaks. Haven't been able to afford a slug of that for years. Next Christmas if I'm lucky."

The palace was a maze of marble. None of the passages seemed to be straight any more. I'd no idea where I was.

Snodgrass opened a door and ushered me in. There was a bed in the room. God it looked inviting.

"The shower and crapper's through there," Snodgrass said. "Pleasant dreams."

The door shut and I was alone. "Hey," I said to the shut door. "Hey, Snod...." I tugged at the handle. The door was locked. No kidding, I said to myself. I trudged across the three metres to the bed and collapsed on it.

Em Talking

At Aunty Nagoya's I lived in a broom cupboard. Not quite, but almost. The room was so narrow there was hardly any space between the bed and the wall. Most of my clothes hung from nails driven into the back of the door. The window was high and, if I stood on my bed to look out, I saw rusting roofing iron, crumbling brick and cats fucking. But it was my room. All mine. If I shut the door, bolted it, I was alone in my own universe. I could have moved into Cicero's huge front room, shared his huge bed, stepped out through the sash windows onto the weathered planks of his balcony and sat and watched the passing parade in the street below, sipping Cicero's hooch. But the price would have been too great. If I shared Cicero's bed, it was only occasionally, and on my terms.

Late one night, after my shift at the Dog had finished, I lay on my own bed and looked at the ceiling. A single light bulb dangled from a dirty wire, but there was a pattern of old smoke stains on the plaster. I knew enough Earth history to know what they were. During the Economic Ice Age the electricity had been shut off for a few thousand years. They'd forgotten how to make electricity. Long dead lodgers had lived and snored and made love in this room by the light of gemco lamps. Trimming the wick, trying to get the flame to burn clean, not always succeeding. There was a knock on the door. I thought it might be Cicero. I didn't want to see him, so I lay still and said nothing. The knock came again. It was a light knock, slightly hesitant. It wasn't Cicero. I got up and pulled the bolt back. Quincy stood in the dim light of the passage, her black patchwork smock made her look like a raven.

"Hiya Quince," I said. "Come in."

"I'm not disturbing you?"

"Hell, no," I said. "I was just studying the ceiling."

Quincy kicked off her boots and we both sat on the bed with our backs to the wall and our knees under our chins. There was nowhere else to sit.

"Where do you reckon Ish is?" she said.

"Dunno," I said. "Taking a short break."

"A holiday in the tracts? It doesn't seem likely."

"There's no point worrying," I said. "He'll turn up."

"I reckon the Scott-Woks have got him," Quincy said.

"It's possible," I said. "But I don't reckon it's likely."

"You know Mrs. Scott-Wok don't you?"

"She's called Sue-Ellen Harrison. Yeah, I met her in Spearchucker, but I haven't seen her since."

"Send her an e. Ask her if she knows anything."

"Why're you so worried, Quince?"

Quincy was silent, looking straight ahead at the opposite wall. Her face was half hidden by her golden red hair, but there was a tear in the eye I could see.

"You're in love with him, aren't you?" I said.

"Suppose so," she muttered.

"I'm pleased for you, Quince. Make the silly boy see sense when he turns up."

"He's in love with you," she said.

"Yeah, I know," I said. "But it shouldn't be too hard to... what's the phrase? The Earthlings have a phrase."

"Alienate his affections," Quince said.

"That's right," I said laughing. "You're almost as alien as I am. Grab his affections."

"Can you send Mrs. Scott-Wok an e? Find out what she knows?"

"They're not secure," I said. "Every bastard and his dog reads other people's email."

"You're talking like an Earthling," Quincy said. "Every bastard and his dog."

"I know," I said. "I listen to Ned too much."

"Don't ask Mrs. Scott-Wok straight out," Quincy said. "Can't you sort of, you know, put it in code."

"Leave it another day, Quince," I said. "If he's not back by this time tomorrow we'll see what we can do."

We talked some more, Quincy and I. We just nattered about the other lodgers, the extent of Quincy's jongma winnings, the politics of the Dog's kitchen. I told Quincy about the rumors from Home.

"Would you like to go back?" Quincy said.

"Yep," I said.

"All those months of travel. All those pirates?"

"I'd chance it," I said.

"I wouldn't," Quincy said. "I wouldn't go to Kovalev, I wouldn't go to Newharp. I was born here, this is where I'm staying. My parents' planets are just the places that childhood stories come from. Sort of make-believe fairy lands."

"So's mine," I said. "But it's real too."

Two days later Quincy and I let ourselves into the room Harri and Ned share. They'd an old e machine, flickering on top of a chest of drawers. Hell it was primitive. It took me and Quince at least half an hour to get the program fired up and then another half hour to run a search for Sue-Ellen Harrison's @.

Dear Ms. Harrison,

I hope you remember me. You were once of great assistance to me when I was overcome by a fit and fell to the ground in a swoon. My health is much better these days, thank you very much, and I rarely keel over any more. I have found gainful employment as Secretary of the Pigeon Fancier's Association.

I am now writing to you on behalf of the Association. As you know, some terrible crimes have been committed against our feathered friends, and it is time that citizens of every creed and color took a stand against cruelty to pigeons. For example, my Association recently heard of a case in which a pigeon was stuffed into the exhaust pipe of a Dogstar and fired violently through the letter box of a school. This sort of thing has got to stop. We are trying to gather as much information about the perpetrators of these crimes, especially the horrendous one I have just mentioned. The criminal in question seems to have disappeared. We need to track him down. Schools should be places of love and tranquility and not hell houses of animal cruelty. If you can help in any way, please let me know.

Gonzalez Della, Secretary

A day later, we got a reply:

Dear Mr. Della,

I do indeed remember you well. I am so glad your health has improved. I'm afraid I can't help you with any information about cruelty to pigeons at the moment, but I am touched by the story you tell. If I ever learn anything about pigeon-baiters such as the Dogstar fiend you mention, I will let you know the details.

Yours sincerely,
Sue-Ellen Harrison

"She's just being polite," Quincy said. "She thinks you're a nutter and she's giving you the brush off."

"Rubbish," I said. "She's just making it look like that. She says she remembers me. She says she'll let me know if she finds out anything about Ned. That's exactly what we want her to do."

"I hope you're right," Quincy said.

"Have faith, Quince," I said. "I know this Ms Harrison, she's hot stuff. Can you keep a secret?"

"Of course."

"She shot that footage of Ned wrecking the runabouts. If the Aliens Board knew which one of their own employees gave that stuff to the telly, they'd fire her, pronto."

"I don't think she needs the money," Quincy said. "Not with her husband owning half the Newharp businesses in town—legal and not so legal."

"I think it's because Astolphe Scott-Wok is so rich that she needs to earn her own dough," I said. "Wouldn't you? Under similar circumstances?"

"Maybe," Quincy said. "Come on, let's go downstairs and win a few measly newbucks."

"You play, Quince," I said. "I'll watch."

"Do you know how to play jongma?" Quincy said.

"No," I said. "And I don't want to."

Ned Talking

My brain was going down the drain. I'll never drink again, I swear to god. I made it through the door to the shower and crapper department. It was more like a museum. Crappers through the ages—take your pick. Showers, baths and whirlpools—marble, brass, glass. I threw up into something—it looked more like a bird-bath than a crapper. Maybe it was, maybe it was for the in-house parrot. Jeeze I felt crook. I went back to bed.

I wasn't feeling much better when cheery gat-boy Snodgrass showed up tugging a trolley covered with dishes of dinner through the door. Blubber boy was pushing it.

"Take it away, Snodders," I said.

"You've got to keep your strength up," Snodgrass said. "We can't have you dying of malnutrition."

"Go away."

"But we've come to keep you company," Snodgrass said. "I'll just lay the table and we can all get stuck in."

I watched through closed eyes as Snodgrass and Blubber

boy transferred the food to a round table that stood in the corner of the room. It wasn't a pretty sight. I turned my eyes towards the window. It was night, the black window reflected the table. Snodgrass placed two candles on the table. Blubber boy produced a lighter with a flame like a bunsen burner and lit them. In the window the reflected candles danced in the night. Snodgrass fished a wine bottle from the lower deck of the trolley and eyeballed the label. "Smooth tannin finish," he said. "Hint of raspberry."

"Bugger off," I said.

Snodgrass drew up a chair and sat down. Blubber did the same. It was a wonder the chair didn't crack. They had laid a third place.

"Come on, Neddy," Snodgrass said. "No party-pooping."

"I'm not hungry."

"All the more for us, then."

For a while there was silence in the room. I closed my eyes. The silence was punctuated by the sounds of chomping, slurping, belching, guzzling and the clashing of knives and forks on plates. Feeding time at the zoo.

"Have some pud, at least," Snodgrass said. "Sticky caramel custard sundae garnished with glacé silverberries and dripping with a thick liqueur sauce. Plenty of added sugar. Cook's excelled herself."

I didn't say anything. I ignored them.

"You'll need a modus operandus," Snodgrass said. "Tradecraft. Very important."

"What are you on about?" I said.

"Your new life as a foreign correspondent."

"I'm not a foreign correspondent. I'm a door-to-door salesman."

"That as well," Snodgrass said. "They are not mutually exclusive callings."

"Snodgrass, I don't move in important circles. I don't know the Tetride bosses. I don't know anything that would be of use to Scott-Wok. I'm not a spy."

"Of course you're not. You're a foreign correspondent. It's all arranged, all agreed. Mr. Scott-Wok said so. All you need is a bit of training."

"Training?"

"You've got a rigorous schedule in front of you. We are your handlers. We're here to handle you. Cheroot?"

"What?"

"Cigar. Would you like a cigar, Ned?"

"No I wouldn't."

"Then I'm sure you don't mind if we indulge. Rounds off the meal."

I managed to sit up on the bed. I looked at Snodgrass. I looked at Blubber. They were lighting huge cigars, leaning forward over the table, sticking the ends of the things into one of the candle flames. They could have been kids drinking with a couple of straws from the one milkshake. They sat back, puffing. Soon the whole place stank.

"Dead letter boxes," Snodgrass said.

"What?" I said.

"They're where foreign correspondents post their letters."

There was no point in arguing. The sooner these guys trained me up as a spy, the sooner I was out of the place.

"All right, tell me," I said. "What do I need to know about dead letter boxes?"

"Ah, that's the spirit, Neddy boy. Already you are keen for enlightenment. What about a slug of tawny port to get us going? Very good year."

"Get on with it."

Em Talking

Dear Mr. Della,

I happened to mention to a colleague your interest in bringing pigeon-baiters to justice. My colleague tells me that he has heard of the appalling Dogstar exhaust outrage, but believes

the perpetrator is currently alive and well in one of the regret-
table no-go areas of our society. However I'm sure the fiend will
sooner or later return to civilization. That will be your chance.

Yours sincerely,

Sue-Ellen Harrison

"So what do you reckon?" Quincy said, pointing a dayglow fingernail at the screen.

"I reckon Ned has been captured by the Scott-Woks. He is alive and well. He'll be coming back to us soon."

"If the Tetride bosses learn that Ish has been mixing it with the Scott-Woks," Quincy said, "even against his will, they won't be too happy. They might reckon Ish is a security risk."

"Well, let's stay quiet," I said.

"I'm not thinking of shouting it from the roof tops. I think I might go downstairs and see what's for lunch. Coming?"

"No," I said. "I've got to go to work in a few minutes."

"How long are you going to stick at it?" Quincy said.

"The Dog? I don't know."

"All those drunks patting you on the bum. All those greasy stoves. Slop buckets. Cockroaches. Rats. Bad pay."

"I do know my own work conditions, Quince."

"Well, what are you going to do about it?"

"I'd like to start my own business," I said.

"Doing what?"

"I don't know—a language school, maybe."

"Illegals like you have to keep a low profile. Even in the wharflands. You can't go sticking up a sign: *The Lingo Center— Emceesquared Gonzalez della Harpenden, Proprietor.*"

"Want to be my front woman?"

"If we start a business, any sort of business, we'll be paying protection money to the Tetrides."

"Goes with the territory, Quince."

"I'll think about it."

Ned Talking

I didn't see Scott-Wok again. I didn't see Helen. But I saw a lot of Snodders and Blubber—and I didn't much like what I saw. But I didn't complain. I listened to what they told me. I memorized the routines. I learned how to place bugs in phones, computers, cars, holes in the wall. They gave me a camera so small you could hide it in the heel of your shoe. They gave me a pair of shoes with hollow heels.

"So what am I meant to use all this crap for?" I said. "What am I meant to photograph? Who am I meant to bug?"

"All in good time, Ned. All in good time."

But they never told me. After three days Snodgrass suddenly announced we were going back to the tracts. Five minutes later we were in the mobile clinic, grinding through traffic we couldn't see.

"Madam sends her regards," Snodgrass said.

"Who's Madam?" I said.

"Mrs. Scott-Wok."

"Sue-Ellen! Scott-Wok told me she was at Spearchucker."

"She is. She sends her regards."

"Did Scotters ring her up, tell her all the news from home?"

"Mrs. Scott-Wok rang up herself. Apparently the secretary of some bird-brained animal rights group is interested in your whereabouts."

"Animal rights?"

"You have a reputation for cruelty to pigeons. You fire them through letter boxes."

"That pigeon! It was already dead."

"If you say so."

They dropped me in the tracts, not far from where they'd kidnapped me.

"Remember," Snodgrass said, "Just go about your daily business, Ned. We'll be in touch."

I stood in the street and watched the clinic lumber away. It was about lunchtime. I was hungry. I found a milk bar and drank some milk and ate a bar of bird seed held together with sugar. I didn't feel like going about my daily business. I felt flat and depressed. To sell organs door to door you need to be hyped up, thinking positive, firing on all cylinders. I looked out of the window of the milk bar. The tracts had never looked so dreary, so tedious. There was a Paul Lean poster on a wall across the street. Somebody had vandalized it. I should have been pleased, but the sight just depressed me. I shouldered my bag of brushes and wandered off in search of a light rail station. By mid afternoon I was back in the wharflands.

There was no one I wanted to talk to at Aunty Nagoya's, there wasn't even a game in progress, so I dumped my brushes and made my way round to the Dog. There wasn't a lot going on there either. But Cicero d'Pettitt was sitting at a table talking to someone I didn't recognize. I nodded to Cicero and kept walking in the direction of the kitchens. On the floor Fido-Fido opened one eye and granted me a greeting with a single thump of his tail.

"G'day Fides," I said, but the animal had already closed its eye and returned to sleep.

"Where the hell have you been?" Cicero called out behind my back.

"Tracts," I said and kept walking.

"Where the hell have you been?" Em said in the kitchens. She was scouring pots at a sink of murky water. Her arms were bare and there was a ring of soap suds around both her elbows. She looked gorgeous—fierce, but gorgeous.

"Tracts," I said.

"Pig shit," she said. "You're in deep trouble, Ned."

"I met an old friend from Tidy in the tracts. An old mate from school. I stayed a couple of nights. It saved on the traveling."

"This old mate got a name?"

"Johnny Wannamarra. He's got a job in a panel beaters. Beating panels. Out in the tracts."

"If that's your story, you'd better stick to it, idiot-boy," Em said in a whisper. Then she looked past my shoulder and said in a normal voice, "Look, this isn't a social club. This is my place of work. I'm at work. Howabout the three of you decamp smartly back into the dining room. You're allowed to socialize out there."

"Certainly," Cicero said. "We've just come to invite Ishmael to join us."

I looked at the pair of them. They meant business. "After you," I said and followed them out of the kitchens. I was getting a bit sick of having my life ordered by pairs of heavies. We sat down at the table.

"Ishmael Codwallader," I said to the guy, extending my hand.

"I know who you are," he said in a cold voice, not shaking my hand.

"But I don't know who you are," I said, and looked at the hand I was holding out as if I suddenly suspected it might be covered in bird shit or something.

"Cut the funny business," Cicero said. "Start talking. And it had better be good."

I went into my spiel. Snodgrass and Blubber had already drilled me in it. Knocks on door in tracts. Door opened by old friend—Johnny Wannamarra. Stays for a yarn. Goes to see another old friend. Everyone gets on hooch. Stays night. Car breaks down on way back to Johnny's house. Has to stay another night. More hooch. All phones out of action because of local recycling.

"Recycling?" d'Pettitt said.

"The wires, the cables, they melt them down."

"Heard of mobiles?"

"They recycle the towers. Cut them up and flog them to scrap metal boys. It's hell out there in the tracts, mate. They don't have infrastructure in the tracts. See, living here in the wharf-lands, with the Tetrides keeping everything under control, you forget what primitive animals people turn into when there's no structure, no social contract, no...."

"Shut up, Earth boy. Did you meet any of the opposition on your travels?"

"The Scott-Woks? No didn't see hide nor hair."

"You'd better be telling the truth."

"Of course I'm telling the truth, what do you reckon? That I've been dining and wining with Astolphe? I think you're getting a bit paranoid, Cicero."

"We'll be watching you from now on, just remember that, we'll be watching you."

Poor old d'Pettitt, he sounded quite desperate. He sounded like a man trying to impress his boss with a display of toughness. I reckoned the other guy was his boss. Maybe the other guy was one of the top Tetride bosses. He was a mean looking dude, but he had no style. Scott-Wok had said the bosses were an ugly bunch with no style. This specimen fitted the description.

"Well, I'll be off, then," I said. "See you around."

I got up from the table, half expecting one of them to order me to sit down again. But they didn't. I was halfway to the door when Cicero said, "Just remember...."

"Yeah, I know," I said without turning round. "You'll be watching me. I've got that bit."

I'd only gone a few hundred meters when I heard a familiar sound: live dogs used as bagpipes. I stopped to listen. If the truth be told, I'd started to like Kovalev music—it's an acquired taste. There are subtleties that escape the casual listener. The noise was coming from an open doorway in a building that had once been The Mission to the Deaf and the Dumb, but was probably now a church. The old sign had been carved into the wall above the door—but a new one in day-glow colors had been painted over it: *Interplanetary PentaNostra Rebirth Meeting, All welcome.* The canine bagpipes were joined by another sound, a twangleodium. This was an outrage—I'm not a purest, but you can't mix Newharp music with Kovalev music. We're talking oil and water, we're talking chalk and cheese, we're talking oil and chalk. A voice started to sing. Smith Mei Lim. Gawdalmighty, I thought they'd deported her. But they hadn't, it was her all right. I walked through the door into a sort of vestibule. A crazy old geezer pressed a pamphlet into my hands and ushered me through a gap in some curtains. What a sight! There was a whole hall full of people. There was a band on stage and there were mad bastards handling baby alligators. I'd heard about baby-alligator-handling: it brought you closer to god. Quincy had told us all about it one night in the Dog. She'd had the whole table in stitches—but no one had really believed her. She'd said her Newharp mum went in for the baby-alligators while her Kovalev dad was a lizard man.

On the stage Smith Mei Lim was twangling and singing. The words were a bit hard to make out, but there was some crap about casting out the gators of desire, and consigning the monsters to the fire. Those loonies who had alligators in their hands were holding them up and waving them about. The alligators were going frantic, snapping at everything in sight. They were only about twenty centimeters long, from tail to snout—they couldn't have been more than a week old. If they'd been any bigger they'd have made mincemeat of all concerned. There was a lot of howling and yelling and people talking in tongues. I could barely believe my eyes—in the old days Smith Mei Lim had been upset when I howled along with her twangling. Now look at her, positively working the crowd into a howling fit. One old goat started to stuff a baby alligator down his trousers. A circle of gibbering onlookers formed around him. Crying out to the lords their gods and all manner of saints and cultural icons. The air was thick with wailings and gnashing of teeth and lamentations in every language spoken in the wharflands— and then some. The trouser stuffer got the animal completely under his belt. You wondered what it was going to bite. But it shot down his right leg and savaged his boot, then it was out of the joint, scuttling like a rat, snapping to right and left. The old boy fell to the floor, rolling his eyes, babbling. The crowd surged in and picked him up, held him shoulder high. Smith Mei Lim yowled about the wordergod, the teeth of sod—or something—who knows what she was actually saying, clarity of diction wasn't her strong point. Great clouds of incense were pouring out of a brazier on the stage. One of the band members threw a handful of something into the brazier, sparks, flames more smoke. A rhythmic chanting started around a young girl with a baby alligator. She held it high, she gazed at it with wild eyes. She might have been a sword sallower, except she held a writhing, snapping alligator in her hands, not a sword. But that didn't stop her, she rammed the alligator down her throat.

"This is a disgrace," a voice said beside me.

"No kidding," I said without turning to look—my eyes were glued to the girl with the alligator tail sticking out of her mouth. The girl spewed, she chundered, she barfed. The alligator and a whole stream of puke and blood shot up into the air and fell to the floor.

"This is no way to find god," the voice said. "Behavior like this plays into the hands of Paul Lean and his followers."

I turned. It was Mr. Sam Yang Rhee. He was standing stock still, a rock amongst the waves of writhing nutters and reptiles. His face was drained of blood.

"You're not wrong, Mr. Sam," I said.

"The lord will wreck vengeance upon these heretics," he said.

"I sincerely hope so," I said.

"They will writhe in hell."

"I think they already are," I said.

"We sorrowed across the cosmos," Mr. Sam said. "For what? For this?" He looked as if he was about to faint.

"Come on, Mr. Sam," I said, "We're out of here."

I took him by the arm and gently pulled him through the crowd, through the curtains, through the door and into the street. We both stood still, getting our breath back, breathing air unpolluted by incense or screams and babblings. Mr. Sam got his eyes back into focus and looked at me properly for the first time.

"Do I know you?" he said.

I was about to tell him that of course he knew me, when I remembered that my whole face had been changed, and I was older by two years.

"It was a long time ago," I said. "Come on."

I led him back to the Dog. He seemed frailer than he'd been at Spearchucker, bewildered, confused, he was quite content to let me lead him by the arm. In the Dog we sat at a table. I looked around. The place was filling up; Cicero and his boss were nowhere to be seen. For which I was grateful.

"Tea," I said. "We'll order some tea." Em appeared, now dressed in her "traditional" costume.

"You again?" she said to me.

"I've brought a friend," I said.

"Mr. Sam," she said in surprise. "I thought they'd sent you back."

"Good heavens, it's Em," Mr. Sam said. "What are you doing dressed like that?"

"It's what waitresses wear in this place."

"And you...?" Mr. Sam said to me. "Forgive me, you seem familiar, but...."

"It's Ned, Mr. Sam," Em said. "He's had a face shift and he's now called Ishmael, but he's the same old idiot boy underneath."

"Of course," Mr. Sam said. "I thought the voice was familiar." Then he said to me, "Your Newharp is excellent, you could almost be one of us."

"He is one of us," Em said. "For all intents and purposes he's an illegal alien hiding out in the wharflands."

"We're not all illegal," Mr. Sam said.

"Did they give you residency?" I said.

"Citizenship even," said Mr. Sam, but he didn't sound very happy about it.

"You're an Earthling?"

"Alas."

Em said, "It can't be all bad. You don't have to worry about the cits. You can vote in elections, and stuff like that."

"Earth is not as I had imagined it to be," Mr. Sam said. "You and Harri were right to be cynical about the gladsome glades."

"Well," Em said, "They're soppy words—that was the real

trouble. Look, I'll bring you tea. I have to keep other customers happy. I'll get all the gossip from Ned later."

Em brought us tea and I gossiped with poor old Sambo. He told a sorry tale. After I'd wrecked the runabouts and Spearchucker had been all but burnt to the ground, the authorities had rewarded those inmates who hadn't rioted by granting them residency. There wasn't much else they could do. Conditions in the camps had become hopelessly overcrowded and the smugglers and their runabouts were getting harder to catch. Most of the PentaNostras had settled in one of the outer suburbs of Jackson's Port. Disillusionment, homesickness, helplessness had set in. Their twangling and hymn singing hadn't been enough. And then some crazy revivalist sect had put up a tent and promised heaven on earth by way of baby alligator handling. Smith Mei Lim, Mrs. Wozlebut and most of the rest had gone to a meeting to stage a protest, to bear witness to their own brand of truth. But they'd been swept away by the madness, consumed by the ecstasy, converted. They were all hard at it now: frightening the wits out of innocent baby alligators.

It was funny to be hearing all this from poor Sam Yang Rhee. I couldn't stop him. He needed to talk, he sounded like a man who had been starved of conversation. All his misery came tumbling from his lips.

"There are rumors about the rock," I said. "There are rumors that it isn't as big as first thought. There are rumors that the Willergod party might be overthrown."

"Let us pray that they are true," Mr. Sam said, but he didn't say it with any hope in his voice.

"If they are true, you could go home."

"I'm too old," Mr. Sam said. "I'd never make it, even if the pirates let us through. And the cost would be huge. Where am I to make that sort of money on this accursed planet?"

"Good point," I said. It sounded inadequate, but I couldn't think of anything else to say.

"I will die on this planet," Mr. Sam said. "But not today. Thank you for the tea, Ned. Now I must go back to that madhouse.

I must arrange medical treatment for those who have injured themselves badly. Good bye, Ned."

I watched the old man leave the Dog, limping slightly, leaning on his walking stick. He could have been something out of the scriptures, a mad old prophet; he could have been a rag seller from the narrowest of the wharflands' alleys.

Em Talking

The relief had hit me like a bucket of water, it had flooded over me. I hope I didn't show it. I hadn't admitted to myself how worried I'd been, but when I looked up from the dirty saucepan and saw idiot boy, the world lit up. All I said to him was "Where the hell have you been?" and I didn't have much opportunity to say more because Cicero and some pug-ugly were hot on his heels. And then, less than an hour later idiot boy produces another shock, Mr. Sam. Who I hadn't recognized at first—he'd aged, he'd gone as frail as a leaf.

I had to work late; it was after midnight when I got off. I wasn't keen on walking home by myself at that hour. I called a wharf cab, a flybynight. It took forever to arrive and when it did it was an off-duty fork-lift. The Skyroan cabbie had built a sort of box with a window and a seat and stuck it on the forks. Some people will do anything for a newbuck. I accepted with bad grace and was driven home in a box. When we arrived outside Aunty Nagoya's the cabbie demanded an extra two point fifty, he said it was an after midnight surcharge. I paid him the normal amount and went through the front door with a stream of Skyroan obscenities following. I wasn't remotely tired and I was keen to talk to idiot boy. I went to the room he shares with Harri. I knocked, got no answer and entered. Harri was asleep in one of the beds, the other was empty. I went to my own room and stuck the key in the keyhole, but the door was already unlocked. I was sure I had locked it that morning. I always lock my door, not that there is much to steal, but I lock it anyway. I pushed the door violently open and sprang back into the corridor. There were two people sitting on my bed. They were collapsed on each others' shoulders with their backs to the wall. They might have been dead.

They were asleep. Idiot boy was the first to open his eyes.

"Come in, Em," he yawned. "Come in and shut the door."

"Oh great," I said, going into my own room and shutting my own door, "Just invade a girl's private space why don't you?"

"We've been waiting for you," Quincy said. Quincy the cleaning lady has keys to all the rooms in the house. "We thought you might like to hear Ish's story. So we decided to wait up for you."

"Well you make the coffee then," I said and kicked off my shoes and sat down on the bed.

"Good idea," Quincy said and got down on her hands and knees on the strip of floor between the bed and the wall. She hauled the coffee box from beneath the bed, took out the utensils and ingredients, turned the box upside down, stood my little gemco burner on it and soon had a ring of flame under the flat bottom of the percolator. If the truth be known there is nothing quite so warming as the late night smells of percolating coffee and cleanly burning gemco mixed with the sounds of bubbling and hissing from the machine itself. Throw in a couple of close friends.

Quince got back on the bed, sitting so close to Ned that it would only be a matter of time before their arms went numb from the pressure. This was the most delightful development, it was the best thing that had happened to me in months. I felt—in so far as my hard and cynical heart can feel these things—total delight and love for my friends. But I wasn't going to be left out in the cold either. I shifted my bum a few centimeters, pressing my arm against Ned's other side. We'd got Ned well and truly trapped, me and Quince.

"OK, idiot boy," I said, "start talking."

Ned Talking

The girls drank their coffee black with no sugar. I couldn't hack the bitterness myself. I poured the sugar in.

"You'll rot your teeth," Quincy said.

"Us salesmen get discounts on teeth," I said. "Goes with the territory."

"About your recent holiday," Em said.

So I told Em what I'd already told Quincy. I told her about my kidnapping, I told her about my conversation with Astolphe Scott-Wok, I told her about Snodgrass and Blubber turning me into a foreign correspondent, I told her about Mr. Sam Yang Rhee's confessions.

"Yeah, well I've been washing dishes," Em said.

"Get a new job," I said, come out to the tracts with me. Flog a few organs. It's all go go go in the tracts."

"Get real, Earthling. What are you going to tell Cicero?"

"I've already had a yarn with Cicero and his boss."

"And you told them you'd been staying with friends?"

"Johnny Wannamarra—great guy."

"But you weren't staying with him. He doesn't even live in the tracts."

"Well...."

"Well what? You've either got to tell Cicero the truth. Or you put me in a very difficult position."

"You sound like a school teacher—*a very difficult position.*"

"Listen, Ned, if Cicero finds out that I know you've been playing footsie with Scott-Wok, and I haven't told him...."

"...it'll be all over between you," I said.

There was a bit of tension in the air. And not just in the air. Em was sitting so close to me that I felt it in her arm. After a few seconds she said, "So what are you going to do?"

"Do?"

"Are you going to spy for the Scott-Woks or not?"

"I don't know anything, Em. There's nothing I can tell them. I'm just a door to door salesman."

"So why did they go to all that trouble?" Em said.

"Search me."

We sat in silence for a while. Then Em said, "Mr. Sam was a shock, he looked ten years older."

"He was as old as the hills to begin with," I said.

We talked some more about Mr. Sam, Smith Mei Lim and the whole PentaNostra mob. Em told Quincy and me about the tedium of traveling half way across the galaxy in the company of a troop of hymn singing twanglers. She remembered little incidents on the smuggler's ship that even I hadn't heard before. I described the scene in the revivalist meeting. Quincy told us more stories from her childhood about baby alligator handling. Some of the stories I'd heard before, but they were all funny in a horror show sort of way. Quincy laughed and settled her head on my shoulder. Em got off the bed and made another brew of coffee. When it was ready we drank it in silence. I felt totally content. I didn't want to be anywhere else. I didn't want to be doing anything else. I just wanted to be sitting on Em's bed in the middle of the night with Quincy's head on my shoulder and Em on my other side, drinking coffee that would rot my teeth.

Em said, "It would never do for you two to go clambering past Aunty's window."

"No it wouldn't," Quincy said.

"Eh?" I said.

Quincy sleeps on a covered-in balcony that overlooks the back yard. The old balcony railings are still there, but the weather is kept out by a collection of second hand windows, sheets of fibro, sheets of roofing iron. It's a snug little place, but to get to it you climb these metal stairs from the back yard. Actually they are more ladder than stairs. They go straight past one of Aunty Nagoya's own windows. She's a good old moll, Aunty, but she's a bit possessive about Quince. She takes an interest in Quincy's well being.

"You'd better stay here," Em said. She squeezed my shoulder, leant half across me and kissed Quince full on the lips. Then she was gone, out of the place. I wasn't quite sure what to say.

I said, "Aunty will think it a bit odd if Em goes up your stairs. People have different footsteps. She can tell by listening."

"I don't think she's going to sleep in my bed," Quincy said.

I felt like a dill for half a second. Of course she wasn't. There was always Cicero's great monster of a bed: all bits of brass and broken china and a rug made of animal skin. And bloody d'Pettitt tucked up in it. For another half second I felt a stab of jealousy so sharp it could have been steel. Then Quincy slowly pushed me down until I was lying flat on my back. She didn't lie beside me, although she could have, Em's bed was just wide enough for that. She lay on top of me, her head blotting out the light bulb, her red hair glowing like a halo of fire. She was warm and alive and her breasts were pressing against my chest.

"Kiss me, Earthling," she whispered. "Put a bit of effort into it."

Em Talking

Reading Ned's account brings it all back. This morning, when the words had materialized out of the ether and I'd read them while sipping coffee, I sat there in my courtyard, my eyes closed against the minor sunlight, feeling again the warmth and love I had felt all those years ago for both of my friends.

When we decided to do this memoir, Ned and I agreed we'd confine ourselves to those three years on Earth, we'd keep the narrative manageable. But, nevertheless, for the record, we were married for a time, Ned and me. It didn't work out—we'd been friends for far too long, we'd been through too much together, we were too fixed in the ways we related to each other. But Ned was lonely in those early days of exile. Reader dear, you will have read the bit at the beginning of this memoir where Ned says he wouldn't revisit Earth even in his dying imagination. A pox on the place, he says. Don't be fooled—in those first few refugee months he yearned for the familiarity of home, he yearned so much that the despair might have been a physical lump in his chest, demanding surgery. I speak with authority; I had felt exactly the same myself. We all do. I did on his planet, he did on this one. So I comforted the lad, took him to my breast, to my bed and to the marriage celebrant. We were happy with the arrangement for six months or so. And then he began to make his own friends, to establish his own place in local society. He got himself a proper education and a proper job. After a while I hardly saw him. There were a few cross words, not many, but we split up anyway. We didn't talk to each other for at least a month. Then one day we met in the street. Hello, Em, he said and kissed me in the Earth fashion—straight on my lips—he did so with the warm, offhand nonchalance of an old friend. The marriage fiasco might never have happened.

* * * * * * *

I didn't sleep in Cicero's bed. I walked quietly through the quiet house. It wasn't that quiet. The odd snore and grunt came from behind closed doors. The clack of the jongma tiles still filtered up from the ground floor. It would filter up till dawn— which wasn't very far away. A couple of feral cats were hard at it on the roof. I opened the door to Harri and Ned's room and quietly kicked off my shoes, slid out of my dress and into Ned's bed. In the other bed, Harri was out like a light. Ned's bed smelt of lavender. I nearly laughed out loud. Bloody Ned, who'd have thought it? But it probably wasn't Ned who had put the sachet between the sheets. Quince! You couldn't really call her the chamber maid, but she had keys to everyone's room.

I lay awake, listening to my brother's deep, even breathing. I said an old Newharp prayer from my childhood. I hadn't believed in god even in those long distant days, but all kids have ditties and spells and incantations. I'd had one that was meant to keep my friends safe. No monsters bite you, no harpies fright you, sleep like logs, dream of fogs. Fogs of golden dust at dawn, fogs of mist and silver worn, worn by the night, worn by the light, a cloak to cover you, and sleep you tight.

It didn't make much sense, but it said what I felt. I wanted

Ned and Quince to know happiness. I wanted them to have a good fuck. Only once had Ned talked to me about his loathsome sexual experiences—that time in Spearchucker when I'd made him tell me about Tidy Town and he'd suddenly started to describe the activities of the Reverend Mr. Robinson call me Rob. I'd been shocked at the time—even after all Harri and I had been through on the smuggler's ship, I was shocked. It wasn't so much the tale itself; sexual abuse is nothing new, any inhabited planet can provide those sorts of stories by the ton. It was the anger in Ned's voice, the depth of it. He spoke of deliberately going back to the Junior Purists week after week, he spoke of being almost completely passive, the plaything of this Robinson. Ned the wild boy, the tearaway, the young hoon, he did what Robinson wanted week after week after week. And then, when he told me about it, he spat the words out, spat them out with so much anger that they could have been bullets. And then he'd never talked about it again. And I'd been too afraid to ask, to ever mention it again. Sometimes I caught myself wondering if we'd even had that conversation. Had I dreamed it? I knew I hadn't. And I knew I wanted Ned and Quincy to be happy as much as I'd ever wanted anything. But I was no fool, I didn't think it would be easy. It might be impossible. And I was worried about this Scott-Wok development. Ned was a small, small fish in deep black waters full of sharks—he could so easily become nothing but a sudden swirl and a stain of blood dissolving within seconds. He didn't seem to know this. Idiot boy.

I fell asleep at dawn.

Ned Talking

Thank you, Em, for not describing in meticulous detail your sex life with Cicero. Even now I don't think I could hack reading that sort of stuff. I'm deeply grateful for your sensitivity in this matter. I'm glad you slept alone in my bed that night. Thank you also for your well wishes re: me and Quincy. And for the record: we did, we did indeed have a good fuck. Very good.

* * * * * *

Things settled down. I went back to work. Sometimes I worked the wharflands, sometimes I worked the tracts. Nobody hassled me, nobody hassled any of the other sales staff. We peddled organs and we peddled them good. Occasionally in the tracts we came across the opposition. We tried not to tread on their toes, we tried not to work streets we knew they'd already worked. I got the impression they were doing the same to us. And why not? The tracts were extensive, they went on and on in all directions. There was room for everybody. I heard nothing from Snodgrass and Blubber. It was pretty obvious that Scott-Wok had seen reason, had got the picture: there was nothing I could tell him. Maybe Sue-Ellen had played a part, told the silly drongo not to go turning her old schoolmate into a spy. I dunno.

Me and Quince became an item. Sort of. Mostly I still slept in the room I shared with Harri. But two or three times a week Quince and I climbed the steep steel steps to her fenced-in balcony. Em had made it pretty clear we weren't getting regular use of her room—that had been a one-off, a sort of honeymoon present. And Aunty Nagoya hadn't kicked up a fuss the morning after the first time I slept on the balcony. Quince and I had climbed the steel steps talking loudly, making it plain we weren't going to be furtive about anything. Maybe Aunty Nagoya liked me, thought I was good for Quince—who knows?

Em Talking

So I was a fool. I'd thought it wouldn't be easy for Ned and Quince. I'd thought Ned would have all sorts of hang ups. I'd thought the pair of them would have to work through all sorts of crap. Wrong! You could tell just by looking, just by watching the way they touched each other when they passed in the passages or the dining room, just by the way they put their arms round each other in the street, just by the way their hands lay on each others' thighs under the table at the Dog: you could tell that at night they were having a great time on the balcony. But I didn't simply trust my intuitions, I asked Quincy straight out.

"Are you and Ishmael sexually compatible?"

"What sort of question's that?" Quince said, startled at first, then giggling.

"It's a straight out question," I said.

"Yep," Quince said, "And that's a straight out answer."

"Good," I said.

"Did you doubt it, Em?"

"Didn't know," I said. "Couples sometimes have trouble. It depends where each partner is coming from."

"Ish comes from Tidy Town where he had a few fumbles with girls," Quincy said. "He once got a girl called Joan to take her bra off in the cabin of a ute—that was pretty big time. I'm his first actual proper girlfriend, Em."

"I reckon you must be," I said.

"What's that meant to mean?"

"Just that," I said. "Ish has lucked out."

"Too right he has," Quincy said.

If Ned hadn't told her about Robinson, it wasn't my job to tell her. Perhaps it was better that way. Maybe all that anger was buried so deep it could do no harm.

Then there was more news from home. Real news. Letters, there were actual letters. Words written on paper. Pictures, scans. Harri and I got long screeds from our parents. They were alive and well, they'd survived the guerrilla campaign in the mountains. The Willergod party had been overthrown. Our parents were back home in Santa Gertrudis. And we heard from friends, from relatives. And the news was good. The rock was closing fast, but all the measurements now showed it to be movable, deflectable. Every ounce of technology the planet possessed was being hurled at the rock. The first bombs had been delivered and exploded. The course of the rock had been changed by a fraction of a fraction of a degree, it's speed had been increased by a fraction of a fraction of a kph.

"Increased?" the idiot boy said one evening in the Dog when I was off duty and sitting at a table with my friends.

"Sure," Harri said. "If we put a bomb behind you, your speed would be increased."

"So your halfwit rellies want the rock to arrive even earlier than expected? They're that keen for oblivion?"

"They want it to pass *in front* of our planet. Get it, Ish? You can avoid a car crash by slamming on the brakes or you can plant the foot. We're planting the foot."

"Too much foot planting," Ned said, "and you slam into a tree, you fail to make the turn, you roll the crate."

"No skin off our nose," Harri said. "The rock can go jump for all we care. Just as long as it misses Newharp."

"Actually," I said. "The best we can hope for is that it will go into orbit. There's no way the rock can escape Newharp's gravity. If we're lucky it will just become a new moon. Go round and round for ever."

"Just a moon in June, you crazy loon," Ned crooned.

"Shut up, Ish," Quincy said. "This is our home we're talking about."

"You were born *here*," Ned said.

"I've got grandparents on Newharp."

"Every bugger's got grandparents on Newharp," Ned said. "Or great grandparents twice removed."

"Except you," Quincy said.

"Say the place survives," Ned said. "Howabout we go and visit your grandolds?"

"Yeah, yeah," Quincy said. "We'll just duck across one afternoon for tea and scones."

"We could get into the silverberry," Ned said. "It's great stuff."

"Dream on, Earthling."

I leaned back in my seat. I looked around the Dog. There

were a dozen other tables of people, there were a dozen people leaning against the bar. And they were all talking about the same subject: the rock. And none of them knew enough to sustain a genuine conversation for more than five minutes. But they kept talking, going over and over what they did know, speculating wildly, retelling rumors and, in the process, starting other rumors. These were strange days. We were all on edge, but the atmosphere was calm—the calm before the storm as the Earthlings put it. And that was only in the matter of the rock. There were times when I almost felt as apprehensive about the spare parts business. Every time Ned went out to the tracts I was worried—there was a knot in my stomach. Not a big one, but it was there. And Quincy was the same—you could tell by the way she watched the clock, by the way she suddenly relaxed and was her old happy self when Ned showed up in the evening.

And Cicero was worried too. He tried not to show it. He didn't talk about it much. But if I was with him late at night, or in the early hours of the morning, he asked me a little too often if Ned had said anything about the Scott-Woks. I always told him no, or just passed on Ned's cheery insistence that relations were amicable.

"That's what worries me," Cicero said one night.

"It worries me too," I said.

"If Earth boy is telling the truth, there is no competition out in the tracts. The Scott-Woks do their thing and we do ours. It's all brotherly love out there."

"Maybe it is."

"You reckon that's how Astolphe Scott-Wok works? You reckon that's the great Scott-Wok tradition? Share up the territory peacefully? You in your small corner and me in mine? We know these guys, Em. We know them from home. Earth Boy wouldn't have a clue."

"Ned says he met one of their salesman in the street last week."

"I know, he told me. He said the pair of them nodded to each other. The Scott-Wok guy crossed the road and began working the even numbers. Ned did the odd numbers. Do you reckon he's telling the truth, Em. Or do you reckon he's done a deal?"

"What sort of deal? He's still pulling in the punters, isn't he? Demand for organs is on the increase. Harri says they are working flat out down there."

"Ishmael could be passing every tenth customer to the Scott-Woks, sending them in the other direction. I reckon that's what's happening. He's working for the other side—on the side."

"And the rest of the sales staff," I said. "Do you think they're all running that sort of scam?"

"It might be every sixth customer," Cicero said. "The bosses would murder me if I let that sort of thing happen."

"Go to sleep, Cicero," I said.

"Maybe I should rough the little runt up a bit," Cicero said. "Get the truth out of him at the point of a knife."

"For god's sake, go to sleep. And don't you dare touch Ned. He's your best salesman. And you know it."

"They'd murder me, Em."

"I doubt it."

"You don't know the bosses."

"Thank god."

I turned over and went to sleep. In the morning Cicero didn't look as if he'd slept at all. But I didn't ask.

Ned Talking

A couple of heavies grabbed me in the tracts. Talk about déjà vu. Been there, done that.

This particular pair of beauties just drove up beside me in a dirty unmarked Dogstar. Well, it was unmarked in the sense that it didn't have Citizenship Police written all over it in big letters. It had *I am filtheey, Wash me now* written all over it by some kid's finger. But the plain clothes guys inside—they might as well have been in full cit uniform. Their daggy suits were uniform enough.

"Get in," the guy in the passenger seat said out of the window.

"Who? Me?" I said.

"Don't get smart with us, sonny."

"ID," I said.

"We know your ID, Ned. That's good enough. Now get in."

I looked up and down the street. There were two more unmarked Dogstars—one at each end. I did as I was told, I opened the back door of the Dogstar and climbed in with all my brushes. The driver took off, squealing rubber like a failed drag-strip johnny. Neither of the beauties seemed inclined to speak. I certainly wasn't. I looked dully out of the window, watching the tracts roll by. Ten minutes later we were roaring down a ramp into an underground car park. Five minutes later I was facing the pair of them across a small table pitted with cigarette burns. There were no windows.

"You are Edward Malley aka Ned Malley aka Ishmael Codwallader wanted for willful destruction of property to wit two sotto-c spacecraft one detention center one fire truck wanted also for illegal use aiding and abetting illegal aliens trafficking in human body parts avoiding arrest breaking a court imposed good behavior bond arson resulting in total destruction of government property to wit one mothers and babies institute illegal use of a tractor while intoxicated with a banned substance to wit fermented and distilled genetically modified canola oil blah blah blah...."

"That would be about right," I said.

"About?"

"I didn't done the Mothers and Babies."

"If you say so."

"I do."

"Tell us about the organ trade."

"This some sort of deal?"

"Tell us about the organ trade."

"I think we're talking a deal here."

"The organ trade, Ned. Tell us about it."

"I think we're talking back scratching."

"Organs."

"You scratch mine, I'll scratch yours."

"Listen, you little squirt, you're in deep deep shit. You're in no position to do deals. Now tell us about the trade in illegal organs."

"You boys got dodgy prostrates? Kidneys shot? Arteries clogged worse than a tract sewer? Meatus trouble? Blood in the urine? Urine in the blood? Decayed...."

"Shut it! Start talking. About the trade."

"Alright, all right, no need for standover tactics. Sure I can tell you about organ replacement. Highly skilled technicians grow the organ in question using the genetic code of the prospective recipient, said code being garnered from a single donated cell which then multiplies under accelerated conditions...."

"We know how it's done, shithead, tell us who does it."

"About this deal...."

"There is no deal."

"The deal is: if I promise to find out who does it, you get off my case."

"You already know who does it."

"I know nothing. I'm a salesman."

"Who's your boss?"

"Cicero d'Pettitt."

"Who's his boss?"

"Don't know."

"Where are the organs manufactured?"

"Don't know."

"Where do your clients...?"

"We prefer to call them punters."

"Where do your godamned punters get the operation performed?"

"Don't know."

"You don't know much."

"Company policy. *Need to know.* I don't need, therefore I don't know. You've got the wrong guy."

"I think we've got the right guy."

"Only if we're talking a deal."

"What do you tell your clients...."

"Punters."

"What do you tell the poor fuckwits who want new organs? You have to give them instructions. Where do you tell them to go?"

"Dog."

"What?"

"Dog."

"What dog?"

"And Harp."

"The Dog and fucking Harp?"

"Yarp."

"That's a pub?"

"An entertainment complex comprising a restaurant, a bistro, two bars, a gaming room, sauna and massage facilities, pool hall, a cultural center and library...."

"Alien?"

"Who's an alien?"

"This brothel you're talking about, this Dog and Harp, is it run by aliens? Is it a snake pit full of aliens drinking and gambling and fighting and singing alien songs? Is it an alien pub?"

"It exudes the ambience of Newharp. There is an elegant Newharp theme to the decor."

"Do you flog real estate as well?"

"Alas, brushes and organs are my sole stock in trade."

"Where is it?"

"Where's what?"

"The Dog and Harp."

"P21XdT-347 Street."

"What does P21etc. stand for?"

"It's a diseased star in the thingo galaxy. Believed to be dead."

"But this street? It's in the wharflands?"

"Where else?"

"And you convince these poor bunnies who want new body parts, you convince them to go into an alien pub in the heart of the alien fucking wharflands?"

"They find it a most attractive...."

"Listen, shit-for-brains, the average tract dweller would no more venture into the wharflands than they'd go on holiday in the Gobi desert."

"If they are reluctant, my company runs a taxi service."

"You pick them up and take them to the Dog and Harp?"

"I don't personally, no."

"So who drives the taxi?"

"Don't know."

"And where do they go after the Dog and Harp?"

"Don't know."

"What else don't you know?"

"Don't know."

"What else *do* you know?"

"Not a lot."

"I think you know a shit load more than you say you do."

"I have been careful to maintain my ignorance."

"Why?"

"Why what?"

"Why deliberately remain ignorant?"

"Ignorance is strength."

"Bullshit."

"True fact."

"Well you tell us about your strength, then. How does being a dick brained ignoramus make you strong?"

"It puts me in a better bargaining position."

"But if you know nothing, what's there to bargain with?"

"I can find stuff out."

"What stuff?"

"Any stuff you want."

"But we have to let you go?"

"Can't find it out sitting here."

"Interview suspended."

"There's nothing to suspend. The data cache hasn't been switched on. We've never had this conversation."

"You stay here. No funny business."

The two beauties left the room. I sat back and looked around. It was true that the cache hadn't been switched on. There was a security camera mounted near the ceiling. You can't tell, of course, but I'd bet that wasn't working either. These two guys were no more interested in going on the record than I was. I wasn't sure of their game, but the buggers weren't interested in cracking down on the illegal organ trade, that was for sure. Too many high rollers had an interest in keeping the body parts trade illegal—politicians, captains of industry, corrupt police, disbarred doctors, civil servants, uncivil servants, every bastard and his or her dog or bitch had a finger in that pie. Make the trade legal—pop!—there goes a lucrative protection racket. Beauty One and Beauty Two weren't fearless fighters against that little earner. I reckoned they were just interested in muscling in on the action themselves, they probably felt a bit out of it, a bit hard done by. Well, they would, wouldn't they—running a suburban cit station out in the tracts, watching some other gang make a fortune on their patch. They wanted their slice of the action. But I guessed one thing, I guessed that they would *claim* to be fighting internal police corruption. That much was certain..

The door opened. The beauties sat down.

"Right, Ned. Start talking."

"I've been talking. I've done nothing but talk."

"Tell us what you can find out."

"Tell me what you want me to find out."

Beauty One looked at Beauty Two. Beauty Two nodded. Beauty One said, "The names of the Tetride bosses."

"Pull the other one, fellas," I said. "If I told you I could get hold of that sort of info, I'd be lying. You know that."

"Just testing."

"Well don't. Get real. What do you want to know?"

"The names of the members of the Citizenship Police who are corruptly accepting bribes to permit this illegal trade to flourish. Who gets paid what?"

"Am I to take it that you gentlemen are members of an

internal investigation unit, dedicated to stamping out corruption within the force?"

"You could put it that way, yes."

"Then I would regard it as my duty as a citizen to help you with your enquiries. But I think bygones should be bygones, don't you?"

"You come through with the goods, Ned. Then we might...we just might have better things to do with our time than chase up old arrest warrants against little pip-squeaks like you."

"I reckon I'd better get back on the street," I said. "I've got brushes to sell, quotas to achieve."

"All right, hop in the car."

Talk about a quick turnaround. Talk about going down market. Within two hours of being picked up I was flogging brushes and organs again. And the buggers hadn't even offered me tea or coffee. No biscuits. It wasn't what I was used to; I was a silverberry man, I expected hospitality plus from my kidnappers. I didn't think Beauties One and Two quite understood the league they were playing in. Still, it left me with a whole afternoon's door knocking, and I used it to good effect. I flogged two Scrub-yr-Hides to an elderly couple and got the first down payment on a thyroid gland from a young lout doing home detention for illegal use.

This time round I decided not to tell anybody about my adventures. I didn't want Em having a go at me for putting her in a very difficult position with old Bundle-of-Charm d'Pettitt. And there was certainly no point in worrying d'Pettitt himself. And Quince and Harri would only tell Em. So I kept my own counsel—kept it good and proper.

Em Talking

So now he tells me. The full story. After all these years. Well, it makes sense of certain subsequent goings on. And Quince hadn't been keeping me up to date either.

* * * * * * *

She found the place. She'd gone out checking real estate without telling me.

"Come and take a look at this joint," Quincy said to me one afternoon when I wasn't working.

"What joint?"

"I'll show you."

She wouldn't tell me what I was meant to see, but the afternoon was sunny and the wind off the harbor was fresh. I pulled on my Newharp poncho and we went for a walk. After ten minutes we were in the dead end of a small dead end street with a harbor view up the live end. The street was enclosed by workshops and warehouses—some working, some boarded up. The harbor view was about two degrees wide, we could have been looking through a vertical letter box. We watched a freighter glide by: first the bows, then the foredeck, then the superstructure, then a succession of rusty hatch covers, sailors and masts and then for a second or two the stern was visible with a mangy flag drooping from a slanting flag poll. Then we were back to a strip of bright, glinting water.

"You'd see life in installments, if you lived here," I said.

"What about working here," Quincy said.

"What as? Fork lift drivers?"

"Language teachers."

"Using what for a school?"

"This place."

Quincy turned to the building behind us. It was narrow, three stories high and all the windows and doors were boarded up. An old, tattered notice said it was for sale. A new sticker said it was already sold.

"Nice idea, Quince," I said, "but it's just been sold and anyway we'd want some place that we could rent, not buy."

"It's just been sold all right," Quincy said. "It's just been sold to me."

"Oh, yeah."

"Yeah."

"And what did you use for money?"

"Winnings."

"Jongma winnings?"

"They're the only sort I have."

"How rich are you, Quince?"

"I've been playing for years. I have this policy of not losing."

"Gawdalmighty."

I stood and looked at the place for a while. Gaunt, that's what it was: gaunt, bleak, spooky. When the weather turned grey, it would become grim, sordid, grimy. The brickwork was crumbling. A gutter was hanging loose. Some graffiti artist had written a series of incomprehensible tags all over the first couple of meters of wall.

"Have you been inside?" I said to Quincy. Quite frankly it didn't look like the sort of place you'd want to go inside.

"Of course I've bloody been inside. You think I'd buy it without looking?"

Quincy pulled a ring with three keys from her pocket. The reinforced door to the place was locked with three padlocks. It took Quince a few minutes to get them all undone.

"After you," she said.

"We should have brought a torch," I said, not crossing the threshold. "There's no light inside."

"There's enough. After you."

We explored the rathole. I'd come to think of it as the rathole within seconds of going inside. Quincy was right about there being enough light to see by, the boards and bits of roofing iron bolted across the windows were full of holes. Shafts of light fell in pools on the floor. The floor was covered in all manner of crap and rubbish. A dead bird. The skeleton of a possum. Glass. Bits of ceiling. We went up the stairs: more of the same. We climbed to the top floor: ditto.

"Concealed lighting," Quincy said. "White boards, language labs, nice chairs that swivel, screens, indoor plants, holograms, views of Earth for the English classes, views of Newharp for the

Newharp classes."

"Newharp classes?" I said.

"Sure, teach these Earthlings how to speak proper. And mother tongue maintenance for second generation types like me. This joint's going to hum. What about the floor?"

"What about it?"

"Carpet? Matting? Polished boards? Parquetry? Sprong-o-mat?"

"Just how much money have you got, Quince?"

"Enough, enough. And I can always win more. Which room do you want for your office?"

"Quince, I'm really not sure about this."

"Yes you are. You told me you wanted to establish a language school."

"I'm illegal. I'm an alien. Even in the wharflands I can't go that high profile."

"I'm the front woman. I'm the proprietor. I own the joint. You just run it and do a bit of teaching."

"But...."

"But nothing," Quincy said. "You can't be a kitchen hand all your life."

"Oh, Quince," I said. There were tears in my eyes. I put my arm around my friend. She put hers around me. We stood there in the half dark amongst the litter and crap, I could feel Quincy breathing. She could feel me. Her hair was against my face, tickling my nose. I sneezed, but I didn't let go of her. "I'm jealous," I said.

"Jealous of who?"

"Idiot boy."

"Ish? Why?"

"He's got you."

"Nobody's got me, Em. I'm ungottable."

"*Ungottable* is not a word in either English or Newharp. I won't have it spoken in my language school."

"Sorry, Miss. I'll never do it again."

"Kiss me, Quince."

Ned Talking

I was getting a bit worried about Harri. I shared a room with the guy (when I wasn't sharing a balcony with Quincy). I saw quite a bit of Harri. He was no trouble as a room-mate, no trouble at all. Most of the time I was hardly aware the guy existed. He said and did nothing. He'd always been a gloomy bastard—but he was getting gloomier still. I reckoned it was the organs. Growing organs from a single cell in a secret laboratory under the Dog; slaving away in artificial light, never seeing the sun; watching weird bits of innards form slowly out of sludge—it couldn't be good for you.

I'd lied, of course, when I told the two beauties that I didn't know where the organs were grown. They were grown in the cellars of the Dog. There was a complete laboratory down there—also a suite of operating theatres. But it was true that I'd never seen the place. I had no need to see it. But I knew where Harri worked. Harri had said the labs were spotless, a vast empire of glass and steel and bright lights and high tech machinery, some of it brought from Newharp. And it was all run using the best Newharp know-how. That's why our spare parts were top-of-the-range. They weren't being produced by bungling Earthlings. And the surgeons knew their trade.

"I reckon you need a change," I said to Harri one evening. We were both lying on our beds looking at the ceiling. We were just having a bit of rest after a hard day's yakka, a bit of quiet time before the bun-fight of dinner at Aunty's. Harri continued to look at the ceiling. He didn't even grunt. I said, "You're going stir crazy, mate. That lab's worse than prison." This time he grunted. I'd achieved contact. I said, "Want to change jobs for a bit? I'll do yours, you do mine."

"We're too specialized. I couldn't sell organs, you couldn't grow them."

"All you do is wash bottles. Gently rock the growing organs. Swab the floors."

"Yeah, but I know which bottles to wash. I know how to tend

the organs. I know where the floor cleaner is kept."

"Em's going to change direction," I said. "She's branching out. You've got to do the same."

"Em's Em. I'm me."

"So?"

"So nothing."

I didn't say anything. I just looked at the ceiling. That's one good thing about conversations with Harri—you don't have to say anything, you can have pauses that last ten minutes, ten hours, ten days if you want. But this time I only paused for a minute and a half. I decided to use Scott-Wok's question. I said, "How do you see yourself in five year's time?"

Harri didn't answer for about three minutes. Then he said, "Lying on this bed, looking at this ceiling."

"Remember the foam gun," I said. "Remember filling the troop carrier with foam?"

"Of course I remember."

"You were alive then."

"I'm alive now."

"A belief open to doubt."

This time the silence lasted about six minutes. I wasn't going to be the one to break it. At last Harri said, "You're right."

"How am I right?"

"That was the high point of my life. Firing the foam gun. I'd never been so alive before. I'll never be so alive again."

"Why do you say that?"

"Because."

"That's not much of an answer."

"It wasn't much of a question."

I didn't think there was much future in this slow motion banter. I said, "When Em and Quince get their school up and running, why don't you teach in it?"

"My English is lousy. You know that."

"Do this mother tongue maintenance stuff that Quince talks about. Teach Newharp to kids who were born here. You wouldn't need to talk any English at all. All the better if you didn't."

"Do you see me as a teacher, Ned? Inspiring students?"

Quite frankly, I didn't. Harri would put the students to sleep. Or cause them to jump out of the window. It amazed me that I'd made such a stupid suggestion in the first place. "Nope," I said.

"Well there you are then," Harri said.

The dinner gong sounded. Aunty was a great one for the gong. She insisted on beating the crap out of the thing herself; even Quince wasn't allowed to have a go.

"Chow down," I said.

The pair of us got off our beds and made for the dining room. I felt I'd just had the most useless conversation of my life. But it wasn't necessarily over. I could restart it any time I liked. You could say that about Harri: he never shut himself off from you, you could always restart a conversation.

Em Talking

I was walking to the Dog one afternoon when Cicero caught up with me. We walked in step for half a minute. We were almost there.

Cicero said, "I'm getting married, Em."

I didn't react at first. I was so used to Cicero saying I ought to marry him, and so used to saying "I don't think so", that it took me a bit of time to adjust. I kept walking, and while walking said, "To anyone in particular?"

"Yes," he said.

There was a silence between us, a tension.

"Does she have a name?" I said.

"Jill."

"Never heard of her."

"She doesn't move in Newharp circles."

"An Earthling?"

"Yes."

"I hope you'll be very happy."

"You're the first person I've told, Em."

We had arrived outside the Dog. I stood on the footpath,

turned to Cicero and said, "Good. Now listen, I've got work to do. My shift starts in a couple of minutes." I spun on my heel and entered the Dog. Cicero didn't follow. For which I was grateful. In the staff changing cupboard I burst into tears. I dried my eyes, washed my face and changed into my traditional waitresses outfit. I looked at myself in the mirror—grow up, I said to myself.

Ned Talking

Quince and I had taken the day off. Everyone needs a holiday now and then. We'd spent the day riding around on the ferries— just looking at the harbor, looking at the ships, throwing scraps to the sea gulls. On one of the ferries we stood on the open bit in front of the wheelhouse and had a bit of a yarn through the open window with the captain. When she was younger, she'd been a navigator on a Skyroan freighter trading with colonies on the moons of Kovalev, but she'd got jack of the long black nights at hyper-c, the weightlessness, the claustrophobia of shipboard life. The same set of faces for breakfast lunch and tea and no way of escaping them. She said it was a mug's life. She'd jumped ship on one of the moons, bribed a smuggler, come to Earth. She said she had Earth residency, but she was a bit cagey about how she'd got it. There are some questions you don't ask, so we didn't ask. The captain said chugging around the harbor with the wind in your face beat the inter-planetary stuff any day.

We docked just down from Quincy's rathole and went to look at the place. The builder she'd hired and a couple of layabouts were drinking tea. But you could see that they had done a bit of work: the floors were clean, the windows had glass in them. Some of the walls had been scrubbed down ready for painting. We drank some tea with the builder and his lads and then set off for the Dog. It continued to amaze me that Quincy had squir- reled away all this money—enough to buy a building, enough to hire a builder. She was only a year older than me, only eighteen.

I earned reasonable money peddling organs, but not enough to save any.

"How come you win so much?" I said.

"Dunno," she said. "Just luck, maybe."

"Not all the time," I said. "Luck doesn't work like that."

"Jongma's also a game of skill."

"Yeah, but some of the old geezers you play against are pretty skilled themselves."

"It's in the looking," Quincy said.

"The looking?"

"Sometimes I just look at the back of a jongma tile and I know what's on the other side. I just know. You have to...sort of...I don't know, it's hard to explain."

"Try," I said.

"Yeah, that's what you don't do," Quincy said. "You don't try to look, you just let your eyes slide over the tiles without effort. Without really thinking about what you are doing."

"Sounds like magic to me," I said.

"Probably isn't," Quincy said. "There's probably some perfectly ordinary explanation."

"Can you do this for other things?" I said. "Can you predict the future?"

"Oh sure," she said and laughed. "I predict that the future will come to pass. How's that for prophesy?"

"No seriously," I said.

"I don't like to think about the future, Ish. I get a feeling of...insecurity...unease...foreboding. I've gone and bought that building; those guys are busy doing it up; it's going to look real flash, but all the time I can't really believe we're ever going to open a language school in there. I keep thinking something is going to happen."

"What?" I said.

"Search me," Quincy said. "I've got no crystal ball."

I didn't say any more, just put my arm round Quincy's waist as we walked along. It was strange, while Quincy had been speaking I'd had a sudden attack of goose bumps, I'd shivered.

The day had gone cold. Up until that point everything had been delightful, carefree.

We reached the Dog, found a table next to a night view of a Newharp street in a snow storm, and sat down. Em was on duty, I hoped the girl would take the day back to its original brightness. She came up to our table, asked us how the ferry rides had gone, took our order and disappeared into the kitchens. The feeling of unease was still with me, slightly stronger, if anything. Em had seemed distracted, preoccupied. She hadn't really been interested in our outing.

"She seemed a bit out of it," I said to Quincy.

"She's been crying," Quincy said.

Em Talking

I shouldn't have been so upset. I'd always known this was possible. I'd made no claims on Cicero. I had no right to make claims. It had been me who'd restricted our friendship, rejected his plans, refused to become his partner for life. So he'd gone and found some other girl, fallen in love and was going to get married. To an Earthling—someone who had never taken a stained pants-suit to a Newharp nonhydronic, never walked along the esplanade at Santa Gertrudis.

And I would never sleep in Cicero's bed again. Even if he asked me, which I knew perfectly well he might—Miss Jill Somebody or no Miss Jill Somebody, blushing bride to be.

Ned and Quincy came into the Dog. Their faces were glowing. They'd been standing around in the sun and the wind at the bows of ferries all day. They were a bit tired, they weren't speaking much, you could even say their mood was somber—but they looked so content in each other's company. They were a couple—pure and simple. I didn't want to chat. I just asked how their day out had gone, took their order and made for the kitchens. I gave the order to Walid the mad cook and took another order to another table. I was busy for five minutes serving others. Then, as I was cleaning the table next to Ned and Quincy's, I saw the action out of the corner of one eye. A guy who'd been drinking alone at the bar wandered unsteadily through the restaurant. He slightly bumped Ned as he passed, steadying himself on Ned's shoulder for a second. Ned hardly looked up—this was the Dog after all, drunks leaned on your shoulder all the time. The drunk said, "Sorry, mate, gotta go buy a paper news, I mean a...a... newspaper." Ned looked up quickly but the drunk was already lurching towards the door. Ned recovered fast and looked back at Quincy who just smiled and said something I couldn't catch. I looked down at the table, gave it an extra swipe with my cloth and went to take another order. The day had been black with the pain of Cicero's news, now it was blacker still. Ned had told me the code the Scott-Woks would use when they wanted to contact him: *paper news*. He was meant to go to something they called a "safe house" in the tracts within twenty four hours.

Ned Talking

The place looked as safe as a barbed wire canoe. There was an awful lot of graffiti in the tracts, but this joint looked like it was held together by its graffiti. Scrape the tags off and the gimcrack little hovel would fall down. I knocked on the door. I nearly knocked the door off its hinges. A voice within croaked, "All right, all right, no need to use a sledge hammer." After a few minutes of wheezing and clattering and muttering behind the door, it creaked open. "Yairs, watcher want?" said an old boy with his fingers sticking out of woolen gloves. There was hair growing out of his nose and ears and his skin was covered in scales. He was about a million years old. Jeez, I thought, I could sell a few organs to this guy—maybe I could kill two birds with one rock.

"Paper news is good for youse," I said.

"No news beats the booze," said the old boy smartly. It was the right response, he knew his lines, he'd probably been practicing all morning. He straightened his back and said. "You

Ned, young fella?"

"Yep."

"OK, get inside quick."

I got inside quick. The old boy slammed the door and slid a few bolts across. Then he set off down the hall at a brisk trot. I followed.

"Were you followed?" he said over his shoulder.

"I'm following you," I said.

"On your way here, thickwit—were you followed?"

"Nope," I said. "I took all the precautions."

"In here," said the old boy, opening a door into a disused bedroom. The curtains were drawn, the floor was dusty, the place stank of mold and rot. There were two chairs—cheap plastic objects—and a briefcase beside one of the chairs. Otherwise the room was empty. The wallpaper was decorated with a pattern of roses. The mold spots could have been ladybirds. "Take a pew," said the old boy. I sat down.

"Who taught you your tradecraft?" he said.

But I'd already tumbled to him. He was trying to disguise his voice, but he wasn't really up to the job. "A drunk called Snodgrass," I said. "Total no-hoper. He thinks spying is all about sticking stupid rubber masks on your face."

"Gee, you're bright, Neddy-boy," Snodgrass said and started to peel the mask from his face.

"I take it I haven't been hauled out here just to watch you play dress-ups," I said.

"Shit!" Snodgrass said as a bit of rubber came away, pulling hair with it.

"You want to use a solvent," I said. "You want to oil your face with gemco before you put the mask on."

"Shut up, Ned. Take a dekko at this," Snodgrass said, opening the briefcase and handing me an album of photographs. I took a dekko. Society dorks stared me in the face. Image after image of goons in formal wear, grogging on, dancing, posing at balls. Glasses of god knows what poison clutched in their hands. Girls with low cut dresses. Girls with no cut dresses. A picture of half a dozen young drunks in evening dress, with their daks around their ankles, pointing their bare bums at the image taker. And that one wasn't flat-to-the-page—the moonie boys had insisted on 3D holographic.

"What are you showing me this crap for?" I said to Snodgrass, who'd finally got the rubber off and was looking a bit more like simple, lovable old gat-boy again.

"They're your countrymen and women," Snodgrass said. "Blue chip, blue rinse, blue blooded Earthlings."

"Not my set," I'm afraid.

"Recognize her?" Snodgrass said, leaning forward and tapping a picture. It showed a peculiarly dippy young woman, reclining across the knees of three young buffoons on a sofa. She was holding up an arm covered in a long glove. In her hand was a glass of bubbles. The look on her face said: *aren't I wonderful, my daddy's got millions*. The same girl was also in half the other images in the album.

"Snodders," I said, "I've told you: this is not my set. I don't mix in these circles."

"One degree of separation," Snodgrass said. "That's all."

"What are you on about?"

"You mix in a set that mixes with this set."

"I doubt it."

"Who's this guy, then?"

Snodgrass leaned forward again and flicked through the pages on my knee until he came to the one he wanted. He tapped it with a fingernail covered in bits of rubber. A pill in formal gear stood with his arm around the millionaire's daughter. Behind them was a stage on which a full Earth dance band were playing instruments that were definitely not dogs or bagpipes. Streamers and dead balloons littered the dance floor—it was late in the evening, it was early morning, the band looked pooped, the happy couple looked unfocused, drunk. The pill's stuffed shirt was awry. The pill was Cicero d'Pettitt.

I looked at the image for a minute in silence. Snodgrass wasn't saying anything, he was savoring the drama of the moment.

Finally I said, "I take it the woman's name is Jill."

"Right in one, Neddy. Miss Jill Lean."

"What do you want me to do about it?"

"Have you any idea who Miss Lean's father is?"

"Yeah, sure," I said. "Mr. Lean."

"People's Deputy the honorable Paul Lean, Convener of the House Committee for Ways and Means."

"Oh, that guy," I said, trying to sound bored, trying not to show the shock I really felt.

"That guy," Snodgrass said. "Once a rabble rousing scumbag from the sticks running the League o' Purity. Now a politician famous for his get-tough-on-aliens stand. 'Give them the sack— Send them back,' is his campaign motto. But he is also owner of extensive land holdings, interlocking directorships in companies manufacturing a diverse range of goods from cam shafts to lottery tickets. Believed to have the Governor of the National Monetary Control Commission in his pocket. Suspected of being the silent partner in a number of semi legal financial institutions specializing in asset stripping and...."

Snodders went on for some time. I tuned out. I couldn't give a rat's arse about the fine details, the man was a go-getting racist, that was all you needed to know about Paul Lean. It was the image of d'Pettitt with his arm round the dorky daughter that really appalled. Appalled and intrigued—how had he got himself onto that dance floor in the first place? How had he ever managed to get his arm round the girl's waist, convince her to marry him?

"So what do you know?" Snodgrass said, clicking his fingers. "Wake up, Neddy boy."

"I don't know anything," I said.

"You knew right away that the girl was Jill Lean."

"Jill is the name of the girl d'Pettitt is going to marry. It was you who told me who her daddy is."

"And d'Pettitt is your boss?"

"You know that. d'Pettitt runs things back at base. I rather like to think he works for me and the other sales staff. You could say he is our accountant."

"A low level functionary? A hireling of the Tetride bosses?"

"I'm afraid so."

"So what's he doing marrying this Lean girl?"

"I think he's marrying money."

"He's doing that all right. He's a nobody, an illegal alien with a history of crime on two planets—he's marrying some stinking rich politician's daughter who's always getting her pic in the social pages."

"I'll bet you daddy's pleased."

"He must be."

"A handsome young son-in-law like Cicero. Little alien babies in the offing...."

"It's not a matter for irony, Neddy boy. If Paul Lean didn't approve of this wedding, it wouldn't happen. It wouldn't happen because the happy groom-to-be would have an unfortunate accident."

"But Cicero is alive and well," I said.

"Why?" Snodgrass said.

"Buggered if I know."

"Find out."

Em Talking

I didn't talk to the idiot boy about that overheard remark. I didn't mention "paper news". The next day I just watched as he finished his breakfast in Aunty's dining room, picked up his salesman's bag of brushes, kissed Quincy, waved a cheery hand to me, and headed off to the tracts. And all day I worried.

I worried because idiot boy was in over his head. *And he didn't know it*. He just thought all this foreign correspondent business was a joke, a failure in the Scott-Wok's camp to understand how things really were. *Oh Ned, oh idiot boy, it's not the Scott-Woks who don't understand. It's you.*

But I wasn't without self-knowledge. I knew this as well: if I'd been feeling happier myself, I wouldn't have worried nearly so much about Ned. But I was miserable, and I felt guilty.

I was miserable because Cicero was marrying some Earth girl I'd never met, had never even knew existed. And I was guilty because this trivial incident meant more to me than the fate of my own planet. I knew, in my heart of hearts, that my own mundane affairs were nothing compared to the possible destruction of Newharp. I knew that my own parents, all my relatives except Harri, most of my childhood friends, were now facing a fate so much greater than my own—but for every minute I spent worrying about Newharp, I spent ten minutes worrying about me, about my loss of Cicero.

I tried talking to Quincy. I made her come to my room before I left for the Dog. I brewed her coffee and sat on the bed next to her.

"I'm obsessed," I said.

"You are," she said.

"I'm obsessed with Cicero and this Jill girl."

"I know," Quincy said.

"I shouldn't be," I said.

"It's natural," Quincy said. "Don't worry about it."

"The rock is only three Earth months out," I said.

"They might have deflected it already," Quincy said. "Every spacecraft on the planet is carrying bombs to the rock. They're not going to waste a single ship, just to carry news to us."

"My parents are there," I said.

"My grandparents are there," Quincy said.

"But all I think about is Cicero. Cicero and this bloody Jill."

"I know," Quincy said.

"I'm a monster," I said.

"Pig's bum," Quincy said.

"I'm worried about Ned."

"Ish will be all right."

"He's a babe in the woods. He thinks the Scott-Woks are a bunch of softies, he thinks they play by the rules."

"He's met Astolphe Scott-Wok. He's played ball with his daughter. He was at school with Mrs. Scott-Wok. He knows more about them than you."

"He knows nothing."

"If you say so, Em."

"I say so."

"Em, if you go on like this, you'll crack up."

"Oh, Quince, I wish today was over. I wish Ned had already come back from the tracts, from this bloody safe house. I wish he were here with us."

"He will be, Em, he will be. Now go to work."

Ned Talking

A plan was forming in my Earthling's mind. The more I thought about it, the more I liked it, the more I liked it, the more I thought about it. Quince was totally pissed off. I lay in her bed on the balcony, plotting. She clicked her fingers in front of my face.

"Yahoo, anybody home? Say something, Ish. Speak to me. Show me you're alive. Give me a sign."

"Hello Quincy."

"Oh thank god! He lives. He speaks."

"Sorry Quince," I said.

"He feels sorrow!"

"I'm just a bit obsessed at the moment."

"Not you as well."

"As well as who?"

"Em."

"Em? What's she obsessed about?"

"What do you reckon?"

"The rock."

"That as well."

"That as well as what?"

"Christ, you're thick."

"Yeah, I know. What's the matter with Em?"

"Cicero's the matter with Em."

"Why?"

"He's getting married to this Jill woman. Remember? So Em's...she's...bereft."

"Bereft? That's one way of putting it. She'll be a lot better off when d'Pettitt sets up house with Little Miss Muffet. I've never understood what Em saw in...."

"I know that. I'm not stupid."

"I never said you were, Quince."

"What do you reckon she's like?"

"Who?"

"Little Miss Muffet of course."

"I think she's a society dork and I reckon her dad is Mr. Money-bags. A corrupt politician who hates aliens."

"Oh yeah?"

"Why not—it's a good...a good...what do you McCall it? Hypothalamus?

Hypothesis is the word you're struggling for, idiot boy."

"That's what Em calls me."

"I can understand why."

"Why?"

"Because you produce totally stupid, halfwit hypotheses. That's why."

"Why?"

"Why what?"

"Why is it totally stupid to think that Cicero is going to marry a society heiress? Think about it, Quincy: Cicero wants to advance himself, get into the big league, start earning serious money. What better way?"

"Because society heiresses don't marry criminals from outer space."

"Oh I don't know...a bit of rough trade...."

"They don't *marry* rough trade, Ish. They have flings with rough trade."

"You're wrong."

"I'll bet I'm right."

"Ten newbees says you're not," I said.

"I'm a professional gambler. You don't want to bet with me."

"I do, Quincy dear. You're on."

"OK. We'll wait and see who this Jill actually is. I reckon she'll be a recovering junkie straight out of clink. Now what did you do all day? What happened in this safe house?"

"I was shown a million images of this Jill woman."

"What for?"

"The Scott-Woks want to know why she's marrying d'Pettitt."

"So what's she look like?"

"Rich society dork with a feelthy rich papa, name of Paul Lean."

"I don't believe it.... That bastard!"

"Ten newbees please."

"I don't believe you. I'm not paying."

"I'll accept a kiss."

"Drop dead. And stop...tickling...me."

Tickle turned to slap. Giggle turned to pant. For a while the whole damn universe was blotted out. Nothing existed outside Quincy's balcony. Her patchwork quilt, her indoor pot plants, the glass prism on the shelf. And then we lay still and dozed and came back to consciousness wrapped around each other, and the world beyond the balcony reasserted itself.

Quincy said, "So who is this Jill? Who is she really?"

It took me five minutes to convince Quincy that I wasn't joking, that she really was Paul Lean's daughter.

"So why do the Scott-Woks want to know about her and Cicero?" Quincy said.

"Just curious, I guess. They probably want to know why Cicero is still alive."

"I'm curious about that myself," Quincy said. "And how did he do it? How did Cicero of all people get to meet the girl in the first place? Why did he do it? Hasn't he got any pride? It's like marrying...I don't know...it's like marrying a viper."

"Love thine enemy," I said. "And as for *how*—it sure wasn't by bringing her here," I said. "Tea at Aunty Nagoya's didn't figure in the game plan."

"True fact," Quincy said.

"Are you going to do it, Ish? Are you going to spy for the Scott-Wok's? Tell them what's going on?"

"It can't hurt," I said.

"You don't like Cicero, do you?"

"Not much."

"It's because you're in love with Em, isn't it?"

"I'm in love with you."

"No, you're not. I'm your friend. You like being with me. You like doing things with me. You like sleeping with me. But you're not in love with me."

"And you?" I said. "Are you in love with me?"

"Not yet."

"But you could be?"

"I'd be mad to fall in love with you, Ish. I'd break things off if it ever looked like I was going to fall in love."

"Jeeze, this conversation is getting heavy," I said.

"Go to sleep," she said. "And here's your kiss, you can have it anyway."

Em Talking

It was about time I had a talk to my brother. We hadn't been doing much of that lately. Perhaps me and Gloom-n-doom had never really talked. Not long and hard and into the night. Brothers and sisters probably don't often do that—they already share too much, they have to preserve their own spaces. But Quincy had told me that Ned was worried about Harri. Ned thought Harri was going into terminal decline. Going down the tubes was the way he put it. And if it was so obvious to idiot boy, it must be obvious. But I'm no fool, I didn't bowl up to Harri and say, "I'm told you're going mad." I went round to his room one evening when Ned was downstairs with Quincy, watching her win mega newbees at jongma. I sat on Ned's bed. It didn't smell of lavender any more—maybe they were keeping the lavender for Quincy's bed. Harri was sitting in the room's only chair in front of the open window watching the life in the street below.

The street sounds came dully to where I sat on Ned's bed. The window was wide open and the breeze was ruffling Harri's hair.

"I'm worried about Ned," I said to Harri.

"What's the matter with him?"

"It's this Scott-Wok business."

"Don't worry about it. Ned's small fry. So am I."

"Why do the Scott-Woks want to find out about Cicero and this...this...Earth girl?"

"Her name's Jill. You know that, Em."

"She's not small fry," I said. "Her father's not small fry. Her father's the most anti-alien politician on the planet."

"Political expediency. Maybe it's not so expedient to be anti-alien any more. Maybe the Tetrides have offered Lean a deal. If the Tetrides and Lean team up the whole balance of power will have shifted. If it has, it's no wonder the Scott-Woks want to know what's going on. Maybe this Paul Lean now represents a threat to Scott-Wok's plans to take over the Tetride organ business." Harri spoke so flatly that you'd think he was explaining that rain made you wet: anybody could see what was going on.

"You reckon Scott-Wok wants to take over the Tetrides?"

"Listen Em, if you are in competition with someone, you can do two things. You can destroy the competition, rub it out, annihilate it. Then you can start from scratch: build up your own business on the ruins of the old one. Or—second option—you can take over the competition as a going concern, swallow it up. Which do you reckon makes more sense? Which option do you reckon they teach in business college?"

"These guys don't go to business college. They're gangsters, not captains of industry."

"These guys are captains of a gangster industry—they're business executives, they believe in cost-benefit analysis."

"How do you know this?"

"Look at what's happening. Why do you reckon everything's so quiet out in the tracts? Why do you reckon no one's bombed the Dog? Do you think Scott-Wok doesn't know where the organ factory is?"

"Ned reckons there's room for everybody. He reckons Scott-Wok is happy to live and let live."

"Ned's a dill. Scott-Wok is just biding his time. When he thinks the moment has come he'll strike and strike hard. But my bet—and it's only a bet, Em—is that he'll try to eliminate the bosses. Chop the head off, keep the body. The organ factories, the transplant clinics, the rank and file lab workers and surgeons, the bottle washers, the sales staff—they'll be left alone. Ned and I are going to wake up one day and find we're working for the Scott-Woks. That's all, a change of bosses."

"So what's the worry about Jill Lean?" I said.

"The worry is her dad. If he's joining forces with the Tetride bosses, the whole equation changes. Maybe Scott-Wok will think again about trying to eliminate the bosses and their Earthling mates. Maybe he'll go for gang warfare instead. Maybe he'll go for the biggest market share he can get; but he won't try for a monopoly. Then there'll be gunfire in the tracts. Sabotage in the wharflands. The bosses will hit back, have a go at the Scott-Wok organ factories and clinics. Ned will need an armed escort in the tracts. We'd all be well advised to stay out of the Dog."

"But why is Cicero marrying this dork?" I said. "Her dad could join forces with the Tetrides without marrying his daughter off to an...an alien."

"I think he wants to change his image—I think he's after the alien vote. People with Citizenship get to vote, you know. Quincy can vote if she wants to. She was born here, she's allowed to be here. Mr. Sam Yang Rhee can vote. The screaming alligator handlers can vote. All this get-tough-on-aliens posture is starting to be political liability. What do you reckon People's Deputy Lean's ambitions are? Just to remain chairman of some committee on ways and means? He probably wants be king of the whole damn castle."

"But Cicero's illegal, like the rest of us," I said. "How can this Lean guy hold a huge wedding? Even he can't be seen to have an illegal for a son-in-law. That won't get him votes."

"Do you think he can't pull strings? I think friend d'Pettitt is going to be Citizen of the Year before Christmas. Hard working boy from outer space makes good. Newharp rags to Earthly riches."

"God, Harri, how did we get mixed up in all this?"

"We're illegals, Em. This is our world."

We were both quiet for a while. I looked at my brother. He was older. We were both so much older than the naive refugees who'd shipped out with the PentaNostra— what?—three Earth years ago, three and a bit years ago. What a way to grow up.

"You need a girlfriend," I said to Harri. I said it spontaneously, I hadn't meant to.

"How do you know I'm not gay?"

"All right. You need a boyfriend."

"I'm OK, Em."

"You need to get out more,"

"Why?"

"Because you are vegetating. You're either in this room or you're underground, growing organs."

"I don't run the organ farm by myself. I have...colleagues."

This was a point. Harri worked all day beneath my feet at the Dog. But I had never visited the labs. Under the floor that I worked on was an ordinary cellar. They kept the booze down there and there was a cool room for food. At the back of the cool room was a small locked steel door. A flight of steps went down into the earth, down to the labs and the operating theatres. Harri and one or two others used the steel door in the Dog to get to work. But there were other ways in and out. There were tunnels to other steel doors in offices or workshops or factories near the Dog. I'd never been down to the labs, I was forbidden to mention them. I had no idea who else worked down there, I didn't know what people made their entrances and exits from the nearby buildings. This office worker, that factory hand, this that and the other shop assistant, anybody I often passed on the street in the immediate vicinity could be Harri's workmates.

"God, Harri," I said, "Have you got a little friend down there? A special girl or boy, close to your heart? Love amongst the organs?"

He blushed. My brother blushed. It was a sight I'd never seen. It was amazing to behold.

"For heaven's sake, why haven't I been told. Why haven't I met her, him or it?"

"She's just a girl, Em."

"What's her name?"

"It's all need-to-know down there. You know that, Em."

"Yeah, but I need to know."

"No you don't."

"Yes I do."

"No you...."

I threw Ned's pillow at Harri. Harri ducked. The pillow went straight out the window and disappeared. Harri stood up and leaned out. He started to yell to someone in the street to pick up the pillow, but gave up.

"Too late," he said, sitting down again. "Someone just ran over it. Tire marks straight across the middle." The door opened. Quincy and Ned entered. "Em's just lost your pillow," Harri said.

"Lost it where?" Ned said.

"In the traffic," Harri said.

"What were you doing with it in the traffic?" Ned said to me.

"Taking a nap," I said.

"Couldn't you use your own pillow?"

"It would get all dirty. Someone might run over it."

"Oh," said Ned, "I hadn't looked at it like that."

He sat down on the bed beside me. He was pretending not to care about his damned pillow, not to be remotely curious. Quincy sat on Harri's bed—she looked at me with an inquiring frown.

"Guess what," I said.

"What?" Quincy said.

"Harri's got a little friend."

"A pet mouse?" Ned said.

"A girl?" Quincy said.

Harri looked down at his feet. He was giving nothing away.

"What's her name?" Ned said.

Harri said nothing.

"Come on, Harri," Quincy said. "Who is this lucky wench?"

"Need-to-know," Harri mumbled, still looking at his feet.

"Need-to-know?" Ned said. "What sort of name is that?"

Harri continued to look at his feet.

"He's blushing," I said. "I've never seen my brother blush, but look at him now."

"So who is this girl?" Ned said.

"Someone from the catacombs," I said. "It's a case of love in the sweatshop."

"I can't talk about the lab," Harri said. "It's secret."

"Yeah, but this girl," Quincy said. "She's not a spare part. Tell us about the girl."

Suddenly Harri was very angry. The whole atmosphere of the room changed completely. "It's nothing to do with you," he shouted. "Just leave me alone, will you. Just leave me alone."

There was a shocked silence for a moment and then Quincy said quietly, "All right, Harri, all right—we were only curious. We're happy for you. We just thought you might like to tell us...."

"Well I don't! Now shut up."

Harri looked close to tears. Or close to smashing something. It was hard to say. I looked at Ned, I looked at Quincy, I nodded towards the door. Without saying anything the pair of them left. When the door was shut I walked over to Harri and squatted beside his chair. I put my arms awkwardly around him. He was trembling. He didn't yield to my embrace. We stayed like that for a minute. My right leg developed a tremor, but only from the strange position it was in. I released Harri and stood up.

"What's the matter?" I said as softly as I could.

Harri said nothing.

"Talk to me Harri," I said.

"There's nothing to say. Just don't keep pestering me. Don't bug me all the time."

"Nobody's bugging you, Harri."

"Please, Em. Please leave me alone."

There was nothing I could do. I left my brother sitting on the chair by the open window, staring at his feet.

Ned Talking

I met Cicero in the Dog for a "business lunch" (his words). We talked business over plates of preserved soyalillo. It tasted OK but was far too expensive. Not that it worried me, Cicero was paying. Apparently lillo is the subtlest of subtle flavors to be found in the whole range of Newharp cooking. But there isn't any lillo on Earth. It doesn't grow here. So they make a substitute out of soya beans. They say it's only a crude imitation of the real thing. I believe them.

"We're dropping kidneys to two thou the pair," Cicero said. "Next month only."

"And that's a thou for one?"

"You don't sell kidneys as one offs, Ish. The punters want kidneys, they can do the job properly and buy a pair."

"Some people can only afford one at a time."

"OK. Fifteen hundred for one. A discount of twenty-five per cent if they buy the next one within twelve months. That'll make it two twenty five hundred the pair. Which is a bargain, seeing as how the surgeons'll have to slice them up twice."

"What about arteries? They're not moving. I only sold six meters fifty last month."

"Seasonal fluctuation. Leave arteries alone."

We went through the whole product range. d'Pettitt was brisk, professional. We called for plates of Jelly Grass and settled back.

"When's the happy day?" I said.

"What happy day's that?" Cicero said.

"The hitching. The nuptials."

"Soon."

"I'm looking forward to it," I said.

"*You're* looking forward to it?"

"There's nothing like a good wedding. Big nosh up afterwards. Funny speeches. There won't be a dry eye in the place."

"I hadn't exactly put you down as prime wedding guest material, Earth boy."

"I was thinking along the lines of best man."

"That position's already filled."

"Ah well," I sighed. "Groomsman will do."

"Why the interest in my forthcoming marriage?"

"We've been through a lot together, Cicero. We've forged a dynamic sales team, you and me. And now you're moving on. A guy would like to raise a glass of bubbles at the appropriate moment."

"Moving on?"

"We're talking rungs on the corporate ladder here," I said. "I understand you will be higher up the pecking order." This was a bit of a punt, I understood nothing at all.

"You understand?"

"That's the word around the office," I said confidently.

"What office?"

"This place. The Dog functions, as you will have noticed, as the headquarters of our dynamic sales team. It's our office. And rumor in the Dog has it that Cicero d'Pettitt will soon be middle management, if not senior management."

"You don't want to listen to rumor, Ishmael."

"Indeed you don't—but it is unsettling for the sales team not to know who their charismatic leader will be in a month's time. Morale may fall, sales figures may plummet."

"Want the job?"

"What?"

"Would you like to take over from me, Earth boy?"

"I'm too good in the field. I'm not really a headquarters man."

"Salesmen burn out, Ish. One of these days you'll have to think of moving yourself."

"I'm not thinking of burning out at eighteen."

"Think about it. Someone will have to fill my shoes."

"How long have I got to think?"

"If you want the job, you'd better apply within a week."

"So what's the time frame? When are you getting married?"

"Couple of months. But they'll need a smooth change over."

"I'd need to know who to bribe. What sort of percentages."

"You'd be given a thorough training, introduced to all the necessary people. It's all pretty straight forward—there's nothing easier than bribing a bent cit."

"I'll think about it," I said.

"You do that, Ish. Give it some thought."

I walked home from the Dog amazed. There was no doubt about it, Cicero wanted me to take over his job. I'd be doing him a favor. It was in his interests to hand over to someone with my undoubted talents. Which put me in a bit of a bargaining position. And it would get me access to all sorts of information: corrupt police, the identities of the bosses. I would be in a position to advance my private plans. I might even get an invite to his wedding.

Em Talking

I needed someone to talk to. Usually, if I was troubled about something, I talked to Quincy. But this time I needed someone older, wiser, someone who could advise me. I didn't know anyone. There wasn't anyone. And I could hardly talk to Harri—it was Harri who was troubling me. And talking to idiot boy would do no good—he was another source of anxiety, he was preparing to take over Cicero's job. He hadn't a clue—he thought it would be all plain sailing: paying bribes, dealing with the bosses, competing with the Scott-Woks. Spying for the Scott-Woks at the same time. They were no fools, the Scott-Woks, they'd known what they were doing when they recruited Ned as a spy. If he took over Cicero's job, he'd have useful information. And the Scott-Woks would want it.

I was lying awake one night. There was hardly any light in my room, but a little moonlight, or lamplight, came through the high window, falling on the wall, dully illuminating the image of Santa Gertrudis I'd taped there. Suddenly I knew who I wanted to talk to. It was a mad thought. It was totally impractical. She was probably thousands of kilometers away at Spearchucker or one of the other camps. But she might be at the Scott-Woks' palace. Ned seemed to think Mr. and Mrs. Scott-Wok spent *some* time together. But I wanted to talk to her. I wanted to talk to Sue-Ellen Harrison. I remembered her leaning across the table and suddenly talking to me in fluent Newharp, telling me exactly what I needed to know. She'd been on my side then. She'd be on my side now.

Late the next morning, when both Ned and Harri were out of the place, I went to their room. I fired up the computer and sent an e.

Dear Ms. Harrison,

I'm writing to you again about the terrible things that are being done to pigeons. I am in despair at the behavior of certain pigeon tormentors. They seem to go from bad to worse. If only I could meet you face to face, I am sure I could convince you to throw your considerable wisdom and resources behind the cause. Is it possible for us to meet?"

Yours sincerely,

Gonzalez Della

Four times in the next couple of hours I checked the inbox. I wanted to get Sue-Ellen's reply and delete it before anybody else read it. On the fifth try, there it was.

Dear Mr. Della,

It would be a pleasure to meet you and discuss pigeon welfare. Would tomorrow afternoon be convenient? If you let me know the Pigeon Fanciers Society address I would be delighted to come and talk to you.

Yours Sincerely,

Sue-Ellen Harrison

She was in town! I'd lucked out. But where could we meet. I didn't want Sue-Ellen to come to Aunty Nagoya's. And the Dog would never do. I sent back a quick e. All it contained was the address of our language school. Quincy's builders hadn't finished yet—they were taking their time. Often they didn't show up for days on end. If they were there tomorrow, too bad. I'd pretend Sue-Ellen was there for professional purposes and find somewhere quiet to talk to her. I felt happier than I had for days. I went to work almost light hearted. I was doing something, I was taking charge, sort of.

It was Saturday night. A heavy shift at the Dog. The kitchens were a shambles. The eating and boozing areas were full of eaters and boozers shouting. The jongma game out the back was so fast and so noisy it was almost impossible to follow the action. Not that I had much opportunity to follow the action, I was serving food and hooch as fast as I could slap the stuff down in front of people. But even in the rush of it all I was aware of Harri. Somewhere down there beneath my feet, Harri was also working the late shift. At least, he said he was. Was that when Harri and this girlfriend person had quality time together? Were they alone down there, canoodling amongst the organs? What was she like? Why was Harri so touchy? Why why why? I supposed that mystery girl was one of the workers who entered the labs through a tunnel from a nearby building. I could have walked past her on the street a hundred times. Was she a pretend office worker, cleaner, fork lift driver? What was her name? And how were she and Harri getting on together? Badly, if Harri's mad reaction was anything to go by. I was still shocked by the way he'd yelled at Quincy, closed himself off from me. If he wanted to keep his girlfriend to himself, well and good—but he didn't have to throw a fit about it.

At midnight Harri emerged from the cellar. He slunk through

the kitchen, which was calming down. He nodded to me and mumbled, "Hi Em," and kept going. A few minutes later I checked the main room, he wasn't to be seen. He'd gone straight home. Even Gloom-and-Doom usually stayed for a few minutes after work, but not tonight. I wondered if I should blame mystery girl: was she a manipulative bitch who enjoyed putting people like Harri through hell? God knows, he'd be easy enough to put through hell if he ever let a girl get close to him. It was hard to say. I couldn't say. I knew nothing.

Ned Talking

I sent progress reports to my various admirers. I used a dead letter box for the Scott-Woks: a lose brick in a warehouse wall. And one day when I was out in the tracts I left a short note at the police station for the two beauties. I told both parties that I was moving right along. I told them all about my job prospects. I told them I'd soon be in a position to tell them what they wanted to know. I told them to stay tuned.

Em Talking

Luckily it was an off day for the builders. I was alone. Our building was coming right along, it was almost finished. I sat on the floor in the reception area behind the front door. We still had no furniture, but the area was carpeted, the walls were painted a pleasant shade of pale yellow. There were blinds on the windows that let in just the right amount of daylight. It was very restful. It was the cleanest, most uncluttered place I had been in since I left Newharp. I hoped Sue-Ellen Harrison wouldn't mind the lack of furniture. I hoped she wouldn't think her journey wasted when she heard my story. I'd been slightly surprised when she said she would come to me. I had been expecting to go to a meeting place of her choosing. I didn't know if it was all that safe for the wife of Astolphe Scott-Wok to venture deep into the heart of Tetride territory, I suspected it wasn't. I lay down on the carpet. I closed my eyes and tried to imagine how the place would feel when it was a functioning language school. There'd be students clattering up the stairs, other staff to have tea with, the smell of the stuff you use to clean white boards. Where would we go for lunch? I supposed most days we'd eat sandwiches in the staff room.

I'd dozed off. The knock on the door jolted me awake. I scrambled to my feet and hurried to open it. A woman in traditional Kovalev costume stood on the doorstep, her face obscured by her hood. There was no gleaming Gamma Crux parked in the street. I wasn't fooled. Harri and Ned had told me how she'd materialized on our rock at Spearchucker, dressed like that.

"Come in," I said.

Sue-Ellen stepped into room. I shut the door and she threw back the hood.

"Have you been asleep?" she said. She was just as I remembered her: strong, completely in command of the situation, totally adult.

"I must have been," I said.

"Nice place," she said, looking around. "A bit flash for pigeons, I'd have thought."

"We're going to start a language school. Me and a friend."

"I might apply for a job," she said.

"Err, I'm sorry. We haven't any furniture yet."

"Don't worry about it. Let's sit on the floor."

Sue-Ellen sat down cross legged. I sat down too. Suddenly I was shy, embarrassed by my own effrontery. What would she think about my half formed anxieties, my problems? Inviting her here had seemed a good idea at the time, I'd decided Sue-Ellen Harrison was the only person in the world I could talk to. Now that I was sitting facing her across a meter and a half of empty carpet, I wasn't so sure. I started to say something about how much I appreciated her visit, how I hoped I hadn't caused her too much trouble.

Sue-Ellen ignored my babble. "Actually," she said. "Your knees seize-up if you sit around too long like this. I think I'll lie down." She lay down and placed her clasped hands behind her head. "Nice ceiling," she said. "The color contrasts well with the wall."

"Ms. Harrison," I said. "I'm worried about...."

"Sue-Ellen for chrisake. Don't be so bloody Newharp."

"Sue-Ellen, I'm worried about...."

"Yeah, yeah. We'll get to your worries in due course. Lie down, why don't you? Tell me everything that's happened since the Spearchucker fiasco. Where have you been living? What have you been doing? Have you got a boyfriend?"

I lay down on my back and looked at the ceiling. I was suddenly glad that I didn't have eye contact with Sue-Ellen. I was very conscious of her lying next to me, looking at the same newly painted ceiling, but I was glad we were not looking at each other. I started to speak. I began at the beginning; I told her about the escape in Waldron's Leo Minor, the misery bus trip down the North-South highway, Aunty Nagoya's, the Dog. Once I'd started talking, I couldn't stop. Sue-Ellen didn't say much, just asked the odd question that went straight to the heart of the matter. I talked and talked. I lost track of time. It was getting dark when I got round to Harri's theories about the Scott-Wok's planning to take over the Tetride organ business.

"He's bright, your brother. But Astolphe's empire couldn't just acquire the organ business on its own. It would have to completely take over the Tetrides. Lock, stock and barrel."

"Could he do this, could your husband...."

"It's possible to merge two business empires without getting a great deal of blood on the boardroom floor."

"Without a great deal...?"

"There's bound to be *some,* Em."

"Like real blood," I said. "Not just metaphorical blood?"

"These are the Tetrides and the Scott-Wok's we are talking about. Not a couple of bookstore owners."

"Harri reckons the small fry will just have a change of bosses."

"I hope he's right."

I talked on and on. I told Sue-Ellen about Ned getting ready to take over Cicero's job.

"Helen likes Ned," Sue-Ellen said.

"Helen?"

"My daughter."

"Oh, yes, of course. I'm sorry, I never met her."

"She and Ned played slogball."

"Is Ned spying for your husband?"

"I doubt that Ned would know anything that Astolphe didn't already know."

"He might when he takes on Cicero's job."

"That's true enough."

"If the Tetrides find out that he's passing information to...to the opposition, they'll...."

"...kill him."

"Oh, Sue-Ellen, I want out of this."

"You are out of it. Just run your language school. You'll have to pay protection money to the Tetrides—or their successors—but it won't break the bank. And as long as you pay up, you'll be protected."

"I want Ned out of it. I want Harri out of it."

"You've got to let other people make their own decisions."

"Ned's a fool. He doesn't know that he's playing with fire."

"I'll tell Astolphe that I don't want my old school mate, or his mate Harri, to come to any grief. Astolphe'll understand—he knows about loyalty to childhood friends."

"Thanks. I feel a lot happier."

"No you don't. Now what's your real problem, Em."

"Those were my problems."

"Rubbish. Got a sex life?"

"Not at the moment, no."

"But in the recent past?"

"I had a...I suppose you could call him a childhood friend. We started sleeping together at Aunty Nagoya's."

"This lad got a name?"

"Cicero d'Pettitt."

Sue-Ellen exploded with laughter. "Nombre de dios! And now he's going to marry that Lean creature. I'll tell you what, Em. Any halfwit who would throw you over for that airhead wasn't worth having in the first place. You're well rid of him."

"He didn't exactly throw me over. I never really committed myself. I kept him at arm's length."

"Not a bad policy. I'm a bit that way with Astolphe."

"No one can work out why...why the airhead is marrying Cicero. He's hardly in her social class. Her dad hates aliens. He wants to keep the bloodlines pure."

"No accounting for taste. And Paul Lean has suddenly gone all pro-alien. He hasn't made a racist speech for six months. It won't do his new-look politics any harm to have a Newharp son-in-law."

We were silent for a while. It was now dark. The only light in the room was street light, filtered by the blinds.

"This Paul Lean," I said. "Is he in with the Tetrides?"

"Someone like Lean tries to be in with as many groups as possible. It's called having a broad electoral base."

"But if he's pro Tetride, he'd have to be anti Scott-Wok."

"Not that I've noticed. He was very friendly towards me at dinner the other night."

"Dinner? You've had him to dinner?"

"Sure. I am Mrs. Scott-Wok after all. If I'm in town I move in that sort of circle."

"And his daughter, this Jill?"

"Yeah, I've met her. Self centered and vacuous. Total lame-brain. So lightweight you wouldn't even call her thick."

"It's nice of you to say so."

"It's bloody true, Em. Christ I'm hungry. Let's go and eat somewhere. You can tell me your troubles."

"I've been doing nothing but tell you...."

"You've hardly begun."

We stepped outside Quincy's building and I locked the door. Sue-Ellen, her hood obscuring her face, put two fingers in her mouth and let out a piercing whistle. There was a blaze of light from a rusted Dorado that had been parked by the entrance to the cul-de-sac. With a growl of enhanced engine noise the car moved towards us.

"What's this?" I said.

"Bodyguard stroke chauffeur," Sue-Ellen said. "Jump in."

Sue-Ellen and I sat in the back. The bodyguard/chauffeur slammed the Dorado into reverse and surged back down the cul-de-sac. The car might have looked like a shitheap on wheels, it performed like a Gamma Crux.

"Snodgrass, this is Ms. Gonzalez-della-Harpenden," Sue-Ellen said.

"Pleased to meet you, Miss," the bodyguard said.

"The Eatery," Sue-Ellen said.

"Very well, Madam."

Sue-Ellen turned to me, "Ever been there?"

"Where?"

"The Eatery. Little bistro in Castello Balmoral. Straight down the line Earth tucker I'm afraid. But good."

"I never leave the wharflands," I said. "Illegals like me tend to lie low."

"You'll be all right in this joint. Very discreet."

It was too. The Eatery was everything the Dog wasn't. The tables were covered with starched white cloth. The silverware was silver. The plates were warmed. The waitress was dressed in demure black and white silk, the maître d' bowed. He didn't bow low, but he bowed. The string quartet had no need to struggle against the shouting and singing of the mob. Nothing but quiet chatter in English competed with their sweet airs. In the Dorado Sue-Ellen had pulled her Kovalev smock unceremoniously over her head the moment we left the wharflands. She'd been wearing a yellow and red sari underneath it. Now, in the bistro, where I could get a good look at her, she looked stunning.

"We'd better talk English in this place," she said. "Do you mind?"

"Not at all. I just wish I'd dressed for the occasion."

"Don't worry about it. These buggers are impressed by nothing but money. I've been here before. They know I've got heaps."

The maître d' and the waitress were most attentive. They knew she'd got heaps.

I suppose the food was good. In an Earthy sort of way. I wouldn't know, we don't eat much of it in the wharflands. The plonk was excellent though—even I could tell that.

"Harri's the problem, isn't he?" Sue-Ellen said.

"How do you know?" I said.

"Because you've been skirting round the issue. Encircling it. All you've told me about Harri is his political analysis of the Tetride-Scott-Wok problem. Now tell me about him."

So I told Sue-Ellen about Harri. I told her everything I knew. I told her about his increasing withdrawal, his sudden outbursts of anger, his touchiness on the subject of his girlfriend. I said I was half-inclined to blame the girl, whoever she was, whatever she was called.

"And you believe she exists?" Sue-Ellen said.

"Of course she exists," I said.

"Why 'of course?'" Sue-Ellen said.

"Because Harri has told me about her. He wouldn't make her up. He wouldn't lie to me. What would be the point of that?"

"But he's never introduced you?"

"People who work in the organ labs aren't meant to talk about their work, they're not meant to socialize outside the labs. The labs themselves are secret."

"They are not *that* secret, Em. Even I know there is an organ lab underneath the Dog."

"He's my brother, Sue-Ellen."

"And if he is making up phantom girlfriends and going all hypersensitive, and pretending that he can't introduce you, then he's got problems. Brother or no brother."

"I'm sure she's real."

"Well, you know Harri better than I do. Trust your own judgment, don't trust mine."

"What sort of remark is that?" I said.

"One calculated to make you question your own judgment," Sue-Ellen said.

"This is just playing games," I said.

"Yeah, it is. Tell me about Quincy."

"Quincy? She's my..err business partner. She bought the building, paid for the renovations. She's Ned's girlfriend."

"Neddy boy! Little Ned's got himself a girl?"

"Why not?"

"Why not indeed. I suppose even total yobs like Ned must exercise a certain charm on a certain type of girl."

"Quincy's got very good taste. They are both my friends. The fact that they are on together is one of the bright, warm spots in my life."

"Are you in love with her?"

"Who?"

"Dear Quincy, that's who."

"She's one of my closest friends."

"You're in love with her. Tell me about her."

I was silent. Sue-Ellen said, "Go on, Em. Tell me about Quincy. Don't worry about whether you're in love with her or not. Just tell me about her."

So I told Sue-Ellen about Quincy. I told her everything I knew. I didn't know that I knew so much until I started to talk. By the time I'd finished talking, the bistro was half deserted, we seemed to have drunk another bottle of plonk and the pudding Sue-Ellen had ordered had been eaten without me being able to remember what it tasted like.

"I've no idea what that tasted like," I said, pointing at the empty dish.

"Earth tucker's like that," Sue-Ellen said. "Don't let it worry you."

"So what do I do?" I said to Sue-Ellen.

"Exorcise your demons," Sue-Ellen said.

"How do I do that?"

"Want to come to the d'Pettitt-Lean wedding reception?"

"No."

"Good. I'll arrange an invite. For you, for Neddy, for Quincy and for Harri."

"Why?"

"You've got to confront the reality of who Cicero is. You've got to watch him get hitched to this airhead for no better reason than social climbing. It'll be a grim spectacle, but it will cure you forever. And you'll have your real friends with you. You'll see Quincy and Ned in a truer perspective. And it will do Harri good to get out and about—simple as that."

"How can you arrange an invite? We're Cicero's friends. But I don't think he is going to invite any of us. And I wouldn't accept an invitation from him even if he did invite me."

"You can come as friends of the bride."

"What?"

"Paul Lean has asked me to find a few aliens to swell the ranks of his party. He wants young people. He suddenly wants it to look as if he's had alien friends all along, that his daughter has lots of alien friends."

"Some-of-my-best-friends-are-aliens! That sort of thing?"

"That sort of thing."

"We're meant to be rent-a-friends?"

"Exactly."

"Stand-ins? Extras? Publicity props?"

"Suitable costumes supplied free of charge."

"This is outrageous, Sue-Ellen."

"It is, isn't it?" she said calmly.

"I'm not going."

"Think about it, Em."

"I don't need to think about it. I'm not going."

"I'll bet you Ned, Harri and this Quincy girl accept. Come too. Otherwise you'll miss the fun."

"Fun?"

"The reception might not run strictly as planned."

"What do you mean, by that?"

"Oh, I don't know," Sue-Ellen said, suddenly going all vague.

"The best laid plans of mice and men."

"This is some sort of quote?"

"They gang awry. Robert Burns."

"Never heard of him."

"Scottish."

"It figures. Ned's told me about them—they eat haggis."

"Come to the reception, Em."

"Where's it going to be?"

"Guess."

"I don't know."

"Some popular dive of ill repute called the Dog and Harp."

"The Dog! I work there."

"I know you do. Be a pampered customer for once."

"No way."

"The marriage ceremony itself will be in the Cathedral in Point Potts—deep in the heart of respectable old Jackson's Port. That will be very tedious, you don't have to go to that. Afterwards the wedding guests will process in a motorcade to the reception deep in the heart of the wharflands where they will be joined by other happy well-wishers such as yourself—a symbolic reconciliation of both cultures."

"This is revolting...."

"After the official party has eaten its fill, and made its speeches and toasted the happy couple and the wedding dance has been danced, the doors of the Dog and Harp will be thrown wide open. The general populace will mingle with the official guests, the party will spill out onto the street. Bands will play. Free hooch will flow. Nibbles will be nibbled. Dancing in the street. A great time will be had by all."

"Oh, for Christ's sake!"

"Be there, Em."

"If the Tetride bosses found out that we'd been...."

"Oh, they'll find out all right. They'll be there too. They own the Dog and Harp after all. Paul Lean could hardly forget his great mates, the bosses."

"I don't understand."

"It's late at night, Em. So, let's get Snodgrass to take us home."

Ned Talking

Well that little bit about Sue-Ellen prophesying that the reception might not go as planned—that was bright of her. I wonder how she knew.

* * * * * * *

Cicero took me to meet the bosses. Or some of the bosses. We met in a dusky room full of heavy furniture and cigarette smoke. It was up a steep flight of narrow stairs, just round the corner from the Dog, above the main hall of the old Mission to the Deaf and the Dumb. There didn't appear to be any action in the hall. No sounds of twangling, no talking in tongues, no baby alligators scuttling across the floor. The PentaNostras were having a quiet day. In the upstairs room all the smoke was coming from the only woman present: an overweight old girl of about seventy with tons of clanking jewelry and a voice like a chain saw. Scott-Wok had been right: this mob were an ugly bunch, they lacked style. They didn't tell me their names and I didn't ask. But they named a few politicians, they named a few members of the Citizenship Police. They told me a lot of stuff about percentages, sweeteners and kickbacks. I learned about slow payers and how to persuade them to become fast payers. I learned about my new salary. It was peanuts. I said so.

"That's your starting salary," one of the bosses said. "You're still on commission. The sales staff bring in the punters, the punters pay up, you get an extra1.5% of total receipts. Rising to 2.5% in increments of 0.5% for every ten thou over the agreed target. Get it?"

I did a quick sum or two. I wouldn't be making much more than I already made. I said, "I'm renegotiating after six months, all right?"

"A year," the guy I'd already met in the Dog said.

"Nine months," I said.

"A year," the guy said.

"All right, a year," I said. "But you are going to see profits and I'm going to see my fair share."

"We'll talk about that in a year."

"Tell us about Mrs. Scott-Wok," said the human chain saw.

"Sue-Ellen? I was a school with her. But she was Year Twelve when I was Year Four. I didn't exactly know her."

"But you met her in Spearchucker?"

"Briefly. She's an interpreter. Cicero met her too. Didn't you mate?"

Beside me, Cicero just nodded. He hardly said a word during the whole meeting.

"Have you seen Mrs. Scott-Wok since Spearchucker?" said the woman, blowing yet more smoke into the atmosphere.

"No. How could I? I've only been in the wharflands and the tracts."

"Know a guy called Snodgrass?"

"Called *what?*"

"Snodgrass."

"Never heard of him. Why doesn't he change his name?"

"Someone saw Snodgrass driving a rust-bucket of a Dorado around the wharflands. There was a woman in the back seat. Kovalev cloak, hood covering her face."

"So?"

"So Snodgrass is a hard man, employed by the Scott-Woks. Mrs. Scott-Wok is known to wear a Kovalev cloak sometimes. Sure she hasn't been to see you?"

"Why would Sue-Ellen want to see me?"

"We thought you could tell us."

"Well I can't. She hasn't been to see me. She wouldn't recognize me anyway. Not with my face shift."

"Well, you'll have to introduce yourself."

"What?"

"We want you to make contact with Mrs. Scott-Wok."

"What the hell for?"

"We want to put a proposition to her."

"What proposition?"

"Never mind. Your job is to make contact. We put the proposition."

"Look, let's get this straight. You want me to bowl up to Sue-Ellen's house, knock on the door, say 'G'day I'm Ishmael but really I'm Ned even though I don't look like Ned any more and my bosses want to put a proposition to you—god knows what it is?'"

"I don't think knocking on the door of the Scott-Wok stronghold would be very wise. We are not all that interested in including Mr. Scott-Wok in these negotiations."

"So how do I get hold of Sue-Ellen?"

"You're a resourceful young man, Ishmael. We are sure you will find a way."

They rambled on some more. Finally the fat old girl said, "We expect great things from you, Ishmael. Let Cicero know as soon as you make contact with Mrs. Scott-Wok. There will be, of course, a suitable bonus." And that seemed to be the end of the interview. But as Cicero and I were leaving the room, the chain saw said. "It's a heavy responsibility we are placing on your shoulders, young man. Don't let us down."

"Not me," I said, and got myself through the door.

"Heavy responsibility!" I hissed at Cicero as we clattered down the narrow stairs. Who does that that old girl think she is, a school principal or something?"

"Don't under-estimate these people, Ishmael. They could rub you out very easily indeed."

On the street, I started to walk back to the Dog, but Cicero said, "This way" and moved in the opposite direction.

"Where are we going?"

"It's no good just knowing the names of the cits you are going to bribe, Earth boy. You need to get personally acquainted. Chew the fat. Have a bit of a yarn. Share a joke or two. You'll find them most hospitable."

"I have met members of the constabulary before," I said.

"But only, I believe, in your capacity as juvenile delinquent. It's time to put things on a more adult footing."

Em Talking

We saw it on the telly. We saw *her* on the telly. Probably the only person in the known universe who could stop a jongma game in its tracks just by appearing on the box.

The box in Aunty's mess is up on the wall, almost at the ceiling. It goes all the time and no one listens to it, although some people do stare at the images. I wasn't staring at any images, I was watching Quincy making money at the jongma table. I'd tumbled to Quincy—she actually played well below her best at Aunty's. She wasn't in the business of taking Aunty's lodgers to the cleaners. She only played with maximum ruthlessness in the back room at the Dog, where the stakes were ten times higher anyway. As far as Quince was concerned, the game at Aunty's was social jongma. She could have been playing snap with a bunch of geriatrics, for all the effort she was putting into it. I watched her lose a pile of newbees to old Mr. Wollongong Wong. She laughed happily, pushing the loot across the table, making a joke I couldn't hear. Mr. Wollongong added the newbees to his little stack, squaring them off, patting them down, possessive as a chook with a new-laid egg. Poor guy, the night was very young, Quince would get it all back when she felt like it. Gee I loved Quince. If I'd been truthful I'd have confessed all to Sue-Ellen in the Eatery. I watched the grace of her gestures; she built a wall of jongma tiles with the speed and delicacy of a master twangleodium player. Her copper hair glinted in the dull light. Someone in a dark corner of the room let out a shriek and pointed at the telly. A few people looked up and shouted for quiet. I looked up myself. Ulrike Lewis was on the telly. And she appeared to be on Earth. She was shown descending the ramp of The Delegate, Newharp's official ship of state.

"Who's this old wreck?" Ned said behind me.

"Shut up," I said.

Someone climbed onto a chair and turned up the sound. Ulrike Lewis was saying that the rock had been diverted. She spoke slowly, one sentence at a time, an unseen translator turned her words into English. The voice was familiar.

"Bloody Sue-Ellen," Ned said. "Trust her to get the translator's gig. Listen to her."

"Shut up," I said.

Ulrike Lewis said the rock was now in near Newharp orbit. All calculations showed the orbit to be stable. Newharp had a new moon. Not a very big new moon, but a moon none the less. The tides were going slightly haywire—it was not known what effect this would have on marine life. Sue-Ellen's voice translated "marine life" as "the habits of fish."

There was no wild cheering in Aunty's mess—everyone was too stunned. Some people were crying. Ulrike Lewis disappeared from the screen. The images were now of Newharp, of the new moon, there was footage of spacecraft placing bombs on the surface of the moon. There were diagrams showing the new orbit. The voice over said—in both languages—that Ulrike Lewis had brought these images with her. She had come as a special ambassador, she would only be staying on Earth for a week. There were other parts of this galaxy she needed to visit, and then other galaxies. Ned leaned over from behind the sofa I was sitting on. He put his arms around me, holding my shoulders, and kissed the side of my neck.

"Oh, Ned," I sobbed, my tears falling on his arms. "I can go home."

"Do you really want to?" he said.

Ned Talking

They were a bit slow, these aliens. They were a bit slow off the mark when it came to partying. For three days they wandered round like zombies. They congregated in the Dog, leaning over the tables, talking intensely to each other in hushed tones. They didn't eat or drink much. Em said the takings at the Dog had actually fallen. It was pointless trying to flog organs in the wharflands—even the Kovalevs weren't buying. They'd glued themselves to telly screens—endlessly watching the same images. This Ulrike Lewis person—apparently she was some sort of poet, a living national treasure although she looked half dead to me—this Ulrike Lewis said the same things over and over in interviews, croaking like a crow. Sue-Ellen sat in the background and translated smoothly into English, she made no attempt to croak. Ulrike Lewis said they'd got the rock under control, likewise the Willergod Party, which was now a spent force. She recited a poem she'd written especially for the occasion. It sounded like doggerel to me—it was doggerel, by any standard. It even had a line about rock around the planet, but the Newharp mob soon learned it off by heart. Ulrike Lewis thanked the good people of Earth for all the generosity and hospitality that they had so selflessly extended to their distant cousins from a distant galaxy in their hour of dire need...blah... blah...blah...and pointed out (in an aside) that no more refugees would be arriving, people smuggling was a thing of the past.

On one occasion the telly showed a shot of the official Newharp ship of State, an intergalactic cruiser called the Delegate. They'd managed to put it down in the desert somewhere without crashing—no Ice Field junkheap this one. It was huge and it gleamed white and free of rust in the sunlight. Ulrike Lewis gave Sue-Ellen a guided tour for the cameras. While she did so she croaked about the great bonds that joined Newharp and Earth—bonds forged in the fire of our common ancestry. Sue-Ellen said the same things in English, she said them with a totally straight face.

It was the announcement that people smuggling was now a thing of the past that got tongues wagging in the wharflands. If there were no smugglers' runabouts flopping down in the desert, how were those people who now wanted to go home going to get themselves deported? There were rumors that a general amnesty was going to be announced: everybody was going to get Earth Residency and Citizenship whether they wanted it or not. Welcome to Earth, monsters from outer space, this is your new home.

It all got too much for me. I went out to the tracts for three days straight and did a roaring trade, the Earthlings were still buying. They were in panic mode. They had their own theories: they thought all the organ transplant expertise was going to drain back into outer space. Soon there wouldn't be any alien surgeons left to do the changeovers. The little matter of no-runabouts, no people-smugglers, hadn't occurred to the average tract dweller. I did nothing to dispel their ignorance. I called in to see the two beauties and gave them the good news about corrupt cits in the wharflands. I named names. I told the beauties to present themselves at the Dog and Harp on Saturday arvo if they wanted to see corruption in action: bent cits and their organ racketing alien mates, carousing and back slapping, hitting the hooch at a mobster's wedding. Compromising images could be captured, I said. This was their way to get a part of the action, I implied.

"We might just be there," Beauty One said.

"If you see a couple of extra press photographers, don't worry," Beauty Two said. "We don't know you and you don't know us."

"Suits me," I said. "But it's good to know that the Internal Investigations Branch has men as dedicated as yourselves."

"Err...yes," said Beauty One.

I arrived back in the wharflands on Friday night. At last the aliens had got their act together, they were starting to party. The Dog was jumping, Em was being run off her feet. People were singing, shouting, dancing on tables, falling down drunk. I had a quick feed. Shouted a few pleasantries at a few happy faces and went for a wander around the wharflands. I ran into Quince, I picked her off her feet and swirled her round, she kissed me passionately.

"See you later tonight, lover boy," she said and ran off. She didn't say where she was going.

I knew where I was going. I went to see my newfound friends the local cits, the ones who were expecting a smooth transition when I took over from Cicero as bribe-master. I found the pair I was looking for in a back room at the local station. They were looking a bit hassled. They'd been hard at it all day fending off illegal aliens who had suddenly started to demand immediate deportation. I told the cits not to worry. I told them a thing or two I thought they ought to know about recent developments in the organ trade. I said I thought the next day's proceedings at the Dog would be interesting. The cits said Cicero had already invited them to the feast, but they were grateful for my information.

Then I partied myself, just wandering round the streets of the wharflands. Every corner had a stall or a brazier doing brisk business. I bought a paper cone with three nine-spice rolls in it. I listened to a makeshift interplanetary band belting out a mixture of Newharp and Skyroan bubble music. A singer howled along to the makeshift sound, singing his makeshift lyrics. I couldn't make out much of it, I didn't try, but the refrain was clear and to the point: *the rock ain't nothing but schlock!* A girl I'd never seen before grabbed me and we danced in the street. Others joined us. A flybynight taxi honked, trying to clear a path for itself. "Get out and dance, you dreary goons," someone shouted. And they did: the taxi driver and her passengers abandoned the flybynight, danced in the street. The girl deserted me for another dancer. I danced with another girl. Then an old woman. Then a wild Kovalev who might have been a man, but who was probably a banshee. Then we all danced in a circle, our arms around each others shoulders. I wandered on, the sweat drying on my skin. I watched some jugglers, a trick cyclist a fire eater. I bumped into Harri.

"Smile, Harri," I shouted above the din of a twangelodia quartet. "It's not that grim."

"Nothing has changed," Harri said.

"That's right," I yelled. "Your godforsaken planet is going to remain in one piece. Unchanged."

"So why celebrate?"

"Hell, Harri, why not? See that girl over there, her with the flowers in her hair, go and ask her for a dance."

"I don't know her."

"Neither do I. Come on."

I dragged Harri by the arm to where the girl stood watching the quartet. "This is not exactly dance music," Harri said.

"Who gives a rat's," I said. I tapped the girl on the shoulder. "Will you dance with us?" I said.

"Both of you?"

"Sure," I said.

"Sure," she said.

The three of us danced in a tight circle, our arms around each others shoulders. The girl with the flowers was fluid, lithe, alive, I could feel her body, sinuous under my right arm. Harri was made of wood. All his muscles were knotted up under my left arm. He was a bit of a worry, Harri. Other people started to dance, forming another, larger circle around ours, going clockwise to our anti clockwise. The quartet got the message and smoothly changed their twangling into a proper dance tune. They worked themselves up to fever pitch. The dancing got faster. Harri remained tense—a victim of terminal arthritis. The quartet reached a climax and stopped dead. Everyone cheered. The circles broke up. The girl kissed Harri and me and raised a clenched fist in mock salute. "The rock ain't nothing but schlock!" she yelled and was gone into the melee.

"I've got to go," Harri said.

"Go where?" I said.

"I'm...I'm meeting someone."

"Who?"

"A friend."

"Her from the depths? Mystery girl?"

"Yes," he managed to say between clenched teeth.

I watched him scurry away, blundering through the crowd.

I wondered if the girl actually existed. Em had told me she had doubts. She thought the girl might be a figment of Harri's imagination. But you couldn't tell with Harri. Maybe he had her chained up in the organ lab. A prisoner, never seeing the light of day, subject to his jealous possession. But then again, maybe the girl was both invented and real at the same time. Harri worked in an organ lab after all. He'd have plenty of bits and pieces out of which to construct her. Probably not—my own imagination was becoming overheated by the tumult in the streets. I went looking for Quincy.

But before I found Quincy, I found Smith Mei Lim. She and three of her PentaNostra mates were preaching the gospel on a street corner. They were handing out tracts. They weren't swallowing baby alligators. Their instruments were in their hands but they weren't playing, Mei Lim was preaching.

"No godless bombs our land forefend!" yelled Mei Lim. "T'was the mighty hand o' the gods that plucked the rock from space and time."

"Yea sister!" the other three yelled.

"And tamed its headlong passage. And bent it to their will!"

"Yea, tell them truly!"

"Revel not in the ways of Satan, dance no dances with unholy bombs. Give thanks for the mercy of the lords thy gods. Unto the lords thy gods alone, give thanks."

One of the Pentas gave a sort of drum roll on his tambourine. A loudmouth in the crowd gave a pious yell: "Thank you gods and odds and sods."

You could tell he was taking the piss. But Smith Mei Lim responded straight down the line. "The gods alone, brother! To the gods alone give thanks. No odds! No sods! brother, sully not the majesty of the mighty ones. Worship not at the false shrines of odds and sods, brother."

The loudmouth yelled some more, but one of the twanglers drowned him out. The other's struck up their instruments, but before Smith Mei Lim could begin, I had seized her by the arm and moved her to one side.

"A message from the gods, sister," I said.

"Who are you?" she said.

"Gods' messenger," I said. "You knew me in another place, another time, you knew me as Ned-the-howler."

"You have Ned's voice," she said. "But not his visage."

"I have been transfigured, sister."

"Praise the lords!"

"Praise them indeed, sister. Knowest thou the Dog?"

"The hound of hell?"

"Worse. A local eating drinking and blaspheming pit. A den of idolatry and false worship."

"The Dog and Harp?"

"Yarp."

"A moral cess pit I have been told."

"You have been told right, sister. And tomorrow Satan will be made manifest. Yea in the Dog itself."

"How come, brother?"

"There will be a great gathering of the unclean, the possessed, the slaves of sin, the bombardiersmen, the...the hound of hell itself!"

"These are unclean times, Ned-the-howler."

"Yea, but they can be cleaned up."

"Only the gods can...."

"Only the gods' earthly servants can.... Them and alligators. Yae, little baby alligators, sister. In the alligator lies salvation."

"True fact, brother."

"Six thirty for seven."

"The number of the beast!"

"The time of the great clash: Satan versus the alligators of the lords. Are you up to it, sister. Are you woman enough for the job? Have the lords themselves chosen well when they chose you? Or do I carry vain messages. Do I cast my words like bread upon the waters, to sodden and drown?"

We carried on like this for some time. I had to keep stressing the date and time of her appointment. Mei Lim was semi hysterical in her ecstasy; it wasn't clear to me how much of what I was saying was sticking in her memory banks. I rammed home the point one last time.

"The accursed Dog, sister. Six thirty for seven, sister. Tomorrow evening, sister. With alligators. The lords anoint thee. Do not fail them!"

Then I was gone, into the human maelstrom, looking for Quincy.

I found her bamboozling a three cup shyster. I've no idea how the three cup trick works, but I know you can never win. You point at an upsidedown cup and it hasn't got the bean under it. It doesn't matter which cup you point at: no bean. The shyster was swirling his cups around on top of an empty gemco drum, babbling his patter. A small crowd was watching. While I watched, Quincy picked the cup with the bean under it three times in a row. A small wad of newbees grew in her hands. The shyster was becoming aggressive in a whining sort of way.

"This is cheating, woman," he said. "On tonight of all nights. You're cheating a fellow refugee, you're robbing a veteran of the space lanes, a survivor of pirate attacks too numerous to...."

"Oh shut up," Quincy said. And stuffed the newbees into his mouth.

Then she turned, grabbed my arm and pulled me through the crowd. I hadn't realized she'd known I was there, she hadn't looked round. We walked about aimlessly, our arms around each other's waists.

"Want to stay up till dawn?" I said. "See the new day arrive?"

"This isn't actually our party," Quincy said. "We're Earthlings, remember?"

"Your grandparents have just been saved from a violent death."

"I think they're already dead—of old age. Last time I spoke to my mum she said she hadn't heard from her parents in years. They used to send messages regularly with the smugglers."

"So what do you want to do?"

"Go home. Make love to you."

"But you don't love me. You said so yourself."

"It's a conventional phrase, Earth boy. A form of words."

"Well—whatever it's called—let's do it."

So we did it. And then slept the sleep of the just. Tangled around each other in Quincy's bed on the balcony. And when I woke in the morning, with Quincy's head warm on my shoulder, I wasn't sure what the day would bring.

"I'm not sure about today," I said into her hair. "I don't know what's going to happen."

"One never does," Quincy said. "Kiss me. Put a bit of effort into it."

I kissed her and put a bit of effort into it. And then we made love—for want of a better phrase—and dozed and got up and climbed down the steep steel steps and showered in the steam and soap of the ablution block in Aunty's back yard, our hands slithering over each other, slick with soap and innocence. And then we ate breakfast in the deserted eating and gambling room. And then we left the house. And I never went back there again.

Em Talking

It might have been a party for some, but the Dog stayed open all night. And all night it needed staff to slosh out the hooch and slam plates of tucker in front of the cheering drunks. I was offered free booze. I was offered various hands in marriage, various hands slid over my breasts, my bum, half a dozen booze-artists wanted to dance with me and one old fart tried to stuff newbucks down the front of my traditional Newharp costume. I slapped his face, drunks cheered and the money went everywhere, to be tramped into the floor, eaten by Fido-Fido. By dawn I was earning triple time. Or so the supervisor said, although I'd believe that when I saw the money and not before. At dawn I'd had enough. I told the supervisor to go jump.

She said, "What about quadruple time?"

I said, "Stuff it," and stood in the staff shower for a period of time that might have been five minutes and might have been half an hour. Then I dressed in my own clothes and picked my way through the drunks and sleeping bodies. I patted Fido-Fido on his sleeping head—although for all I knew, the dog could have been drunk to the point of oblivion—I'd seen a number of revelers feeding shot-glasses of fake-silverberry down his throat at some nameless hour of the proceedings.

On the way home I wondered how this day was going to end. Cicero d'Pettitt was marrying Jill Lean in the Cathedral at Point Potts—and then they and a vast herd of go-getters and politicians and society nerds were going to descend on the Dog. As a joyous gesture of reconciliation. Anything could happen. But I knew this: Newharp, my beloved Newharp, birthplace and childhood haven, was safe. My parents and all my family and friends were safe. And I was a galaxy and a half away—with no chance of going home for years and years. I was too tired to cry, and I don't know what I would have cried for even if I'd had it in me to shed tears. Joy, sorrow, something else? I reached my room. I lay full length on my bed without bothering to undress. And was instantly asleep.

Ned Talking

Of all the mad things. Em was going to work as a waitress at Cicero's bunfight. She told us this while Quincy and I were having a lunch of sorts in the Dog, Em had joined us. All around was total devastation; some of the other staff were mopping up, throwing out the broken furniture. They'd have to work like stink to get the place neat and tidy by six thirty for seven. I told Em not to be a halfwit.

"It's my shift, Ned. I work here, remember?"

"You're invited, you're meant to be a guest."

"I've turned the invitation down. I have a prior engagement, I've got to go to work."

"Em, this really is a bit silly," Quincy said quietly.

"No it's not."

"Let's go somewhere where we can talk."

"We can talk here."

"Ish," Quincy said, turning to me. "Bugger off. Girl talk time."

I went outside. The street party hadn't really finished, it was still ticking over nicely, it would pick up again at nightfall. A lot of regulars were going to be peculiarly pissed off that the Dog was reserved for a private function. I walked down to the wharfs and went for a ferry ride for no good reason. I had time to kill. I was quite content. Somewhere out there in the respectable upper class suburbs, Cicero d'Pettitt was getting ready to meet his fate, first in the echoing deeps of some Cathedral and then in the Dog. I sat in the sun near the ferry's bows and watched the water sparkle. Seagulls wheeled and swooped and squabbled in the wake of a fishing boat. The crew were hard at it, already gutting and beheading fish, throwing the entrails to the birds. I didn't know what the day would bring. I closed my eyes. The sun was warm on my eyelids. I didn't know what the day would bring, and I didn't care.

Em Talking

They arrived in a great motorcade. Invading the wharflands in a gesture of reconciliation. Motorbike outriders, press photographers, bridesmaids, groomsmen, chaps in hats like sewer pipes, women in dresses that could hardly fit through the door of the Dog. And the bride, airhead herself. A mass of white satin and lace. And Cicero, togged up in old fashioned Earth gear. I was right, I knew I was right to have resisted Quincy's pleas. There was no way I was going to be part of this mob. I was an outsider, a humble waitress—and that's the way I wanted it. I felt slightly pissed off that Ned, Quincy and Harri had joined the throng so readily. Sue-Ellen had provided them all with flash wedding guest gear. They were indeed extras, stand-ins, human publicity props. All the tables and chairs in the Dog had been formed into a hollow rectangle. The tables were covered with white cloth, there were flowers all over the place. The scent of flowers almost smothered the scent of cleaning fluid, the scent of cleaning fluid almost smothered the scent of puke from last night's festivities. Myself and the other waiters flowed smoothly around the outside of the rectangle. We plied the guests with plonk and nibbles.

"Care for a top up, sir?" I said to Ned, leaning over his shoulder, pouring bubbles into his glass.

"Care for a punch up the konk, madam?" Ned said pleasantly.

"There's no need to call me madam," I said.

"Cool it, you two," Quincy said. "We respect your decision, Em."

"Good of you," I said and refilled Quincy's glass. "I don't respect yours."

Harri put his hand over the top of his glass. "Water will do," he said and reached for a bottle of expensive mineral water that was decorating the table.

Hell, I thought. Harri really is in a bad way. I wafted around, deftly side-stepping my fellow waiters, opening bottles, pouring plonk, mopping up the odd little spill, changing plates. I leaned over Sue-Ellen's shoulder. "Try the darkfish," I said. "The chief has surpassed himself."

"Want to go back to Newharp?" Sue-Ellen said.

"Of course," I said.

"Good. You leave tomorrow. Tell your brother."

I nearly dropped the bottle. As it was it clanked against Sue-Ellen's glass, spilling bubbles onto the cloth.

"Are you serious?" I said.

"Dead serious. You and Harri are cabin crew on the Delegate. You'll have to dance attendance on that awful Ulrike Lewis woman and her cronies—but it couldn't be worse than working here."

"I...I...this is a shock."

"Don't worry about it now. Talk to me when the mingling starts."

I was in a bit of a daze for the next half hour. I did what waitresses do: served people, but I was on automatic pilot. I even managed to serve something to Cicero without any feeling for the event. My mind was elsewhere. I filled airhead's glass without even bothering to look at her face from close up—she was nothing to me. I was going back to Newharp, I was going home. I realized I hadn't yet spoken to Harri. I plonked some food in front of him.

"I'm full," Harri said, trying to get me to take it away.

"We're going home," I said. "Sue-Ellen's got us onto the Delegate."

"Stuff that," Harri said.

"What?"

"I'm never getting into another spacecraft, Em. That's flat."

"Harri...you can't. You've got to come."

"I'm staying here, Em."

"Why?"

"Why not? One place is exactly the same as another. This place isn't paradise. Newharp isn't paradise either. Paradise doesn't exist."

"Who wants paradise?"

"Em, you go home if you want to."

"Not without you."

"Then let's both stay here."

My mind was suddenly blank. I could think of nothing to say. I didn't know what I felt. The room was silent. The loathsome Paul Lean was tapping an empty glass with the side of a fork. God, he was a revolting specimen in the flesh—all oily sincerity and good cheer. I stumbled out to the kitchens and left the mob to their speeches.

Ned Talking

Talk about weird behavior. There'd been some sort of dust-up between Harri and Em, words hissed that I couldn't catch. Em reeled away, looking like the walking dead.

"What was all that about?" I whispered to Quincy who was sitting between me and Harri.

"Shush," she whispered. "Listen to this guy."

This guy was Paul Lean and he poured forth bilge. What he was saying was interesting only for the sheer buffoonery of it. The man oozed brotherly love, he exuded tolerance and respect for all personkind no matter what their color, creed or planet of origin. No one in their right mind would believe a word, but on went Lean: we were on the brink of a new day, a mighty bridge was being forged, Earthling and alien hands were clasping and no one could dissolve them, for in diversity is strength and unity makes things stronger still. And all this was symbolized by the joining together in holy matrimony of Jill and Cicero, two young people who came from different ends of the universe to find true blah...blah...blah....

Did this guy want the alien vote? Did he what. Anyone would have thought he'd personally arranged citizenship for every broken down refugee in the land. Maybe he had—maybe the rumors of a general amnesty with the vote thrown in were all true. It was beyond me, I tuned out. I let my eyes slip sideways. I wanted to know what was going on beyond the doors and plate glass windows. Things in the street were getting interesting. The security guy guarding the front door appeared a trifle agitated.

There were more speeches and clapping and clichés. Some guy—an Earthling, of course—was introduced as the best man and Cicero's best friend. He rambled on about what a great guy Cicero was and how they'd both had a super time at university together. University! To my quite certain knowledge the only university Cicero had ever attended was a certain institution on Newharp called Re-Ed. We were well into cloud cuckoo land here.

And then there was the dance. Cicero and this Jill woman waltzing around in the square in the middle to the sound of the Dog's resident combo who had all been given spiffy new suits for the occasion. Then everybody else streamed onto the floor, tripping the light fantastic.

"Come on idiot-boy," Quincy said. "Get your carcass into gear."

Quincy and I circled the floor, moving which ever way Quincy decided we should move. Navigation was beyond me, I just followed where she steered. We passed Cicero and Jill.

"Congratulations," I said to Cicero. "A long and prosperous life to you both."

"Thank you ever so much for your wonderful wedding present," Jill said to me and Quincy.

"What present was that?" Quincy said to me as we swirled away.

"Search me," I said.

"Maybe we should have given them something," Quincy said.

"Maybe we will," I said. "The night's still young."

"What's that meant to mean?" she said.

But the dance had ended and Paul Lean was once again calling us all to order.

"And now, dear friends," he said. "Let us open our hearts to all humankind, let us not try to contain our overflowing happiness, but let it pour forth in joyful abundance to encompass the whole wharflands and beyond the wharflands the world without end and beyond the world without end the very stars from which so many of you, dear friends, have come starving, huddled, massive, yearning for a free beer...."

Perhaps he didn't say that. I wasn't listening properly. I was watching the security bloke open the doors and spring back. In came the pack, Smith Mei Lim in the lead. For the first time in my life I saw her without her twangleodium. She'd swapped it for a baby alligator.

"Fornicators and adulterators," she yelled, "bombardiers!" The alligator snapped on thin air, thrashing its little tail. Someone shrieked. I think it was the Jill woman. Behind Mei Lim other PentaNostra held their alligators high and surged forward. The alligators didn't faze the Dog's regulars—they'd heard the rumor about free hooch, and they'd been kept out of the Dog for too long as it was. They leapt tables, knocked over chairs, fronted the bar three deep, shouting out their orders.

Paul Lean bellowed for quiet, screamed for peace. Beauty One tapped me on the shoulder, he held a camera and was wearing a badge that said Press.

"This place normally like this?" he yelled.

"Quiet night," I said.

"Bloody aliens. So who are the local boys? Our opposite numbers in the force?"

I didn't point at the bent cits, I pointed at a couple of Tetride bosses who had retreated to a corner, their right hands in their pockets. "Those two," I said. "Deputy Superintendent of Licensing, bent as a paper clip. Detective first class O'Flaggon, known as Mr. Ten percent."

"Might just have a yarn," said Beauty Two next to my other shoulder. They moved through the throng, sidling up to the bosses.

"What the fuck's going on?" Cicero said, spinning me round to face him.

"Ask your father in law," I said. "It was his idea, letting the mob in."

"These crocodiles...."

"Alligators," I said.

"Get them out, Ishmael. Just get them out!"

"Easier said than done."

"Do it!"

I moved away with purpose. But my purpose was to advise the local cits. I found the three of them being jostled by the rabble near the bar.

"Over there," I said. "Other side of the room. Outsiders muscling in. Disguised as press photographers. Look at them, talking to the bosses. I reckon they're arranging a deal."

"We might just re-arrange it," one of the locals said and the three made tracks through the mob.

"Turn to the lords thy gods," yelled Smith Mei Lim behind me. "Cast out the gators of desire, consign the monsters to the fire."

I turned round. Mei Lim was rapidly going into a trance,

chanting over and over again about desire and fire.

Three or four other PentaNostras took up the chant, twirling about, holding their snapping alligators above their heads. A couple of Pentas without alligators had brought their instruments. The rhythmic chant had a hypnotic quality, it could put you to sleep. The word "fire", however, had an enlivening effect on many present.

"Fire!" screamed an old boy in a stuffed shirt.

"Fire!" screamed three or four other people.

"Fire!" screamed dozens of voices.

"This your handiwork, Ish?" Quincy shouted at me from half a meter.

"Who me, officer?" I yelled back.

"I thought I told you to get rid of them," Cicero snarled, reappearing through the mob.

"It's beyond me, mate."

"You're fired."

"Fire!" screamed a bridesmaid and made for the door, knocking Cicero to his knees as she passed. She led a small stampede, a human tide. It met another tide coming in, punters with the smell of free booze in their snouts. With a crash the two waves met. A rebound wave made for the kitchens, carrying all before it, tables chairs, the combo in their new suits.

In the far corner was a most regrettable sight: the bosses and the two teams of cits were slugging it out. Punching, kicking, trying to arrest each other, handcuffs were being flailed around. As yet, no gats.

"The hound of hell!" yelled smith Mei Lim, pointing with her alligator.

Blow me down. There he was, the hound of hell himself: Fido-Fido lumbering through the melee with a snapping baby alligator firmly clenched in his rotten teeth.

"Out, hound, out!" yelled the Pentas.

Fido took no notice, just lumbered towards his normal snoozing place. The baby alligator snapped wildly, grabbing hold of a passing table cloth, bringing the whole contents of the table crashing to the floor. Including an opened bottle of pseudo silverberry and an ashtray with a smoldering cigar. Silverberry is a toxic, fiery little drop, as I know from experience. The fake stuff is even fierier. I experienced no surprise when the smoldering cigar ignited the spilt liqueur—the flame was pale blue, delicate to behold, it could have been a southern aurora dancing above an Antarctic snowfield, so dazzling and white was the tablecloth.

"Look at that," I said to Quincy.

"Put it out," she said.

But before anything could be done the baby alligator had escaped from Fido's jaws shot through the flaming silverberry and dashed up an ornamental drape that framed a view of Santa Gertrudis by night. The reptile was lightly burning, its scaly hide had acquired the palest of pale blue flickers. The drapes now produced more robust flames.

"Shoot it!" someone yelled. "Shoot it before it fires the whole place."

There was a volley of small arms fire from the corner where, moments before the Beauties, the bosses and the local cits had been slugging it out. The whole mob of brawlers now had gats in their hands. They had turned their collective attention to the flaming alligator. The noise was deafening. Halfway up the blazing drape, the blazing alligator—quite unharmed by the shots, which merely punched jagged holes in the wall—took a flying jump and disappeared into the human tide. The Beauties and the bosses had started a fashion. Gats started to appear from every second pocket, every third armpit. Dear Christ! Even Jill Lean the blushing bride was waving a delicate little weapon about.

"Heavy scene," I said to Quince. "Let's get out of here."

But most other people now had the same idea. People rushed in all directions.

Em Talking

The speeches droned on in the dining room. Then there was the sound of the combo playing dance music. I sat on a stool in the kitchens, torn in half. I wanted so much to go home. I wanted to go home with Harri. Sue-Ellen appeared.

"What's up?" She said.

"Harri doesn't want to go home."

"You can't make him."

"But he's my brother."

"Brothers and sisters have to make their separate ways eventually."

"I'm worried about him."

"You'll worry about him if you stay on Earth with him. You'll worry about him if you go home."

"What shall I do, Sue-Ellen."

"Toss a coin."

"Seriously."

Sue-Ellen didn't reply. A silver newbuck appeared in her hand. "Heads you go home, tails you stay," she said and flicked the coin into the air. She caught it and slapped it onto her wrist, she took her hand away. "Tails," she said. "You stay."

I gulped, stifled a sob.

"What do you feel?" Sue-Ellen said.

"Devastated," I said.

"Well that's got your true emotions out into the open. You're going home. It's settled."

There was a sudden sound of yelling and stampeding feet from the dining room. There was a volley of shots.

"What's that?" I said.

"The mingling has started," Sue-Ellen said.

Harri appeared in the kitchen. "I think I'll do a bit of work," he said. "I've stuff to do."

"You work in the labs, right?" Sue-Ellen said.

Harri didn't say anything.

"You remember Sue-Ellen?" I said.

"Yes," said Harri.

"Look, Harri," Sue-Ellen said. "Go down to your labs, but leave the steel door open. OK? If people come down the stairs, show them to the tunnels that get them out of the place."

Harri hesitated, he still didn't say anything.

"Do it, Harri," I said. "Do it for me."

"OK," Harri said, and made his way to the cellar.

"How do you know about the steel door, the tunnels?" I said.

"Astolphe told me. There's not much about this place he doesn't know. When I said I was coming here, he gave me a geography lesson. Just in case."

A few seconds later crazed people yelling "fire" started surging through the kitchens. A few were waving gats around. One went off, puncturing a soup cauldron.

"Go down those stairs to the cellar. Go through the cool room. Go through the steel door and down the next flight of stairs. Ask directions when you reach the organ lab," I said. I said it over and over like a talking clock. I just sat on my stool in the kitchen, set back slightly from the human tide. I was calm, drained, talking like a clock. Sue-Ellen leaned against a stove. She didn't say anything at all. After a few minutes the smell of smoke began to make itself felt. Then the ceiling became obscure. The dining room was crackling. Wailing sirens could be distantly heard. Ned and Quincy arrived in the kitchen.

"The face is an improvement," Sue-Ellen said to Ned.

"We all change," Ned said.

"Nobody left in the dining room?" I said.

"Nope," Ned said. "We're the last."

"Well, let's go." I said. "Let's check out these famous labs."

We descended to the cellar. As we were walking past the racks of plonk, Ned introduced Sue-Ellen to Quincy. The two women shook hands without breaking stride.

"I've heard about you," Quincy said.

"I've heard about you too," Sue-Ellen said. "I'm delighted to meet you."

We entered the cool room. The small steel door stood open,

we passed through it one by one. I was the last. I shut it with a clang. In single file we went on down a narrow flight of stairs deep into the ground.

Ned Talking

The organ labs were a bit of a shambles. There was a main, brightly lit, chamber with benches and racks down each side. Other, smaller, chambers ran off at right angles. The main chamber looked like a herd of buffalo had passed through. There were bottles and jars and dishes broken and smashed and lying about all over the place. Also organs. The floor was awash with organs, broken glass and culture mixture.

"This place is gross," Quincy said. "How could Harri work here?"

"It had a quiet order to it," Harri said from the far end of the main chamber. He was sitting on a lab stool, waiting for us. "This place was a retreat from the chaos of the world."

"Not any more," Quincy said, picking her way past a pile of kidneys and a half-grown tripe replacement kit.

We all arrived at the far end of the main chamber.

"Don't worry about the mess," Sue-Ellen said to Harri. "Astolphe is moving everything to the north shore anyway."

"Astolphe?"

"My husband."

"I know who he is," Harri said. "I didn't know he owned this place, yet."

"As from last week. He's in partnership with Paul Lean, they've bought out the Tetrides. Peacefully. Paid top dollar. No one got rubbed out. Unless that burst of gunfire upstairs had any casualties."

"Not that we saw," Quincy said.

"Which way did you send everybody?" Sue-Ellen said to Harri.

"That way," Harri said, pointing to a side tunnel. "There are steps up to a dental clinic in P21Xetc. Street."

"I believe there's also an exit into St. Mary's Lane."

"Yeah. Barber's shop."

"We could get a haircut on the way out," I said.

"No time, Neddy boy," Sue-Ellen said. "We've got to make tracks."

"I wasn't thinking of going anywhere special," I said.

"You're going to Newharp."

"Who says?"

"I do. I'm personally deporting you. You can have Harri's job, he doesn't want it."

"What job?"

"Cabin boy on the Delegate. Come on, let's go."

Harri led the way along an undamaged side tunnel and up another steep flight of concrete stairs. He unlocked another steel door and we stepped out one by one into the staff toilets at the back of the Mary's Lane barber shop. A few minutes later we were standing in the street. Sue-Ellen put her fingers in her mouth and let out a piercing whistle. A dark green Gamma Crux, turned the corner into the lane and slid smoothly to a halt. There was nobody driving it.

"What the...?" I said, staring at the empty driving seat.

"It's got automatics," Sue-Ellen said. "Stop staring. Start saying the fond good-byes."

"I'm not so sure about this deportation lark," I said. "I'm an Earthling."

"You've got no choice, Ned. You've run out of protection on Earth. After tonight's little caper everybody will want you in jail. Cits, Scott-Woks, Tetrides, the insurance companies, the municipal dog-catcher, everyone. They'll breathe a sigh of relief when you're put away. For years and years and years."

She had a point.

Quincy put her arms around me. Hugging me tight. Kissing me. She was in no doubt about my fate. This was a goodbye kiss. We finally broke from the kiss. She continued to hold me. She looked at me. There were tears in her eyes. There were tears in mine.

"I love you," Ish," she said.

"It's a form of words," I said.

"No it's not," she said. "I love you."

"You once said you'd run a mile if you ever fell in love with me."

"It's you who've got to run, Ish."

"Time to go," Sue-Ellen said.

I turned to say goodbye to Em and Harri, but they were locked in a wordless embrace. Staring into each other's eyes.

"What's going on?" I said.

"Em's going with you. Harri's staying here," Sue-Ellen said.

"No one tells me anything."

"OK, onboard. Now! The whole wharflands will be crawling with cits." Sue-Ellen said.

I shook Harri's hand. Embraced the guy. Em and Quincy kissed. Then we were away. We were out of the place. Sue-Ellen didn't trust the automatics to get us out of the wharflands, she sat at the controls herself and took off like a madwoman. Em and I both turned in our seats and looked out of the back window. Harri and Quincy stood in the lane watching us leave, their arms were around each others' waists.

Em Talking

The Delegate was parked in the desert a few hundred kilometers out of town. As soon as we were clear of Jackson's Port, tearing down a straight deserted highway, the car's lights tunneling endlessly into the endless night, Sue-Ellen put the car on automatic and swiveled her seat sideways.

"Guess what," she said to Ned.

"What?"

"We go straight through Tidy."

"The old home town," Ned said.

"We're not stopping," Sue-Ellen said.

"Can't we just show Em the sights."

"She'll see all she needs to see out of the window."

"The pub will still be open," Ned said.

"We're not stopping." Sue-Ellen said. "Cheer up, Em."

"I'm worried about Harri," I said. "He's got no real friends."

"Harri will be all right," Ned said. "He's in good hands."

"Whose hands?"

"Quincy's. They were round his waist as we left."

"She was just being supportive. Anyone would be at a time like that."

"She's very good at being supportive at all times," Ned said.

"Well, you'd know."

For an hour or two we said nothing. The three of us were lost in our own thoughts. The car surged along the highway, occasionally overtaking a canola roller lit up like a Christmas tree. Then Sue-Ellen said, "OK, don't blink."

We didn't blink. We saw the battered sign:

Welcome to This Year's Winner of the Tidy Town Award.

We saw a lighted truck stop with a few canola rollers parked in front of it. We saw a pub with a drunk lurching out of its suddenly bright doorway. We saw a few darkened houses and shops and a square building with a flag pole in front of it. Then we were rolling on across the endless plain.

"The buggers have rebuilt it," Ned said.

"You can't have a town without a Mothers and Babies," Sue-Ellen said.

"Civilization as we know it would cease without a Mothers and Babies," Ned said.

"About civilization," Sue-Ellen said. "A word of advice. When you get to Newharp, Neddy boy, try, just try, not to burn the whole damn planet to the ground. They've got a very nice civilization up there. They won't want it completely rearranged by you. Your job is to respect other people's culture."

"I'm well acquainted with alien civilization," Ned said. "After the wharflands, a whole damn planet full of aliens will be a piece of cake."

"Actually, there are very few aliens on Newharp," I said. "You, Earth boy, will be a member of a very select, persecuted, minority group."

ABOUT THE AUTHOR

Rory Barnes was born in London in 1946, but was immediately transported to Africa where he learned to walk and talk in a mud hut in a tribal village (the normal childhood for the children of anthropologists). By the time he was ten his family had moved to Sydney and he has lived in Australia ever since. He studied Philosophy at Monash University where he met Damien Broderick. Over the years these two have written seven or eight novels together; the latest joint-production being *Human's Burden*, published by Borgo Press. By himself Rory has written another seven novels for both adults and teenagers. He can claim the usual list of writers' other jobs: teacher, farmhand, journalist, builder's labourer, book reviewer, publisher's reader, lecturer etc. etc. He once delivered a baby. Once, when hitch-hiking, he was given a lift in a hearse. On another occasion he walked from Jerusalem to the Dead Sea without getting shot. These days he lives in Adelaide with his wife, Annie, who has a proper job. His website is located at:

http://www.rorybarnes.fatcow.com

www.ingramcontent.com/pod-product-compliance
Lightning Source LLC
Chambersburg PA
CBHW050406260626
47156CB00003B/891